360 Degrees

A Novel by Regina Neequaye

ACKNOWLEDGMENT

I would like to give thanks to my creator. Lamar Crowell, my husband, thanks for still believing in me. I would like to thank my mother, Marjorie Renee Monnighan Reynolds who gave me the gift of compassion. To my children, Reynolds, Jordan, and Monnighan, you guys have been my inspiration. To my sisters, Denise, Shela, and Vonetta your support and love is abounding.

*RN*eequaye *P*ublishing

Zero Degrees

I heard a loud, hollow pop followed by an eerie, echoing silence. I slowly walked into my parents' room. Momma was a folded heap in daddy's arms. Blood oozed out of her head and slowly dripped down daddy's bare shoulders. Daddy sat still; his mouth was wide open, but there was no sound. Tears rolled down his face one at a time. The house was so silent the quietness was more frightening than the morbid vision of my momma and daddy. I was numb and in shock. I did not feel anything. I was twelve years old; I knew I was supposed to be scared, crying or something, but I was numb. I left my parents' room and walked down the hall. Khalid stood still in the threshold of his bedroom door. His eyes spoke what his mouth could not. His eyes were blank, looking at me but not actually seeing me. He knew something happened that would end our lives the way we knew it. I ordered him back inside of his room. He walked backwards into his room, climbed onto the bed, and curled his body tight in a fetal position. I tip toed to his room and closed his door. I walked back into my parents' room and picked up the phone.

"911 operator."

"My daddy hurt my momma!"

"How did he hurt her?"

"I think he shot her with a gun."

"Honey stay on the line! Help is on the way!" The operator sounded frantic. I thought she was supposed to remain calm and reassure me. Instead, I felt the need to reassure her.

"Does your daddy still have the gun?"

"I don't know."

"Is your mom...?" I placed the phone down and squeezed my head between daddy and momma. The room was so quiet I could actually hear our hearts beat.

Blue lights flashed through the curtains. A faint knock echoed through the house. I could not move. I wanted to answer the door, but I sat still. I could not move. A loud bang reverberated through the house. I heard an army of footsteps coming down the hall towards momma and daddy's bedroom. There was what seemed like a thousand policemen in full riot gear standing in my parents' room.

"Turn the girl loose!"

"Let the girl go!"

Daddy did not move. He appeared oblivious to the small army occupying the bedroom. He continued to hold momma and sat quietly with tears rolling down his face. The police had guns drawn and pointed at daddy's head. I heard the click of a gun and squeezed out of daddy's arms. An officer abruptly grabbed me and rushed out of the room; the police officer did not wear the standard blue uniform. He was dressed in faded jeans and a sweaty, dingy, gray t-shirt. I felt cold, hard metal on my leg, as he held me over his shoulder and ran with me out of the house.

Everything went fast. The ambulance's spinning red lights made me dizzy. I thought they were coming to take my mother to the hospital and make her better. I did not realize she was actually gone until I saw her neatly wrapped in a thick, black, plastic bag. I remember thinking; *I wish they would open the bag, so she can breathe.* I wanted to scream. I wanted to shout to momma *here I am please come and get me; I'm over here.* I wanted to cling to her and feel her soft chest close to my face one more time. I wanted to feel her warm arms tightly wrapped around me. I wanted to see her beautiful smile; her smile was always reassuring. I knew this was not going to happen ever again.

I don't know how long I stood outside before the police officer brought Khalid to me. The sullen look on his face made me cry. It was a sadness I have never seen on anyone's face before. A deep, penetrating melancholy pierced my heart. I have never felt sadness like this before. Khalid and I were both crying. He ran to me. He jumped into my arms, tightly wrapped his arms and legs around me, and buried his face in my neck. He was almost as tall as me; I cannot believe my skinny legs were strong enough to hold the both of us. We stood outside for what seemed like an eternity while the policemen were talking to one another, going back and forth, inside, outside, and around the house before they took us to the police station.

Grandma was at the police station when we arrived. She sat in a dingy room; the musty smell of mold permeated the air. The walls were made of cinder blocks covered with chipping, gray paint that appeared centuries old. The room was sparsely decorated with a light that hung down from the ceiling over an old, wooden table. Grandma seemed small sitting at the table. Her eyes were puffy. It seemed as if her whole body was shaking. Khalid immediately ran to her. I stood motionless, unable to move. Grandma came over and gently touched my shoulders. She attempted to pull my rigid body close to her. I put up as much resistance as my thin body would allow.

"Don't worry baby; Grandma will take care of you. I am going to take good care of you." I could not respond. It was as if I were dreaming; the kind where at the end of the dream you figure out it's not real, but you still can't wake up and leave the dream. This was not a dream. I would not wake up and run to my momma and daddy's room and snuggle close between them where even if they didn't wake up, feeling their warm bodies made everything okay.

Grandma's house is no longer the same to me. My relationship to this house has changed; it was a place I used to come and visit but then return to my own house. Now I would have to live here. I was no longer going home to my own house to my own things to my momma and daddy.

I was lying in the bed tired but trying not to fall asleep. For the first time in my life, I was afraid. I was afraid, but I did not know what I was afraid of; it was not an object but a feeling I could not touch. I could not describe this feeling. I could not call it a name. There were no words to describe a feeling so sad. This was the first time in my life when I woke up, I would not know what the day would bring.

Momma was ritual. I knew every morning she would come into my room and gently touch me. Though I would already be awake, I would not get out of the bed until she came into my room. She would either make oatmeal or French toast on weekdays, or she would make a three course breakfast on the weekend, but I no longer knew what would happen. I was fearful, and I was hurting. It was an abysmal hurt that cut deep, a continual pain without relief.

The sunlight peeping through the blinds woke me. I scanned the bedroom looking for something familiar when I saw the blood stains on my shorts. The rose colored splatter brought me back to the present. I pushed my head back and deep into the pillow and cried. I cried because my momma would never hold me again. She would never part my hair straight when I cannot see the back of my head. She would never come in the bathroom and wash the part of my back I cannot reach. She would not see me grow into a woman and see herself in me. I cried because I wanted to be in my own home. I wanted to be in my own room in my own bed. Grandma came into the room. She attempted to touch me. I did not want her to touch me. She tried to hold me. I wiggled out of her arms and ran out of the room.

"Thandisha! Thandisha!" She looked helpless, but I was too absorbed in my own pain to feel her pain. I ran down the hall crying and screaming, "I want my momma." Grandma looked broken. She looked tired and worn. She came closer to me with her arms spread and her hands open in a come to Jesus stand like Reverend Deal does on Sunday at the end of church service when he invites the congregation to come to Jesus.

"No! Don't touch me Grandma! Don't touch me! I want my momma!" I did not want to feel anyone's hands but momma's. I did not want to feel old, hard, wrinkled hands. I wanted momma's soft, perfect, and loving hands to touch me.

"Thandie, baby, your momma is with God. God has called her home." She slowly walked towards me. I walked backwards and away from her moving my head from side to side in disbelief at Grandma's words.

"I hate God! Why didn't he call you home? You are old and tired! I want my momma! Where's my daddy? I'm calling him to come and get me out this house!" She walked towards me, a stream of tears flowed from her eyes and down her bronze cheeks. Her hands were together as if she was praying. I walked towards the phone screaming so loud I could hardly talk. My throat and neck were hurting. I picked up the phone and began to dial. I hoped daddy would answer the phone, come to grandma's house and take me back to my own house with my own things. I wanted to be in my own bed.

"Thandie, remember last night Thandie!" She screamed while snatching the phone away from me. "Your daddy killed your mother! He killed my daughter!" Her words were piercing; they cut deep. They took away my final hope last night was a dream and That Day really didn't happen.

"You're a goddamned liar Grandma! Don't say that

to me! Don't you dare say that to me! Don't you lie to me Grandma! You're a liar! Where is my daddy?" She slapped me so hard my neck popped. Her face was tight. It seemed as if every blood vessel in her face was at the surface of her skin.

"Don't you ever mention that man in this house again!" I ran to the kitchen, opened the backdoor, and ran out of the house. I ran hard and fast; Grandma could not keep up. She shouted to Mr. Nance, her neighbor, for help. Grandma and Mr. Nance ran after me. I ran faster. They were behind me. David, Mr. Nance's son, joined them. He caught me and tackled me to the ground. I kicked and screamed. They held me down, and I passed out. When I woke up, I was in bed with Khalid still in Grandma's house.

The funeral was quiet and quick. We were dressed to the nines in our mourning wear. Aunt Mary wore a black pants suit almost identical to Grandma's suit; the difference was Grandma wore a skirt instead of pants. Khalid wore his favorite black suit with a clip on tie. Daddy tried to teach him to tie a necktie, but Khalid could never get the hang of it. I wore a black dress and black nylons. People I have never seen before walked to the front of the church and said nice things about my momma. Older women in the church walked by Grandma and firmly placed their hands on her shoulder. I tried to be strong until Aunt Mary touched me. Tears begin to form in my eyes. I closed my eyes as tight as I could to keep the tears from flowing. I bit my lip in a futile attempt to stop the tears. I could not stop them. They quickly escalated from a slow drip to a full flow.

"Please God bring her back." Aunt Mary gently squeezed my shoulder. "Aunt Mary, please ask God to bring her back." The church was quiet. The minister stopped speaking and looked at me in a sorrowful, powerless way.

"Baby, the Lord gives, and the Lord takes away."

"No, don't tell me that! I want my momma! Tell God to bring her back, please. I will be so good. I will take communion every first Sunday. I will say my prayers. Tell God I will do anything just bring her back."

No one had answers. The church was dead quiet. Then Mrs. Gigs, an usher who has been at St. James A.M.E., as long as there has been a St. James A.M.E., placed her arms around me and escorted me outside. Aunt Mary followed behind us. I stayed with Aunt Mary while everyone, including Grandma, went to the burial site. I sat on Aunt Mary's lap curling my torso so I can place my head in her chest. The sound of her heart was a calming lullaby. I wanted to stay on her lap wrapped in her arms forever until God called me home. After the funeral, we returned to Grandma's house. We did not go to the church for the huge dinner at the repast.

Everyone, including Grandma, stayed in their rooms for a week. Khalid and I ate cold cuts, cookies and potato chips the entire week Grandma was in her room. We had not gone to school in almost two weeks. I was not ready to go to school. I did not care if I ever saw another school again. Aunt Mary came every morning and stayed late in the evening to take care of Grandma. Khalid and I took care of each other.

"You know guys, we're going to register at your new schools tomorrow."

"Aunt Mary, I am not going to school."

"Sure you are Thandie."

"Oh no I am not. Besides, I don't know anyone at the new school."

"Yeah me neither. I am not going to school either. Am I Thandie?" Khalid repeated everything I said.

"Look guys do you think your mother would want you to behave this way? You know Riley wanted very much for you guys to have a good education." Aunt Mary

11

had a point. Momma taught Khalid and me to read before we went to school, but I really didn't care what Aunt Mary said. I wasn't going to school, and in my mind, no one could make me.

Khalid and I refused to get out of bed and go with Grandma and Aunt Mary to register at our new schools. We were both plagued with a terrible stomachache and blurred vision. We were determined we were not going to school. I was sure Aunt Mary and Grandma knew our sudden illnesses were unreal, but we were allowed to stay home.

When Aunt Mary came back with our class assignments and bus schedules, Khalid and I were speechless. The thought of going to school terrified me. We had grown comfortable staying in the house all day. We had become accustomed to basically doing whatever we wanted. Grandma usually stayed in bed all day, and we basically had to fend for ourselves. Aunt Mary tried to get us to go outside to play, but we were not having it. There were a lot of children in the neighborhood. The children appeared friendly, but I really did not feel up to playing with children. My life was not a child's life anymore; my childhood was stolen in one second with one bullet.

Aunt Mary nagged Khalid and me daily about staying in the house. She constantly reminded us of the need for fresh air. After daily pressure from Aunt Mary, Khalid and I finally went outside. There were kids outside playing, but we stayed with each other safe in Grandma's yard.

"Hi I'm Ayanna. What's your name? You want to play Double Dutch?" We were standing outside when Ayanna jumped rope all of the way up the driveway. She looked silly. She had two ponytails, one on each side of her head, that flopped up and down every time she jumped the rope.

"No she doesn't want to play with you." Khalid stood military style; a menacing look covered his face. "Do you Thandie?"

"No," I looked at her and wondered why she wanted to play with a dead woman's child anyway. She had a glow and an aura of innocence I no longer possessed.

Khalid and I walked back inside of the house, leaving her standing alone in Grandma's yard. I looked out of the window and watched Ayanna play with some of the other neighborhood children. They played double dutch and filled the street with laughter and pre-teen conversation. I was envious of their happiness and jovial dispositions. I closed the blinds and played card games with Khalid until it was time for bed.

The next morning, Aunt Mary came for Khalid and me to take us to school. When she came into my room and woke me up, my eyes met her eyes with an intense blank stare.

"Come on Thandie, you and Khalid have to get up. It's time to go." I propped myself on my elbows and continued to stare at her. I thought to myself. *Where in the hell does she think we're going? I told her I am not going to school.*

"What time is it Aunt Mary?"

"Six o'clock now get up!"

"For what?"

"You are going to school."

"No, I am not going to school."

"Yes you are! Get up!" She came over, grabbed my arm and pulled me out of the bed. I tried to grab onto the side of the bed to stop her. She snatched me up and firmly demanded I get dressed. "Don't upset your brother. You have to go to school, and that's all there is to it."

Aunt Mary was right. Khalid would become upset if I am upset. He used my emotions to define his own. If I was happy, he was happy. If I cried, Khalid cried. So I knew if I put on a show, Khalid would join me.

"Come on Khalid; it's time to get up. You're going

13

to school." She woke Khalid.

"Thandisha, are we going to school?"

"Yeah, I guess so." I didn't want to upset Khalid. Besides, Aunt Mary was serious. We were going to school.

Aunt Mary made oatmeal and toast with a bowl of fresh fruit on the side. We ate breakfast in silence.

"Thandisha, do you need help with your hair?"

"No, I can do it myself." I didn't want anyone's hands to touch me but my momma's.

"Well it's time to leave the table and get dressed, so we won't be late." A wide smile covered her face; I hoped she was not expecting one in return. I did not see anything to smile about. I was not ready to go to school and really didn't care if I ever went again. I wanted to stay safely tucked away in my room with my brother forever.

We took Khalid to his new school first. I did not want to upset him, so I smiled a lot pretending I was okay. I wanted him to believe he would be okay. Actually, if he felt anything close to the way I felt, it was amazing he went inside of the building. Surprisingly, Khalid was smiling when he got out of the car and gleefully waved goodbye to me and Aunt Mary. I felt betrayed. After we dropped Khalid off, it was my turn.

"Thandie, you will be okay. I know it has been hard for you and your brother, but you will be okay." I ignore Aunt Mary. At this moment she is not exactly my favorite person in the world. I sat staring out of the passenger side window holding my book bag tightly to my chest.

The building was humongous. It looked more like a prison than a school. I sat in the car with my head turned away from Aunt Mary; I didn't want her to see me cry. I wiped the tears away from my eyes and opened the car door. I wanted to step out of the car and run, but I knew Aunt Mary could probably catch me. I grabbed my book bag and got out of the car without saying goodbye. I walked in the building and followed the directions to the

14

guidance counselor's office as Aunt Mary instructed. I have never gone to school alone on the first day before. Momma always came with me on the first day.

The guidance counselor gave me a class schedule, a school map, and sent me on my way. I was on my own. I walked down the hall looking straight ahead with my belongings held tight against my chest. I didn't want to see faces, and I didn't want anyone to see my face. I wanted to melt and disappear into the yellow, cinder block walls. I wanted to become an inanimate object that did not feel, like the round, brown clock that hanged lopsided above the counselor's desk. The halls were crowded. I was scared. I wanted to go into the bathroom and stay until it was time to go home until I saw Ayanna.

"Hey girl," Ayanna acted as if we were the best of friends.

"Hi," I didn't look at her. I continued to walk staring straight ahead with my book bag held tightly against my chest.

"Where are you going? What class do you have this period?" She grabbed my schedule from my hand. "Okay let me see. Girl, we have English together; come on let's go." She took my arm and dragged me down the hall.

That was five years ago. Ayanna and I have been friends since. She has been my anchor to the outside world for the past five years. My grandmother says that we are conjoined twin because we do everything together. In junior high school, we were inseparable. Now in high school we are still best friends. I love Ayanna and Ayanna loves me because I love her. I thank God for this relationship. She never asks questions about my momma and daddy, but I am sure she knows. The fact she never asks is an indication she knows.

Ayanna is very popular in high school. I stand in the background. She is a cheerleader; she runs track. I go to the games to see her cheer, and I go to the track to see her run. I attend church with her some Sundays to see her sing in the youth choir. Ayanna is the younger of two children. Her life reminds me of what my life would have been if I still had my parents. She is happy and enjoying her life. I was happy enjoying her life that is until I met Andreas. Before Andreas, I didn't really have a life of my own. My life was Ayanna's life and whatever made her happy made me happy.

When I first met Andreas, I felt like he was an angel sent directly to me from God. He is tall and muscular with perfect, white teeth. He had a fellow classmate by the collar pressed against the wall. There was something about the way he gritted his teeth that caught my attention; they were pearly white, straight and perfect.

"Come on man, let me go." The guy was not resisting.

"Hell no! If you fuck with my sister again, it's me and you!" Drake, another classmate, tried to separate them.

"Come on man, let him go! You don't need to get in trouble. Your sister gone do what she gone do." Drake manages to pull him away, and they walk down the hall passing me as I stood by my locker. He didn't notice me; I started playing detective. Andreas was the subject of my investigation. I learned he is a senior; and as fine as he is, he didn't play school sports. He lives on the south side of Atlanta in Zelphie Phillips Homes, one of the toughest government housing neighborhoods in Atlanta. It is rumored the police will not go there. Andreas Booker works after school for one of the factories to help take care of his mother and younger sister, Jazmyne. I dreamed about him day and night, and he does not know I exist. I have already decided when we will marry, the number of bridesmaids, grooms, and the number of little Andreases I will have; and he doesn't even know my name or that I occupy a spot on the planet.

Ayanna, who was conducting an investigation of

16

her own, found he did not have a girlfriend. One day during lunch, she invited him to our table. I begged her not to, but she wouldn't listen.

"Thandisha, I am tired of your ass asking me about the damn boy; it's time y'all met." She stood and motioned for him to come to our table. I tried to pull her back down to her seat. I grabbed her arm, and she quickly snatched away.

"Oh my God, he is coming." Initially, I couldn't talk. He sat down at the table; I noticed his arms were very muscular. He looked like a grown man as opposed to a high school senior.

"Hey, I'm Andreas." I was mute. "Ayanna said you wanted to meet me." I looked down at the table too afraid to look up. Ayanna nudged my side with her elbow.

"Oh yeah I've been seeing you around, and I wanted to meet you." I looked up and was blinded by his pearly white teeth. I was so mesmerized I didn't see a complete face but a blurred image. I tried to control my breathing because I felt as if I would pass out at any moment.

Before I could continue the conversation, his classmate, Drake, came over.

"Hey man what's up?" Andreas stood and turned around to greet Drake. "Hey I'll see you around, and what did you say your name was?" I couldn't speak; I smiled and stared at him until he was out of my view.

"Come on Thandisha; let's go before we're late to class." I walked to class with Andreas on my brain. I sat through English, Math, Science, and Social Studies daydreaming about him. I saw him in the senior hall while changing classes for about two months. He would speak to me but that was it. He did not engage in conversation with me or show an interest in me.

I didn't have a conversation with him again until I saw him at Ayanna's backyard pool party. My grandmother is strict; I couldn't wear a swimsuit. I felt awkward as everyone was dressed for the occasion but me. Fortunately, I found a pair of almost too short shorts, so I did not look like a complete odd ball. He glided over to me. I looked down at his muscular thighs and bulging calves up to his six-pack stomach and then at his pearly whites.

"Hey Thandisha, what's up girl?" I couldn't say anything. All I could do was smile.

"Where is your swimsuit?" He looked down at my legs.

"I'm too skinny to wear a swimsuit in public." I lied; I couldn't very well tell him my grandmother wouldn't allow me to wear one.

"You're small framed, but you're not skinny. You're what I call slim-fine. I bet you look good as hell in a swimsuit." He looked at me from head to toe. I didn't say anything; I couldn't say anything, so I smiled. Then the DJ played my favorite slow jam. I surprised myself by asking him to dance.

"Sure but Thandisha I have never slow danced before." I was shocked; I imagined he was mature and experienced in all things that had to do with males and females.

"Well I remember hearing someone say you simply sway to the rhythm of the music." We swayed side to side. I placed my arms around his bulging shoulders. His big hands felt light as a feather on my waist. The song was over, but my face was still buried in his chest. He stepped back and away from me.

"You're a good dancer." I was still mute. I simply smiled. I remember this night as if it were yesterday. I felt happy and sad at the same time. I know that sounds oxymoronic. I couldn't explain this feeling. I walked back to the table and sat with Ayanna; he followed me.

"You want something to drink?"

"Sure," he glided to the refreshment table. I didn't take my eyes off of him until he was back at the table and sitting next to me.

"Thandisha, you belong to someone?" I didn't know what to say; I simply smiled.

"No, she doesn't have a boyfriend." Ayanna intervened just in time.

"That's good." He smiled. It was getting late; I knew I had to be home by 11:00, but I didn't want to leave.

"Girl, it's 10:45; we told your grandmother you would be home before 11:00. Come on let's go; I'll walk you half of the way home." Ayanna is always responsible. She stays out of trouble. I guess that's why Grandma was happy when we became friends. Ayanna is my first and only friend since I lived with my grandmother. Other children in the neighborhood simply stared at me. They were never mean, but it was obvious to me they knew about That Day. I didn't blame them or become angry with them. I am sure they were afraid to befriend me. Maybe they were afraid my daddy would kill them or their mommas. They stayed away and simply didn't talk to me, but not Ayanna. I was mean to her and rebuffed her initial invitation for friendship. But when I saw her on my first day at the new school, she was exactly what I needed. If it were not for her, I probably would not have made it through the first day.

"Where do you live?"

"Around the corner."

"You want me to walk you home?" I stand, start walking, and he follows me. I am so mesmerized I do not tell Ayanna I am leaving. I try to walk as slowly as I can to savor the moment.

"You live in a nice neighborhood."

"Thanks," Grandma took some of the insurance money and paid off her house. Momma was so smart. She had over $200,000 in life insurance plus a good bit in a savings account. She left Khalid and me $50,000.00 each, but we cannot touch it until we are twenty years old.

"You're very pretty Thandisha." When we reach the driveway, I want him to kiss me; instead, he gently reaches for my hand. "I would like to spend more time with you."

"Thandie! Thandie!" I look over my shoulder; Grandma is standing in the threshold of the door in her robe and slippers. She does not have to say anything. I know she means for me to come inside of the house.

"Coming Grandma."

"Hello Ma'am." She quickly slams the door without acknowledging Andreas' greeting.

"Thandie?" He smiles torturing me with his beautiful, pearly white teeth.

"That's what my grandmother and brother call me. Actually, when my brother was small, he could not say Thandisha, so he would call me Thandie."

"Well Thandie what are you doing tomorrow?"

"I'm not sure. I have to see what Ayanna says, but we will probably go to the mall and catch a movie."

"What time? Would you like for me to give you guys a ride?"

"I would love that, but Grandma doesn't allow me to get into cars with boys." I wait for him to say something about the strictness my grandmother imposes, but he does not.

"If you want to meet us at the mall, we will be there probably around 11:00."

"I'll meet you guys at the Taco Stand say around 12:00."

The door opens again. We both look at one another and smile.

"Thandie, get in here!"

"Coming."

"Now!" I look at him.

"I'll see you tomorrow." I walk up the driveway. Grandma stands at the door waiting for me.

"Who is that boy?"

"Andreas," I walk into the house and pass Grandma who is still standing in the threshold of the door. I really do not want to elaborate on Andreas. I know she will find something wrong with him.

"How old is he?"

"He is 18 Grandma." I am trying to get away from her. I walk down the hall to my room. She follows me into my room and continues to ask questions.

"He looks like a grown man."

"Grandma, he is18."

"Where does he live?"

"Down the street."

"I have never seen him in the neighborhood." She is getting on my nerves; I really am not in the mood for twenty questions.

"He works after school Grandma; that's why you never see him. Besides, you never come outside anyway." I know not to tell her he lives in the projects; she would go nuts. She stands in the hall outside of my room. I walk pass her and go to the bathroom. I turn on the water, so I can get away from her. I am careful not to wash both of my hands. I want to smell the scent of his hands on mine. I look forward to tomorrow, so I can see him again. I go to bed praying I will see him in my dreams.

When I wake up, Khalid is laying at the bottom of my bed. Khalid is 13 almost 14 years old. He hasn't been able to sleep all night alone since we lived with Grandma. Grandma used to punish him for crying when it was time to go to bed. I made a deal with Khalid when we first moved to Grandma's house; after Grandma went to bed, I would come to his room and get him, so he could go to sleep in my bed with me. I used this to bribe him all of the time. When he wouldn't do as I asked, I would threaten to make him sleep alone in his own bed. The truth is I needed him close to me probably more than he needed me.

When I open my eyes again and look over my

shoulder, he is laying behind me with his head propped in his hands.

"Morning."

"Morning." I fall back on the pillow.

"Did you have a good time at the party last night Thandie?"

"Yeah I had a great time. I talked to a really nice guy. I think I'm in love Khalid."

"I'm going to tell Grandma."

"You better not!"

"Thandie, can you take me to the arcade today?"

"No, I am going to the mall with Ayanna."

"There is an arcade in the mall."

"No, I'm not taking you." I get up and push him off my bed. He hits the floor hard. I proceed to make my bed. He gets up from the floor with his arms folded across his chest.

"If you don't take me with you, I'm telling Grandma you're in love with a boy." I hit him on his shoulder with my fist.

"Grandma, I have something to tell you." He walks towards the door threatening to disclose my secret. I grab the back of his T-shirt, pull him back inside of the room, and quickly close the door.

"You better not tell!"

"I'll be ready in twenty minutes." He stands with his arms folded across his chest; an annoying smirk covers his face. I am mad as hell. My little brother is now bribing me, and he has me.

Ayanna and I walk down the street to the bus stop; Khalid follows close behind with a victorious smile. He does not seem to mind we are totally ignoring him and excluding him from our jokes and laughter.

Although the bus takes its usual route, it seems as if it is taking hours for us to get to the mall as opposed to the usual thirty minutes. I am anxious. I look forward to seeing

Andreas again. When we finally arrive at the mall, Ayanna and I take Khalid to the arcade. I actually enjoy the arcade. It is filled with teens, but I am uncomfortable with Khalid's new found power, I cannot enjoy it. I do not want to play my favorite games.

Ayanna is engulfed in a conversation with Darryl, a boy in our chemistry class. They are playing video games, but I am busy obsessing over my anger at my little brother taking control to join in their conversation. It is 11:50; it seems as if it is taking hours for the clock to reach 12:00.

"Come on Ayanna, let's go." She brushes me away. I fold my arms across my chest and roll my eyes; I am mad as hell. I want her to leave Darryl and come with me to the Taco Stand. She flips her hand again, turns her head, and continues to talk to Darryl. I sit on the bench outside of the arcade. I look at my watch. It is 12:04. I am increasingly angry and irritated with Ayanna. I walk back inside of the arcade. Ayanna is playing Trooper with Darryl standing close behind her with his arms around her waist.

"Ayanna!"

"What?"

"It's 12:04."

"So?"

"So let's go; Andreas is meeting me at the Taco Stand at 12:00."

"He isn't coming here to see me fool; he's coming to see you. You go ahead; I'll stay here with Khalid." It was 12:05. I walk Olympic style to the Taco Stand until I reach the entrance to the food court. I slowly look around the corner, and I see him sitting at a table sipping on a soft drink. I use my fingers to brush my hair back before I turn the corner. When he sees me, he smiles showing all of his perfect, white teeth.

"You want something to eat?" He stands and greets me, as I reach the table.

"No thank you; I am not hungry." I lie; I have not

eaten all day. I was too excited; I didn't eat breakfast. I am actually famished.

"How about a soda?"

"Cool that will be nice."

"What kind?"

"Strawberry," he walks to the counter and orders the food. I watch him from the time he leaves until he returns to the table with four tacos, a taco salad and a burrito.

"Are you going to eat all of that?"

"Girl, this is a snack." He smiles. *God those pearly white teeth.* I laugh. "Why don't you help me eat?" He removes the wrapper from the burrito, and puts a small portion inside of my mouth; some of the refried beans fall on the side of my face. He quickly takes a napkin and wipes the beans off of my face so gently I barely feel the napkin touch my skin.

"So what movie are you going to see?"

"I don't know something mild since my little brother came with us."

"You're very pretty Thandisha." He sits still and stares at me. I blush so hard all 28 of my teeth are showing.

"Thanks you ain't so bad yourself." The words are coming now. I can actually speak.

"How old is your brother?"

"He is 13, but he will be turning 14 in a couple of days."

"You only have one brother?" He looks surprised.

"Yes I have one brother; it's just me and Khalid."

"What about you?"

"I have four brothers and three sisters. I'm the oldest at home. You know my sister, Jazmyne, don't you?"

"Yes, I have English with her."

"She told me." My heart flutters. Now, I know he is interested because he is discussing me with his sister.

"She says you're very smart and one of the uppity girls."

"I would not say I am uppity." I laugh.

"Hey ain't anything wrong with that. If you got it, you got it. Me, I don't have it, but I am trying like hell to get it. I work the second shift full-time, Monday through Friday. I'm trying to get my own business."

"Really!" I try to sound interested.

"Hell yeah. You don't make money working for the man. The man gets rich, and you still struggle."

"What kind of business do you want?"

"A lawn service. Oh it is more than cutting grass. See I'm taking horticulture at school. I have four commercial clients already. I'm trying to save up for a riding lawn mower, so I can get some big accounts. I want a zipper. Have you ever seen one?" He is so excited he does not allow time for an answer. "Well they go about 30 mph. You can cut a football field in about an hour. That's what I am saving for." He sits back in his chair with his head cradled in his hands. "So what do you want to do when you graduate?"

"I want to be an artist. Grandma says it is a waste of time. She says I'm going to college."

"So you can draw?"

"Oh yeah. I drew all of the art in our house. I've even sold paintings to members of our bible class."

"I'm not saying anything against your grandmother, but I don't see anything wrong with wanting to be an artist if you have the talent."

"Really?" I smile. No one shows genuine interest when I speak of my goals not even Ayanna. Though I tell her I want to be an artist, she brushes it off. She has already made plans for us to be college roommates and pledge the same sorority. She hasn't decided on which sorority she wants us to pledge; she will decide when we get to college.

"Hey look at Cynthia St. James, Charles Bibbs those are some pretty cool artists. My favorite is Paul Goodnight." He actually knows about art. I am impressed.

"I love DT Turman."

"I never heard of him."

"Grandma bought one of his original paintings for my 15th birthday. He's great. He uses raised oil paint mixed with fine granules of sand splattered on canvas."

"Wow I'd love to see it." For some reason, I didn't picture him being the kind who enjoys art. Though he has a gentle spirit, he looks hard. I think it's his eyes. They look old and kind of weary as if they have seen a lot of pain and disappointment.

"Hey Bro, what it is?"

"What's up?" It is Jazmyne, his sister.

"Give me some money Bro; hell I need to get my damn nails done." She is dressed in a bright orange, tight fitting jumpsuit, bright orange matching shoes, and big tarnished, gold plated, hoop earrings. Grandma would call her a ghetto hoochie.

"I told you to stop putting that fake shit on your nails."

"Niggah, just give me the damn money." She props herself on one leg. He gives her twenty dollars; she smiles showing three gold teeth in the front of her mouth. Her gold teeth look odd and off centered. I have seen people with one gold tooth. I have also seen them with two, but I have never seen three. I stare into her mouth as she talks trying to figure out the pattern, but I realize there is no pattern.

"You need to tell Keekee to get a damn job." She sucks her teeth, rolls her eyes, and walks away.

"Damn that girl drives me crazy. This boyfriend that boyfriend and that damn Keekee; I don't even want to go there." He rolls his eyes toward the ceiling and shakes his head. "How many boyfriends do you have?"

"I have never had a boyfriend."

"Baby, you don't have to play me like that. You are way too fine not to have a boyfriend."

"Seriously, I've never had a boyfriend." I don't understand why he finds that so surprising. I mean I am not ugly, but no one ever talks to me except for Ayanna. I always thought people were too afraid to talk to me because of That Day.

"That's hard to believe, but you don't look like a liar to me."

"I need to check on my brother." I look at my watch; it is 1:33. We stand at the same time. I wait for him while he cleans the table. He gently places his hand on the middle of my back and escorts me through the maze of tables and out of the food court.

"Where is Khalid?" Ayanna is sitting in front of the arcade on the bench with Darryl.

"He is still in the arcade winning tickets trying to get a prize." I walk into the arcade; he follows me. Khalid is playing a video game with a long line of tickets flowing from the machine.

"Khalid!"

"Yeah?" He never looks up.

"Come on it's time to go."

"I'm not ready."

"I don't care. Let's go." I look down at the tickets running out of the machine and notice another bag full of tickets next to him.

"Boy, did you spend all of your money?"

"Not yet."

"How much did you spend?"

"Thandie, will you leave me alone?" I snatch him away from the game. He jerks away from me. When he touches the button again, the game ends. "Thandie, look what you did!" He sits on the floor and rolls all of his tickets into a doughnut shaped circle. He smiles from ear to ear as if he has found gold. He turns, looks at me, and then looks at Andreas. He doesn't speak to Andreas; he looks at him with a long stare.

"Hey man what's up?" Khalid takes his tickets and walks away.

"Khalid, come here!" He continues to walk as if he does not hear me. "Now!" He slowly walks over to me.

"What?"

"Let's go and get something to eat. I know you're hungry."

"I want to play some more; I'm not hungry." Andreas reaches into his pocket and pulls out five dollars. "No thank you," he looks at the money and walks back to his game and insert more coins into the machine.

"Khalid, I'll be sitting on the bench in front of the arcade entrance. When you finish, come out here." Andreas and I sit on a bench, across from Ayanna and Darryl. He tells me his story and shares his dreams. I listen; at the time, I wasn't able to tell him mine. I have not dealt with my story yet. I still have nightmares about That Day. I made a conscious decision a long time ago not to deal with it, not to think about That Day. I rationalize if I don't think about it then the memories can no longer hurt me. I didn't realize tucking the memories away, deep inside of me, without dealing with them almost cost me my life. It is only now I know life is 360 degrees, a full circle. You have to complete the circle. There is no escape. There is no diversion from feeling the pain. The pain cannot lay tucked away forever. The memory will resurface, sometimes at the most inopportune time, and if you don't have the tenacity to deal with them, they could kill you. Not quick, but slow and painful. You have to look at them veraciously, and if you don't, you will have to go back 360 degrees until you truthfully face them.

"Andreas is such a unique name. I have never heard of a black person with that name."

"It comes from my daddy. He's the best gambler in the world." He smiles as if this were an admirable trait.

"Are you like your daddy?" His smile quickly disappears.

"I don't really know because I try like hell to be the opposite. I work hard; I help take care of my mother and younger sister. I don't have a bunch of baby mommas. I figure my dad has to be pretty sick. He says he loves women, but I don't see it. I figure if you really like women, you would want to savor one particular woman. You love everything about one particular woman. Besides, you all are too complex to deal with more than one at a time."

"What do you mean by complex?" I laugh, but I am slightly annoyed at the generalization.

"I have three sisters and a mother. Women are something to deal with. Once you think you know what it takes to satisfy a woman, she changes to something else. Women are very hard to please." He pauses and looks directly at me. "Are you hard to please?"

No one ever asks me anything. So I really do not know how to answer this question. All of my decisions are made for me, or people make decisions and do not care how they affect me.

"I don't know. No one ever told me I was hard to please; no one ever said I wasn't."

"Thandie, I'm hungry." Khalid walks behind the bench and taps me on the shoulder.

"Okay wait a minute." He waits all of three seconds.

"Thandie, I'm thirsty." I look over Andreas' shoulder. His arm is around me. Khalid walks in front of the bench. "Man, get your hands off of my sister!" He gives Andreas a mean, nasty look.

"Okay bro. I'm sorry; I don't mean any disrespect." Andreas moves his arm.

"Let's go Thandie!"

"Sit down Khalid, or I will never take you to the arcade again!" He sits down on the bench next to me pouting. I try to ignore him. I am embarrassed. Khalid is 13 two days shy of 14, but he is very immature. I know other 13 year olds that are much more independent. I have always tried to be patient with him. I believe he regressed about five years after That Day. There are times when he acts his age, but at other times, I swear he acts as if he is nine or ten years old.

"Hey bro, do you want me to walk down to the Taco stand with you? That is if you like tacos. If not we can go someplace else?" Khalid's demeanor suddenly changes; a big smile covers his face.

"Give me some money Thandie." I reach in my pocket and give Khalid five dollars. Khalid and Andreas leave me and Ayanna on the bench in front of the arcade. When they return, Darryl is gone, and Ayanna and I are sitting on the bench in front of the arcade.

"Girl it is 3:00; we missed the movies."

"Yeah I know; we better get ready to catch the bus."

"I can take you home."

"We don't have to be home until 6:30." I told Grandma I was going to the movies. If we come back too early, she will know I lied.

"We can go to the park, and then I'll drop you guys off at your bus stop." This is a good idea; we still have time to hang out before Grandma expects us home. Besides, I really want to spend more time with Andreas.

"We walk to the end of the parking lot to his car. He drives a candy apple red, 67 Thunderbird. As old as it is, it does not have dents or scratches, and it is clean inside and out. He walks to the passenger side of the car and opens the door for me. I have never ridden in a car with a boy. I feel grown up and mature. I reach over the seat and unlock the rear door for Khalid and Ayanna.

"Put your seat belt on Khalid." He rolls his eyes and fastens his seat belt. He used to do everything I told him to do without rebuttal, but now he is beginning to challenge me.

We drive by his home in Zelphie Phillips Downs. His grandmother's apartment is two buildings over from his, and a cousin stays two doors down from the grandmother. There is what looks like a thousand children playing outside. Women, young and old, are sitting on their porches, and a couple of men with worn faces stand bent over looking under the hood of a rusty, old car that appears too old to consider repairing. There are a lot of people that live in his apartment complex. I have never seen so many people in one place before.

We drive onto highway 85 then on highway 20; I can see the outline of the park from the interstate. It is beautiful from this view. The trees are green. From this angle, the litter blends in well with the landscape. The abuse of the park is undetectable until you get up close. Then you can see the park's vulnerabilities. The remnants of paper bags half filled with food are obviously litter and not part of the landscape. A faint scent of urine hovers in the air. I really don't understand how people can abuse something so naturally beautiful. There are empty trashcans all over the park, yet the landscape is filled with litter.

In spite of being surrounded by litter, I enjoy this time with Andreas. We find an old, oak tree that generously provides shade from the sun. We park under the tree and listen to reggae music. Reggae really is not my thing, but I am enjoying Andreas' company.

Khalid has fallen asleep; we leave him in the car. Ayanna finds some people she knows from church and leaves Andreas and me alone. We sit on a picnic table next to the car. I sit next to him and stare into his eyes. He kisses me without warning. It feels good. His lips are soft and damp but not too wet. I have never kissed a boy before

31

and am surprised at how natural this is for me.

"I've wanted to do that all day." He smiles while licking his lips. I could stay with him all day. He is fun and kind. He is easy to talk to and very considerate. His conversation is not the kind of conversation I am accustomed to. He is totally different from anyone I have ever known.

I am having fun, but I have to get home before it is too late. I see Ayanna and yell for her to come back to the car. Khalid is still asleep when we reach the car. He alternates between watching me and watching the road. I am glad he is a good driver because as often as he glances at me, he does not drive off the road. He drops us off at the subdivision entrance at 6:45; we are late. I coach Khalid on what to tell Grandma. *The movie was good and scary. We went to see Dinosaur Horror. It was about big scary dinosaurs. It was so scary; I can't talk about it.* When we reach the driveway, I remind him one more time what to say to Grandma.

"If she asks anything else what are you going to say?"

"Grandma it was so scary; I don't want to talk about it."

"Okay that's good." When we get home, Grandma has already made dinner. I am normally the cook. Grandma never seasons her food. Her food is always bland. Grandma cooks out of obligation. You cannot taste the love in her food. She made fried chicken, rice, and broccoli. The chicken tastes like chicken and flour. The rice is crunchy and needs more time to cook. The broccoli is plain, no butter or cheese. I hate her cooking because it makes me miss my momma. Momma enjoyed cooking. You could taste the love in momma's food. She always took her time and seasoned the food perfectly. The table is quiet as usual. We never really talk to each other, and when we do, it was never about anything meaningful. Our conversations are always forced and superficial.

After dinner, I wash dishes, take a shower, and go to my room. I watch television and wait by the phone praying Andreas will call me. I sit on the bed and look in the mirror often glancing at the phone just in case he calls. I observe my facial features. I am a mixture of momma and daddy. My skin is paper bag brown like daddy. My hair is jet black and thick as a rope like momma. I was so glad when Grandma finally allowed me to chemically straighten my hair. Now if I could only convince her to allow me to cut it. It does not have a style. I always wear it in a bun in the back of my head. I put a rubber band in my hair to make a ponytail then twist the ends into a bun. Grandma once said when I took my hair down, I look like momma. After she said this, I did not wear my hair loose again for years.

"Oh my God Thandisha, you are waiting by the phone." I pick up the phone on the first ring; it's Ayanna. I can hear the television show Grandma is watching in the den. I hate when she listens to my conversation before she hangs up.

"Grandma, I have it." She knows the phone is for me. The only person she ever talks to on the phone is Aunt Mary, and that is not often because Aunt Mary is usually here.

"Thandisha, today was so much fun."

"Yeah Ayanna I had a ball."

"That Darryl is a trip with his fine self."

"He ain't fine as Andreas."

"Child please, Andreas is not that fine; he's too black."

"What do you mean too black?" Ayanna's phone clicks.

"Girl, that's Devontae. Ooh I love him."

"I thought you loved Darryl."

"I do."

"Well you can't love both of them."

"Why not? I am not trying to marry nobody. Thandisha, we are in high school. We're supposed to have fun." My phone beeps. I quickly press the flash button to answer the incoming call.

"Hello."

"Hello, may I speak to Thandisha?"

"This is she."

"Hey, what's up?" His voice is low and deep, yet soothing.

"Nothing I am just sitting in my room watching television."

"I was waiting on you to call me. I decided maybe you wouldn't call, so I called you. Were you busy?"

"No, I told you; I was watching television. I was waiting, kind of hoping you would call." He laughs.

"I really had a nice time today. I really dig you girl."

"I kind of like you too." We talk on the phone for over an hour when my line beeps. It is Ayanna.

"Girl, I am sitting and waiting to see how long it would take you to call me back. You know you are through." She laughs, but I can tell she is annoyed.

"I'm sorry Ayanna. I'll call you back in 20 minutes." Twenty minutes turn into an hour. I cannot get enough of Andreas.

Forty-Five Degrees

Everything in my life has changed. In fact, it is hard for me to remember when my life was not like this. I feel as if I have been an orphan forever. My other life is buried deep inside of my memory, and I can't touch it. I can't go back that far to reach it. This new life is odd and peculiar. I feel as if I will wake up at any moment and find I have been dreaming. The foundation is shaky in this new life. My life does not feel real. It is as if I am looking in a mirror or an audience member in a theatrical play watching the different characters in my life performs. I have no friends in my life from before That Day. Perhaps if I did, they can remind me who I used to be. I have totally forgotten. I have not gone back to my old house since That Day. I don't know what became of that house.

I found a way to survive in this new life. With the exception of my relationship with my brother, all of my relationships are superficial. It did not matter because I need the people in my life to keep me anchored. My sanity is shaky. Ayanna is my superficial best friend. She is happy with our friendship because she is the center of my attention. Living Ayanna's life is appealing to me because I don't have to live my own life. I do not have to think about That Day or myself. I don't think I would have survived if I didn't have Ayanna; she is the center of my attention. Actually, she is the center of everyone's attention including her own.

She is definitely the center of Mr. Williams' attention even at the expense of her older sister, Dee. Ayanna's father gives her a lot of extras. She has the best of everything. Clothes, jewelry you name it; Ayanna has it. She says it is one of the perks in being the baby of the family. Her parents are still together. Her oldest sister, Dee, and her two children moved back home after a nasty divorce. I am sure Dee feels like a failure. Ayanna has a way of making all of Dee's faults known. In spite of her self-centered nature, I love Ayanna. I know her significance to my life.

Ayanna's home has a peaceful ambiance. I enjoy visiting Ayanna's house. I believe if That Day had not happened, my family would have been like Ayanna's family. Ayanna is very close to her father. She is a straight A student. Her primary goal in life is to make her daddy proud. Their relationship is beautiful to me. It is as if he is a king and she is his princess. When her father drives us around to the many events Ayanna is involved in, he always opens the door for Ayanna to get in the car and opens the door for her to get out of the car. Ayanna does not consider this treatment special or out of the ordinary. She expects it.

Ayanna's mother is like a shadow. Not only is she in the background in Ayanna's life, but she is in the background of Mr. Williams' life as well. Ayanna rarely speaks of her mother. I think it is shameful. She obviously does not understand the special nature of a mother. I pray she will never feel my loss. I enjoy sitting in the kitchen talking to Mrs. Williams. It wasn't often I spoke to her. Ayanna would always want to go into her room when Mrs. Williams came into the kitchen, our normal hang out. She acts as if she does not want me interacting with her mother as if she is ashamed of her mother. I do not like the way she speaks to her mother. It is as if Ayanna is the mother, and Mrs. Williams is the child. The sad thing about their relationship is Mrs. Williams appears to accept it. I don't remember my mother being as docile as Mrs. Williams, but her soft nature is very appealing to me. She is inviting and kind, and I often want wrap my arms around her skinny, frail body. I never did it, but I always wanted to embrace Mrs. Williams, and I would sometimes imagine what it would feel like for her to hold me close with her arms tightly wrapped around me.

Grandma says women make the best friends. Though our relationship is superficial and centered on Ayanna, she is my best friend, and I love her. Not the way Grandma loves Aunt Mary. Grandma never told us she and Aunt Mary love each other the way a man and a woman love each other, but we know. Aunt Mary and Grandma have loved each other for years even before I was born. Their relationship began shortly after my mother was born. I never met my grandfather. Grandma never spoke of him. I have a picture of him with momma when momma was little girl. But I never saw him face to face. I have never seen Grandma love a man.

Aunt Mary never spends the night. They do not display physical affection, but I know. It is the way they look at each other. Aunt Mary is very masculine not because of her hair. Grandma wears a short natural too, but Aunt Mary does everything like a man. Grandma is tall and slim like momma and me. Aunt Mary is just as tall as Grandma, but she is heavier. She always wears jeans and male shirts. Aunt Mary never carries a purse. She carries a man's wallet that fits snuggly in her back pocket. Grandma is more feminine. She carries a purse, and unlike Aunt Mary, she is soft and graceful. She is very meticulous about her appearance. Aunt Mary and Grandma's relationship is beautiful to me. They are lovers and best friends. They are very respectful of their differences, and they equally embrace their commonalities. Grandma does not appear as comfortable with their relationship as Aunt Mary. Maybe it is because Khalid and I are now living with her. I think Aunt Mary has been a lesbian forever. She was probably born this way, as there is not a feminine bone in her body.

In fact, she is often mistaken as a man.

Though Grandma is my blood relative, I feel more comfortable with Aunt Mary. She makes me feel I am okay. She harnesses all of my talents. She loves me and loves my art. She frames all of my paintings. Aunt Mary makes me feel it is okay I do not want to go to college. Grandma plans for me to attend college after I graduate from high school. I think it is because she wants me out of the house.

Grandma and Khalid get along great. But Grandma and I are always guarded with one another. She never says anything mean. She is not unkind, but it takes a lot of effort for us to communicate. I wish Grandma was more like Aunt Mary. I enjoy doing special things for Aunt Mary because she always notices the most latent things in me. She discovered my gift for cooking; and because of this, I enjoy making special desserts for her. I make pastries, cheesecakes and any kind of dessert they make in the bakery. She always brags on my cooking. When members of our bible class comment on her weight gain, she attributes the extra pounds to me. Sometimes bible class members place orders for my sweets and pay me to make them.

Once a week, Aunt Mary orders a cake or pastries for someone on her job. Aunt Mary says I am a natural artist, but Grandma is determined I am going to college. I could go to college. My grades are good, but I want to go to culinary school to master the art of cooking, and I am determined I will be a renowned visual artist. My paintings are abstract. I never enter competitions, but I know my art is prize winning. My art comes from my soul.

At times, I feel as if Grandma is jealous of my relationship with Aunt Mary. Aunt Mary does not have expectations of me. She never pressures me to be anything or anyone I do not want to be. Our only disagreement is my choice of Ayanna as a best friend. Aunt Mary acts as if she hates Ayanna. She complains that Ayanna bosses me around too much. She refers to Ayanna as *"the Bitch."* Grandma loves Ayanna because she is Grandma's idea of what a girl should be. She constantly comments on Ayanna's stylish clothes and modern hairstyles. Aunt Mary gets angry with Grandma when she makes comparisons between Ayanna and me, as she often does. She wants me to have Ayanna's outgoing personality and her confident disposition, but I do not have those qualities. Maybe I used to, but I don't have them anymore.

I do not feel Grandma's love. I know she loves me. She has to; I am her only daughter's daughter. But I feel she hates me for being my daddy's daughter. Although I cannot remember a lot of detail, I do remember a strong feeling for daddy. I believe we were very close. I remember I was labeled a daddy's girl, and I remember every Friday he would bring Khalid and me presents.

Initially, I tried to please Grandma. I tried to make sure the house was always clean. I was extra careful to season the food properly when I cooked. No matter what I did, it was never good enough; whereas, Aunt Mary is simply cool about everything. I love Grandma in spite of how she makes me feel. I love her because we share the same grief. I love her because her daughter was my mother. Momma was her only child, and I know she is still in pain. Sometimes at night I can still hear her crying, especially on June 9, momma's birthday, but we never talk about That Day. Everyone came to their own conclusions and made their own reality.

I often worry about Khalid. He has no male role model. I have been hearing people talk about black boys needing good, male role models, and I am concerned. This is one of the reasons I am glad I met Andreas. Aunt Mary is masculine, and she can shoot a basketball as good as any man. Aunt Mary is not a man, but she is the closest thing to a male role model Khalid had until I met Andreas.

Andreas is definitely something good in my life. He makes me feel good. I feel alive again. I enjoy talking to him. Unlike most of my relationships with people, my relationship with him was real from the start. I am very comfortable with him. Although he does most of the talking, he is not self-centered. He often asks questions about me. He is genuinely concerned about my thoughts and feelings. Although I rarely have much to say, he at least asks me questions. Unlike Ayanna, he does not give me the answers to the questions he asks.

Andreas and I are diametrical. Unlike me, he is centered. He knows what he wants. I come from a background of excess; Khalid and I have every material thing we want. With all of the material things I have, I am not anchored. Andreas' family is poor. He works a full-time job to help support his momma and younger sister and still attends school daily. Andreas describes a life full of needs, but he is happy and confident. He knows what he wants to do with his life.

His mother, unlike Grandma, is nice and pleasant. She always answers the phone with a kind voice. His sister, Jazmyne, is a different story. It's hard to believe they are related. Andreas is calm and subtle. Jazmyne is loud like an explosion. Not only does she talk loud, her whole demeanor is very attention getting. She is always over accentuated. Instead of one nose ring, she has two, one in each nostril. She has a gold stud earring in her chin and a silver stud in her tongue. She wears those awful crochet braids; her braids are colorful and move like a mop with the slightest movement of her head. I am not against braids. Actually, I like braids, but the crochet braids are cheap and tacky. I am not trying to put Jazmyne down; we are actually quite similar. Like me, Jazmyne is deprived of something she strongly feels she needs. Unlike me, Jazmyne screams loud for what she needs.

Andreas is very protective of Jazmyne. He is

willing to throw a punch at anyone he considers a threat to
her. He loves Jazmyne the way I love Khalid. Andreas
attempts to be a father figure to Jazmyne just as I am trying
to mother Khalid. I know it's crazy, but sometimes I find
myself jealous of Jazmyne's relationship with Andreas.

.

Ninety Degrees

The summer is excruciatingly hot. I still don't understand how people live without central air. Before meeting Andreas, I spent my summers in the house until sun down, which was usually around 7:00 p.m. The only time I left the house was to visit Ayanna. If her daddy was in his energy conservation mode, I would go home where it was always cold. But this summer is different. I am in love, and I try to get out of the house every chance I can. Grandma is never concerned about my whereabouts as long as I am with Ayanna. So when I asked to go to Phillips High School's graduation with Ayanna, she agreed without her usual twenty questions.

I am happy to see Andreas graduate. He went to a special graduation because he was on a technical path diploma. He graduated from our school too, but he was not in the college bound class, which is what Emaline Bowen High School is notorious for. The school produces more college bound students than any school in the county. The legislators in Andreas' district were concerned because some of the tax dollars from their districts were transferred to our school. So the school had to open its doors to a more economically diverse group of students, which is how the kids in Andreas' neighborhood were able to attend. Emaline Bowen High School does not have a technical tract, so the students that were on a technical tract attended Phillips High School for their specialized technical classes.

He is handsome in his red gown. I have to agree

with Grandma; he does look more mature than the other graduates. Normally, she would not allow me to visit this part of town. She feels inner city Atlanta is too dangerous. Actually, I did not find it any more dangerous than any other part of the city especially since they are now building new buildings throughout the city and renovating the old ones. Actually, they are moving the poor people out of the city and replacing them with an upper middle class to upper class income population. Even the solidly middle class cannot afford to live within the city limit.

Grandma has a class-conscious ideology. She rationalizes that as long as the homes are pretty, the lawns well manicured, and the cars in the driveways are up to date models, the neighborhood is nice. It does not matter what goes on inside of the house or whether or not the people in the house are of good character.

Phillips High School does have a reputation. It is the first school in the city to have armed policemen patrolling the hall, which is strange because Phillips High School never had an instance of gun violence at school. Yes, there are a lot of fights but nothing as extreme as what happened at Shelly G. Reynolds High School last year when a rich white kid shot at everyone in the gymnasium during a Physical Education Class. Everyone knows the reason the police patrol Phillips High School is that the population is one hundred percent black.

After Andreas' graduation, we spend time together almost every day before he goes to work. I am an upcoming senior, so Grandma reluctantly allows me more freedom. I am sure she knows she has no choice, but it drives her crazy. I thought we would be talking about safe sex and birth control the way Ayanna's parents did. Ayanna's father made her mother take her to the teen clinic and gave her the choice of getting birth control pills. Instead, Grandma is nagging the hell out of me about college.

"You're spending too much time with that boy Thandie. How are you going to study for the SAT if you are always with that boy?"

"Grandma, he is nice. You don't have to worry; I'm okay." I hate having these conversations with her because no matter what I say I cannot convince her Andreas is nice and harmless to me. She only allowed him to come inside of the house twice since we've been dating.

"Where did you say he lives again?"

"Around the corner," I hate lying to her, but I do not want more stress from her about Andreas. If I tell her he lives in the projects, she will have a fit. She is proud of the fact she raised my mother without child support or government assistance. She would always say she qualified for assistance, and then she would become angry and say no white man was going to dictate the quality of life she could give her child. Grandma feels people should, *work as long as they have two arms, two legs, and half of a back.*

"Why don't you go over to his house and meet his parents?" I pray she will never call my bluff; I know asking her to meet Andreas' parents is a good way to make her leave me alone. She turns away and washes the same clean glass three times.

"I don't want or need to meet his parents!"

"Why not?" The sick thing about this game I play with Grandma is I didn't want her to meet his parents, but I am mad because she says she didn't want to meet his parents.

"I don't want to because I don't want to." She drops the glass, and it shatters all over the floor. She reaches down and picks the broken glass off of the floor. I continue to clean the table.

"Grandma, I'm going to Ayanna's house. I'll be back before it's too late." I walk out of the door and was half of the way down the street when I see the red thunderbird.

"Hey girl, who you belong too?" He drives the car close to me.

"No one."

"You think I can get those papers?"

"I don't know; it all depends."

"On what?"

"Do you think you can love me forever plus five years?"

"Forever is a long time." He laughs showing his beautiful, white teeth. "Come on baby, get in the car." I slide in the car and lean over to kiss him before fastening my seat belt.

"What do you want to do today?"

"I don't know." Actually being with him is good enough. "I can't stay out too late; Grandma thinks I am at Ayanna's."

"Hell it's too hot to drive around. You want to get a room?"

"Yeah that's cool." Andreas and I have not had real sex; I sometimes lay on my back, and he gets on top of me and grinds his manhood against me until he climaxes. I never worry about getting pregnant; we keep on our underwear. Most of the time we rent a hotel room to be alone. I do not feel comfortable with him coming to my house, and there are too many people who come in and out of his. Today feels different. I am relaxed and very much at ease. We lie on the bed, drink sodas, and eat hamburgers.

"Thandisha, do you remember the first time we went on that pseudo date at the mall?"

"Yeah."

"I asked if you were hungry, and you said no."

"Yeah and so what?"

"Why you lie? I heard your stomach growling loud as hell." I punch him in his chest to stop his laughter. He playfully grabs me and pulls me close. "Girl, I sure do love you."

"I love you too." He kisses me strongly and passionately while rubbing between my thighs. I used to lie still, but I find myself opening my thighs and moving my hips with the rhythms of his hand. He pulls my panties off. I raise my arms as he pulls my dress over my head. He pulls down his shorts and underwear at the same time.

"You have a beautiful body Thandisha." I look at his massive chest and six pack abs. My eyes stop; I do not want to look further. He leans over to the nightstand and pulls a condom from his wallet. He sits on the edge of the bed with his back to me and slips it on. He rolls back on the bed and covers my body with kisses while gently massaging between my thighs. I jerk in pain when he inserts his finger inside of me. "It's okay baby. I'm going to be so gentle with you. I'm going to love you forever plus five years." His kisses are soft and gentle.

"Oh my God! Is all of that going inside of me?" I look down, see his erect penis, and sit straight up in the bed. He smiles and continues to kiss me. I cry out in pain, as he slowly pushes his manhood inside of me. My body is wreathing in pain, but I love him so much; I want to give him all of me.

"Bite my shoulder baby; hold on to me." I sink my teeth deep into his shoulder. Every time he moves, I scream.

Finally, he is inside of me. He moans while slowly gyrating his hips. I cannot move. I am too afraid of breaking something. He moans, makes a funny face, and tightens his eyes before collapsing on top of me.

"I love you Thandisha."

"I love you too." I roll over, lay my head on his chest, and fall asleep...

"Thandisha! Thandisha!" I wake up with him shaking me. "Wake up baby." I am crying; he pulls me close wrapping his legs around my entire body. "It is okay baby whatever it is; it's okay. I'm here." I cry for so long I become light headed. It is 5:30. I know I should be getting home, but I do not want to leave. I feel alive. I want to talk about That Day, but the words will not or cannot come. They are lost in a five-year psychosis that allowed me to exist without feeling. They are hidden somewhere deep inside of me, and I cannot find them. He probes for answers I do not have. I do not know where to start if I could tell him. We sit still and tightly hold one another.

"Thandisha, it's getting late. I'd better get you home." He is right. I am probably already in trouble and should get up and go home.

"I'm not ready to go. I want to stay here with you."

"Okay baby get dressed; I want to show you something before I take you home." We wash up, put on our clothes, and go to the car. We drive to the West End, a very cultural part of Atlanta filled with African American owned shops, restaurants and sturdy antebellum homes. We drive past Abernathy and then turn onto Mayflower Avenue.

"What do you think?"

"Of what?"

"This is it; this is my apartment." We get out of the car and go up the stairs to a studio apartment. The apartment is spacious with hardwood floors, big windows and a small kitchen. The bathroom is small, equipped with a shower, small sink, and toilet.

"I paid for it this morning. I can't get the lights turned on until tomorrow. My sister has to get her bill out of my name."

"It's beautiful Andreas."

"Can I hire you to decorate it?"

"You don't have to hire me."

"You're an artist; you should be paid for your work."

"Please I can draw, and I can cook. I am not an interior decorator." He takes a second key off of the key ring and places it in my hand.

"I don't have to work tomorrow. You think I can get you to come and help me?"

"Yeah, how much do you want to spend?"

"It's just me, so I don't need to spend but a grand or so."

"You have a thousand dollars?" I am shocked; a thousand dollars seems like a lot of money to have at one time.

"I have been working full-time for two years. I should have some money." He locks the apartment door, and we go back to the car.

As usual, Andreas lets me out of the car down the street, and I walk to the house. Grandma opens the door before I can place my key in the keyhole. She grabs a handful of my hair and pulls me into the house. She slaps me so hard my ears ring.

"Where were you?"

"I was with Andreas." I know not to add fuel to the fire and lie. With a hand full of my hair in her hand, she drags me down the hall to my room, and curses me at the same time. She obviously knows I was not with Ayanna.

"Damn you Thandisha! You told me you were going to Ayanna's house."

"I changed my mind." I want to do some cursing of my own, but I cannot say anything; she had me. I did lie.

"How many times have you lied to me?" I can see the hurt on her face, but there is nothing I can do about it. I know she is afraid for me. She has already lost her only child; she does not want to lose another one.

"You will not see that boy again!"

"What are you saying Grandma? I will see him again!"

"You will not! That boy is bad news! He is a bad

influence!"

"I love him, and I will see him again!" I surprise myself by screaming to the top of my lungs professing my love for Andreas.

"Don't you talk to me like that young lady! I have the final word, and you will not see him again!"

"You don't talk to me Grandma; I am just here. You haven't had one honest conversation with me since I have been here. I love him. He talks to me. He cares about what I think. He loves me."

"Shut up girl!" She stands with one hand on her frail hip and the other with a finger pointed in my face. "You better not say another word!"

"Stop Thandie stop!" Khalid stands between me and Grandma. I am more of a mother to Khalid than Grandma, and she hates it. She hates she could not totally infiltrate my relationship with Khalid.

"Khalid, take your bath and get ready for bed! Thandie, don't get on the phone at all. You're grounded!"

"For how long?"

"Maybe until the next millennium!" She walks out and slams my bedroom door. I hear the phone ring and run in the kitchen.

"Thandisha is grounded, and don't call here again!" Andreas and Ayanna are the only people who call me. I know she will not talk to Ayanna harshly. She loves Ayanna. I know it is Andreas.

"Grandma, why did you do that?" I stand in front of her crying with mucous flowing from my nose.

"Girl, you better get out of my face!" I go back to my room and slam my door. After Grandma goes to sleep, I creep to Khalid's room.

"What took you so long Thandie? I'm sleepy."

"Well stay in your own bed." I turn around and leave his room.

"No." He quickly gets out of his bed.

"Shut up and come on if you're coming." I then tip toe into the kitchen to get the phone. I connect the phone in my room. Khalid takes his usual place at the foot of the bed.

He answers the phone on the first ring.

"Thandisha?"

"Yeah it's me." I have been crying. My nasal passages are inflamed.

"Are you okay?"

"Yeah Grandma placed me on restriction. She knows I lied about visiting Ayanna. She knows we were together. I miss you."

"Yeah me too, I guess you can't go tomorrow?"

"I'll meet you at the corner at 9 am."

"I love you."

"I love you too." I hang up the phone and call Ayanna. She answers the phone on the second ring.

"I know this is you Thandisha. Girl, your Grandma came down here mad as hell. Where were you?"

"With Andreas; Guess what? I did it."

"You did what?"

"It."

"No girl! Are you for real? What did it feel like?"

"Ayanna, you never did it before?"

"Hell no." I am surprised. "I flirt with niggahs, but I ain't ready to give up the booty. My daddy would die. What did it feel like?"

"Nothing," I regret telling her. I thought she had done it before.

"Did it hurt?"

"Hell yea, like pure hell, but it was a sweet pain."

"What you mean sweet?" Ayanna laughs.

"I don't know; it was sweet. Oh yeah guess what? Andreas has an apartment."

"Get out of here."

"Yeah. I'm supposed to go shopping with him

tomorrow to buy furniture to decorate it. He said he is going to spend $1000.00 on decorating."

"Where did he get that kind of money?"

"He works."

"Oh yeah; I forgot."

"I have to sneak out of the house. I am already in trouble. I lied to Grandma today and told her I was with you."

"Yeah I know; she came over looking for you. I tried to lie for you, but momma was right behind me. They don't let you lie for your friends even though they used to when they were our age."

"I am not going to bible class with them on Sunday. I'll tell her I am sick."

"What are you going to do if she gets back and you're not home?"

"She won't; I'll make sure I get back before she does. She won't get back until 2:30 or 3:00. They fellowship with other members after bible class anyway." We talk about nothing for an hour before hanging up the phone. I creep back in the kitchen and reconnect the phone.

At 7:00 a.m., as usual, Grandma knocks on the door; and as usual, she scolds Khalid for not sleeping in his room. Although I hate when she yells at Khalid, I understand he is too old to sleep with me. Though he sleeps at the foot of the bed and I sleep at the head, at fourteen, he should be comfortable sleeping alone. Khalid leaves my room and drags himself to the bathroom to shower. She comes back in my room and demands I get ready for bible class. I grab the bottom of my stomach, kneel over, and roll across the bed.

"Grandma, I'm sick. I don't feel well."

"I don't care if you're sick; get up!"

I sit on the bed. I am slow doing everything. I am determined to make her angry, so she will leave me. Grandma is never late anywhere. At 7:15, I am making my bed. I am in the shower at 7:25. I know she will be ready to leave at exactly 7:30. When she comes in my room, I begin to iron my shirt.

"You ain't ready yet?"

"I'm almost ready."

"Come on Khalid; I am ready to go. Thandisha, you will just have to stay home. I am not going to be late because of you!"

"Grandma, I'm almost ready." I whine as if I am devastated as if I really want to go.

"Well we're not waiting." An *I don't believe you're doing this to me* look covers my face. She falls for it. She and Khalid leave without me. I quickly call Andreas to tell him to come to the house instead of meeting me at the corner. I clean my room, complete my chores, and get dressed. I put on a pretty beige linen sundress that is loose fitting but still shows what little figure I have. I feel glamorous like a movie star. It is a change; I am coming alive. Actually, I am now feeling instead of simply being. I am now sharing a life with someone, and it feels good. I know I am being dishonest, but I have to go.

The doorbell chime startles me. I quickly twist my hair into a bun and run to the door. I open the door and greet him with a kiss, as he enters the house. He walks in the house, looks around, and instantly focuses on the paintings on the wall.

"Did you draw these too?"

"Of course," I smile; I am proud of my art. The pictures are beautiful. Some of my pictures are colorful; others are dark and gloomy. I don't know how I started drawing, but my art is an expression of feelings I cannot verbalize.

"I have pictures for your apartment, but they need frames." I grab my portfolio, and we leave.

"Where are we going?"

"Let's go to the north side. I know I will not get

very much, but I don't want a cheap look."

"What kind of look do you want?"

"I don't know just nothing cheap."

"I guess you want a masculine, macho look?"

"Well I really don't know. I'm sure you will be spending time there too. So whatever you decide." I smile. I like that he includes me and makes me part of his world.

I went with a neutral tone; we found a beige sofa bed for $500.00 and a matching cream rug. Though we shop at a discount store, we purchase quality, metal blinds and a nice dinette set.

"Baby, you're a good shopper."

"I got it from my momma. My momma was an economical shopper, and she had good taste in furniture." I surprise myself. I never speak of my mother. She is always on my mind, but I can never verbalize my feelings for her. I try very hard to put That Day, and everything associated with it, out of my mind.

"How much do we have left baby?" He gave me the money to pay for the merchandise. I open my bag. We had been to a few stores, and I lost count of the money.

"We have $236.00 and some change." We drive across town to Coy Country Thrift Store. He does not want to go, but I love thrift stores. Upon entering the store, I see the chair. "That's it." He looks as if he does not see it.

"Where?" He looks around the store and still does not see it.

"Over there," I walk towards the antique chair and matching ottoman. He reluctantly follows me. The chair is mauve with big claw feet. The matching ottoman is oversized with claw feet. "Look it's only sixty dollars." It is obvious; he is not impressed. I remember momma used to say every room should have an antique. "Trust me; you're going to love this." We pay for the chair and place it in the trunk of the car.

"What about dinnerware and linen?"

"I have dinnerware and linen. I have been planning to move for quite some time, so I have been buying stuff here and there. I plan early baby." He places a gentle, moist kiss on my forehead. The shopping makes us hungry; we walk next door to a fast food restaurant for lunch. I am midway into eating my burger when I notice it is 1:00. I am already in trouble. I do not want to make it worse.

"Andreas, look at the time." He looks at his watch.

"Damn baby, I have to get you home." He flags down the waitress and pays our bill. He drives so fast I am sure he will get a speeding ticket. Surprisingly, however, we make it back to Grandma's house without being pulled over by flashing, blue lights. "Babe, I am going to go home and put up the blinds. I guess I'll clean up and put that ugly chair in the apartment." I treat him to a long, passionate kiss before I leave the car. I am always sad when he leaves me. I walk into the house, put on my baggy jeans and T-shirt, and go back to sleep.

I hear the door open; it is Grandma, Khalid, and Aunt Mary. Khalid comes to my room as usual. He opens the door without knocking.

"Thandie."

"Yeah!" I snap at him.

"Nothing," he closes the door. I immediately feel guilty. I know Khalid is dependent on me; sometimes I like his dependency; at other times, I hate it. Sometimes it is more than I could handle. I get up and walk in Khalid's room. I rarely go in his room because he is always in mine.

"Khalid?" He does not answer. I walk to his bed and push his shoulder. "You want me to make you some French toast?"

"You gonna put some cream cheese filling in it?" He faces the wall with his back to me.

"Yeah, I will make it any way you like." He turns over and faces me. "I'm sorry Khalid." We walk to the kitchen. Khalid immediately grabs the French bread from the cupboard. I cut the bread into four, thick slices. Khalid is excited. It takes very little to make him happy, but sometimes, I don't have a little to give. He cracks the eggs while I mix the vanilla flavor and cinnamon into the cream cheese and sugar.

"Thandie, can you make banana syrup?"

"See if we have bananas." I hope we don't, but of course, Khalid finds some. I melt the brown sugar and butter then slice the bananas and add them to the mixture.

"What are you guys making?" I should have known Aunt Mary would come into the kitchen. She always comes in the kitchen when she smells my cooking.

"French toast with banana syrup. Would you like some Aunt Mary?"

"That sounds good."

"It sure smells good in here." Grandma comes into the kitchen. She must have been lying down because one side of her afro was flat, and her face had the imprint of her bedspread.

"What is that white topping you are spreading on the bread Thandie?"

"It is a mixture of cream cheese, vanilla, and frozen cool whip." I finish making the French toast in the midst of Grandma, Khalid, and Aunt Mary and top it with the banana syrup.

"Thandie, this is delicious."

"Thanks Grandma."

"Baby, do you mind making these for the bible class brunch next Saturday?"

"Sure Aunt Mary," I love when Aunt Mary eats my cooking; she makes me feel special. Khalid is quiet. He is busy filling his mouth. I love cooking desserts, pastries, and cheesecakes because I enjoy the compliments I always receive when they are eaten.

After we finish our French toast, I wash dishes and clean the kitchen. I read the newspaper in the den while

Aunt Mary, Khalid, and Grandma watch television. This is a nice rarity, as I am always in my room when Grandma is in the den because she is usually getting on me about something; sometimes so harshly Aunt Mary has to intervene.

"Grandma, can you drop me off at the mall tomorrow morning? I want to get a job."

"Thandie, you really don't need a job."

"Yes I do Grandma. I want to make my own money."

"I think it's good she wants to work; some of these kids today don't want to do anything but drink and use drugs." Aunt Mary agrees with me. Grandma is not convinced. "Well Thelma, baby, I can drop her off."

"I can ride the bus back Grandma." She really does not have a leg to stand on because she does not have to do anything to help me get this job I will fictitiously look for.

"You better not be up to anything."

"I'm not Grandma. I need a job."

"No Thandie, you want a job."

"I'm 17 years old Grandma, and I need to save my own money. I will not do anything I am not supposed to do."

Aunt Mary came to pick me up at 10:00. Andreas and I made plans to meet at the Taco Stand at 10:30. The ride with Aunt Mary is peaceful. I enjoy spending time with her alone. She is very easy going. She does not mind when I change her radio station from the oldies to my favorite hip hop station. Though she is older than Grandma, she is more modern thinking. She has a much more realistic view of my teenage life. She does not place unrealistic expectations on me.

"I hear you have a boyfriend."

"Yeah I do. His name is Andreas. He graduated last month."

"Really that's good so many of our young, black

men don't even make it out of high school." I truly get tired of the negative comments people make about black youth. I don't know "the young black men" Aunt Mary speaks of. Everyone I know graduates from high school when they are supposed to. "Is he nice?"

"Oh Aunt Mary he is so sweet. He talks to me about everything, his dreams, goals and his family."

"You think you love him don't you?" I do not want to tell her too much. I know she will tell Grandma any and everything.

"I don't know if I love him." I lie. "But he is very nice. Grandma will not even talk to him."

"She'll come around." When we arrive at the mall, I inconspicuously search for Andreas' car in the parking lot.

"Aunt Mary, let me out at the front entrance." She steers the car to the curb, reaches in her hip pocket, removes a twenty dollar bill, and passes it to me. I grab my backpack that contains my jeans and T-shirt and thank Aunt Mary for the money.

I walk to the Taco Stand; Andreas is sitting at a table sipping on a soft drink. He stands and greets me with the usual peck on the lips. He takes my book bag, and we walk to his car. As always, he opens the door and secures my seat belt.

"Guess what? The furniture is already in the apartment. We need to arrange everything. I found one of those tall floor lamps." He sounds excited.

"Oh you did? So you went shopping without me huh?" He does not respond; he simply looks at me and smiles.

The apartment is cool from the window unit. I can tell he attempted to arrange the furniture. Everything is totally out of balance. He placed all of the furniture on the same wall.

"What do you think?"

"I can tell you tried." He laughs. "Go and get the

pictures framed, and I'll have a surprise when you get back."

I move the sofa, so it separates the breakfast nook from the living area. I place the lamp on the back of the couch to provide light for the dining area as well as the sitting area. I place the antique chair cater-cornered on the wall and position it for easy viewing of the television. The throw rug in front of the sofa completes my first experiment with interior decorating. It is beautiful. He comes back with the framed prints and Chinese food.

"Wow, this is great; thank you baby." We eat the food and watch television. I feel a hard bulge in his pants. We both ignore it. We lie down and take a brief nap. At 2:00, he wakes up and dresses for work. I change back into my skirt.

We drive to my house in silence. Initially, we pass the house to ensure we do not see Grandma.

"I get off work at 11:00; call me at 11:30." I kiss him, go in the house, and call Ayanna.

"Girl, where have you been? I have been calling you all morning."

"I went to decorate Andreas' apartment; he had some of my drawings professionally framed for his apartment."

"Girl, I bet it's nice."

"It's real nice. You want to see it?"

"I would love to see it."

"Ask your mother if you can use the car."

"Where is the apartment?"

"It's in the West End."

"I am not allowed to drive on the freeway. My dad says I need more experience." Ayanna is obedient and honest. Unlike me, she is grounded. I look for things and people outside of me to make me whole. She is solid on the inside and very secure with herself. Ayanna is not influenced by peer pressure. In fact, she is always the trendsetter. "I'll ask Dee to take us."

"Will she tell your momma? I don't want Grandma to know. If she knows Andreas has an apartment, she will really be on my case."

"Girl, please, as much dirt as I have on Dee. I think not." Dee and Ayanna pick me up, and we ride to the West End. We can tell Dee is mad, but we do not care. Ayanna and I sit in the back seat with Dee's two kids in the middle. I pass the twenty-dollar bill Aunt Mary gave me to Dee.

"Excuse me, but it does not take twenty dollars to go from here to West End!" Dee tucks the bill in her bra, rolls her eyes at Ayanna, and presses the accelerator down to the floor of the car.

"Check this crap Thandisha!" She looks at Dee and then at me. "This is why she ain't got nothing but a crazy ass ex-husband and two bratty ass kids because she is so low fucking down." Dee totally ignores Ayanna. Thankfully, she eases up on the accelerator.

We talk about Andreas and Devontae, her new love. We gossip about who is pregnant and who is cheating on whom; we are totally oblivious to Dee and her attitude. We are engulfed in our own world.

It is a twenty-minute drive from Grandma's house to Andreas' apartment. I am excited and proud showing it off.

"This is it?" Ayanna is totally unimpressed.

"Ayanna, wait until you see the inside." The apartment is still cool although it is ninety degrees outside. Everything is orderly, and in its place.

"This is nice. Are those your drawings?" I knew Ayanna would see the beauty once we were inside.

"Yeah and you know it."

"Thandisha, you have real talent."

"What can I say?" I am flattered by the compliment. Ayanna has always known I am an artist, but we spend most of the time talking about her and what boyfriend she likes the most, or what she is going to wear to this party or that party. I have shown her my work many times; I guess the fact I am a great artist never sunk in.

We are startled when Dee comes inside with the kids.

"This is nice."

"Thanks Dee."

"This is your boyfriend's apartment?"

"Yes, this is it."

"He has nice art. I bet he paid a fortune for it."

"Thandisha painted all of them."

"Thandisha, this is good."

"So what does he do?"

"Who?"

"Your boyfriend, what kind of work does he do?"

"He works at Tyler Manufacturing, and he has his own lawn maintenance business."

"I hear they make big bucks at Tyler."

"And he has a girlfriend named Thandisha. You know the girl standing next to me with the key to the apartment." Ayanna points at me while rolling her eyes at Dee. I do not know how to take Dee's comment, but Ayanna obviously does.

After showing Dee and Ayanna the apartment, Dee drops both of us off at my house. Grandma's car is gone. I look forward to enjoying a peaceful house. As I enter the house, I hear the television in the den. Khalid is stretched out in the middle of the floor watching television. I hate when Grandma leaves him alone. I know he is old enough to stay home alone. But sometimes he is still uncomfortable in the house alone.

Grandma enters the house with a big smile on her face. She is always happy when Ayanna visits. It is a rare event because I am usually at Ayanna's house. I take advantage of her happy demeanor and ask permission to spend the night with Ayanna. I cannot believe it; she allows me to spend the night. This is quite unusual. Although she is okay with me visiting Ayanna, she never likes for me to spend the night. I lied and told her we are going skating.

"Just come home before 11:00. I have an appointment at 12:30 tomorrow, and I don't know how long I will be gone."

"Okay Grandma." I have no intention of spending the night with Ayanna. Immediately after leaving the house, I ask Ayanna if Dee would take me to Andreas' house if I gave her more money for gas.

"Girl, are you crazy? You're going too far Thandisha."

"Ayanna, I love Andreas. He loves me. What's wrong with that?"

"Thandisha, don't you think you're going too fast? What about college? You know we are supposed to be roommates and pledge a sorority together."

"I don't want to go to college. Ayanna, I want to become a world-renowned artist. I'm very talented. Andreas says we're going to sell some of my paintings on consignment."

"Why is everything Andreas this and Andreas that? Whatever happened to having fun, enjoying life, liking boys and going to backyard BBQ's?"

"Nothing aren't we going skating? I still like having fun and hanging out with you."

"Oh, we're really going skating?"

"Yeah," Ayanna eyes light up like a child's on Christmas day. She smiles and hugs me.

"Oh my God I don't have anything to wear. You should have said something earlier; we could have gone to the mall. Come on girl let's go on over to my house. I need to wash my hair and find something to wear." Ayanna pauses and stares at my hair. "Why don't you ever wear your hair loose?" She rubs her hand over my head and grabs my bun. "I'll wash your hair and wrap it. Girl we're gonna be so fine tonight."

We open the door and find Dee in the den talking on the phone and blowing puffs of smoke in the air.

"Dee, you know you're not supposed to smoke in here." Dee brushes Ayanna off and continues her conversation with the cigarette in her hand; she blows the smoke directly towards Ayanna.

"Ain't no use some folks just won't do right." We go into the kitchen where Ayanna begins the tedious task of washing my.

"Thandisha, you have a lot of hair...Hey Dee." She screams Dee's name so loud I have to cover my ears. I hate the way Ayanna talks to Dee. It is very obvious Ayanna does not have the respect for Dee reserved for an older sibling. The lack of respect is evident in the tone Ayanna uses when she speaks to Dee, and she never has anything nice to say to or about Dee.

"What?" I can tell by the way Dee responds to Ayanna she knows she is not respected.

"Where's your gel?" Ayanna stands and waits for Dee to respond. "I know that heifer heard me." I am sure she heard Ayanna too. I want to tell Ayanna that maybe if she speaks to her with a little more respect, she may respond. Dee does not respond; she totally ignores Ayanna. "Sit here for a second Thandisha." She dashes out in a huff with major attitude as if she is on route to a street fight. She comes back into the kitchen with a large jar of hair gel. I hope she does not plan on using it on my hair. I hate putting gel in my hair. I honestly do not see the point. It cakes up and leaves dark flakes.

"Thandisha, you need to cut some of this stuff." She washes my hair and totally ignores my protest against applying the gel. She wraps my hair around my head. I sit under the dryer for over two hours before my hair is dry. Ayanna combs it down and uses a flat iron to straighten it. I look in the mirror. I hate my hair loose because I look too much like momma.

"Ayanna, I really don't like wearing my hair loose."

"Girl please, it looks nice." She makes a small part on the side allowing hair to fall on both of my shoulders. "Thandisha, you should wear your hair like this more often." We go into the den. Dee looks at me with evil eyes, gives me an unwarranted eye roll, and a ghetto girl neck jerk. Ayanna notices the theatrics. "Don't pay her any attention. That child has some serious issues."

I put on tight, hip hugger jeans and a cute snug fitting crop shirt. If I may say so, I look good. Although I am still slim, my hips are rounding and my behind is beginning to stick out more. The jeans truly accent my developing figure. Dee drops us off at the skate center. She does not say a word to us during the entire trip.

"Dee, I will be ready at 11:30."

"Yeah whatever."

"Don't be late Dee!" Ayanna slams the car door; I am surprised the window does not shatter. "I hate that bitch. Damn, if she wasn't my sister, I would not even talk to her stupid ass."

"You really don't hate her Ayanna. I think they call it sibling rivalry."

"I guess I really don't hate her dumb ass, but she gets on my damn nerves."

We walk inside of the skate center. The music is full of bass and so loud you can feel the vibration in your chest. Everyone from school is here. We skate to the latest rap songs and old R&B. I cannot keep up with Ayanna. She is very popular with the boys, and she likes the fact a lot of boys like her. I could care less about being popular or hanging with the in-crowd. Andreas is the only guy that interests me. I only want to hang out with him. In fact, I am bored looking at Ayanna and her entourage. I call Andreas and leave a message on his cell. He calls back at 11:10; I tell him I am at the skate center and Grandma thinks I am spending the night with Ayanna.

"I'll be right there."

Andreas and Dee both arrive at 11:30. Dee gets out of the car walks to Andreas' side of the car in hoochie shorts and a two-size, too small, tight tank top. I do not like the way she looks at him. She introduces herself while blowing the smoke from her cigarette in his face.

"Hi I'm Dee, Ayanna's older sister." She emphasizes *"older."* "I saw your apartment, and it really looks nice. Do you mind if I ask you something?" She pauses, batting her fake eyelashes while blowing smoke in Andreas' face. "How much is the rent?" Andreas looks at me then back at Dee. "Is it expensive?"

"$550.00, but that includes some of the utilities."

"Are there any vacancies?"

"Yeah I think so."

"Call me and give me the number to the leasing office." Dee writes her number on a small torn piece of paper and passes it to Andreas. Andreas does not take the paper.

"I'll give Thandisha the number to the owners, and she'll give it to you."

"I really appreciate that; I appreciate that a lot." She gives him a seductive smile before she slowly turns around and walks to her car. Andreas does not appear to notice her darkened cheeks that subtly hang from her tight shorts. We leave the parking lot. The car is abnormally silent.

"What was that all about?"

"I wanted Ayanna to see the apartment. She's not allowed to drive on the freeway, so Dee gave us a ride." He continues to drive. "Are you mad? I mean did I do something wrong?"

"I could never be mad at you." He takes my hand and places it against his cheek. I remove my seat belt and sit in the middle of the car with my head on his shoulder.

The apartment, as usual, is clean and orderly. We

walk in, and he immediately turns on the air conditioner. We eat cereal, chips, and drink soda while watching television.

"The only thing missing is groceries. You need some food in here."

"Why? I can't cook."

"I can. I can cook for you." I snuggle close to him. "How about we get up in the morning and go to the store."

"Okay but I have to be home at 11:00."

"We'll get up extra early."

He puts on a jazz CD and pulls out the sofa bed. Soft music is exactly what I need. I love Andreas so much. I feel loved again, and it feels so good. We are kissing passionately; he turns on the light and reaches for his wallet.

"Damn!"

"What?"

"I don't have any more jimmies." I pull him back on top of me and grind against his manhood kissing him with a passion I didn't know I had. I am scared, but I desperately want him to touch me. I feel so alive when he touches me. He kisses my breast and massages the mound between my thighs. He enters me, and this time it does not hurt.

"Baby, you feel so good." He kisses me everywhere. He pulls out of me and then gives me pleasure with his mouth. When he enters me again, I am on fire. Then something happens; I feel something I have never felt before. The sensation between my legs is powerful, and it feels good. I moan, scream his name, and pull him closer without being totally cognizant of my actions. Andreas moans and shivers. Perspiration pours out of him, drips onto my face, and rolls down onto the pillow. "I love you baby; damn I love you." He pulls out of me and climaxes rubbing his manhood against my stomach. We lay silently in each other's arms several minutes before we speak again. "Your hair is pretty loose; well it was pretty." He laughs. It is soaked with his perspiration. The ends are beginning to curl totally destroying the new look Ayanna gave me.

"I'm sorry about today. I can tell you were mad I brought Ayanna and Dee here."

"I wasn't mad."

"Yes you were."

"Well I was uncomfortable but not mad. I have lived in the projects all my life with nothing but people around. I like my space away from people that's what that was about. I wasn't exactly mad."

"It won't happen again." We kiss, talk, make love and talk some more.

"Did I tell you I got a small business license yesterday?"

"No you didn't tell me."

"Now I can bid on city contracts. They have a bid list at city hall for different government contracts. If I can get two bids next year, then I'm in there. I'll buy more equipment. These are year round contracts too. I'll save the checks from my business and live off my paycheck. I know your grandmother still probably won't like me, but she'll see I am a hard working man. She will see I will treat you right, and I can take care of you as good as any man." I really do not know what all of that means, but it sounds good to me. "Did you get any more of your paintings ready?"

"Yeah I did."

"I'll take them to be framed, and we'll try and sell them on consignment." I love Andreas because he makes my life a priority also. He makes the things important to me important to him. We talk until we fall asleep.

"Thandisha wake up; baby wake up!" I wake up to him shaking me. "Hey when are you going to trust me enough to tell me about it?"

"About what?" I wipe the tears off my cheeks with my hands.

"About you." I sit up in the bed; I am crying. I do not know how to say it. I do not have the words anymore. I don't even know if I can remember it all. It seems as if That Day happened a lifetime ago. I did everything in my power to put That Day out of my mind, and now he wants me to tell him about it.

"Say it anyway you want to say it." He looks at me waiting for more.

"Something very bad happened when I was a little girl. When Khalid and I were younger, somebody killed our mother. I was there. I saw her. I saw the blood. The blood was on me. I saw him." I cannot talk anymore; the words will not come. I look at him hoping I have given him enough information.

"That must have been hard. Did they catch the guy who did it?"

"Yeah he is in prison. I don't know which one, but he is in prison."

"Well you don't need to know where he is. At least you know he can't hurt you anymore." He lay on his back, pulls me close, and softly rubs my hair. I lay my head in his chest. The rhythmic sound of his heartbeat is hypnotic, inducing a sound sleep.

I wake up at sunrise, but I am so relaxed I go back to sleep. When I wake up again, it is ten o'clock in the morning. I push Andreas' shoulder back and forth about five times before he wakes up. I quickly put my clothes on, pull a rubber band from my purse, and pull my hair back. He makes the bed, sits on the sofa, and watches me.

"You're pretty Thandisha." His smile is wide and bright. "I wish you didn't have to leave." I walk to the sofa and give him a long, passionate kiss.

"Me either."

"You said your grandmother has an appointment."

"I have to hang out with my brother."

"Why don't I pick you and your brother up after she leaves? We can go grocery shopping and have lunch before I go to work."

"That will work, but I have to go now."

He let me out of the car at Ayanna's house. I check to make sure Grandma has not called then I quickly walk home. As usual, Khalid is waiting in the den for me. He opens the door before I can insert my key in the lock.

"Did you have a nice time Thandie?"

"Yeah it was real nice." I go into my room, watch television and wait for Grandma to leave.

"Khalid! Get dressed!"

"Why?"

"Because I said so." He goes to his room and changes into a pair of baggy shorts and matching over-sized shirt. I call Andreas to come and pick us up. Khalid is more responsive to Andreas than before. They talk about the Bulls, the Pacers, and the Lakers, Khalid's favorite basketball team. I did not know Khalid knows so much about basketball. I am impressed.

We go to the grocery store and then to the apartment to put the food away. We drive downtown and eat lunch. This time with Khalid and Andreas feels so right like the three of us are one big happy family. I order a grilled chicken salad. Andreas orders steak and baked potato, and Khalid has his usual, cheeseburger and fries. By the time we finish our meals, it is time for him to take us home and go to work. I always hate when he has to take me home. Andreas and I sit in the car. Khalid goes into the house.

"I hate leaving you Thandisha."

"Me too. Pick me up tonight after you get off work."

"What?" He looks surprised.

"You heard me. I'll sneak out of the window."

"You sure?" I take his hand and place it inside of my panties.

"Um huh." We both laugh.

Ayanna comes over, and we watch television and engage in our usual teenage gossip. Actually she does all of the talking. I am listening but not really paying attention, but since she talks so much, she does not notice.

"You talk to that boy today?" I do not like the way she says *that boy.*

"Yeah of course."

"Why did I bother to ask?" She rolls her eyes. It is obvious she disapproves of my relationship with Andreas. "Thandisha, you're changing." What she really means is she is concerned because she is no longer the center of my attention.

"Ayanna, I'm in love. I want to be with him every moment all of the time. I miss him right now even. I love the way he smells even when he's just coming from work. I just love talking to him."

"Thandisha, you're way too young for all that. When we go to college, you'll meet so many people Andreas won't even matter." I am tired of her telling me I am going to college. I have told her a hundred times I have no intention of going to college. I'm going to be an excellent cook and a great artist. Art is natural for me. I don't have to go to college to be an artist.

"I don't think so; I need him."

"Whatever, look at Dee, she was the same way stuck on some boy. She got married and had those damn brats. Now look at her." I am waiting to hear more. I want to tell her the only thing wrong with Dee is she has a very judgmental sister and a harsh daddy who wants to make her feel bad for the rest of her life because she got married without his approval.

"And?"

"And? Hell, she's living back at home. Momma and daddy begged her to go to school. Oh, but not her grown ass! She had to marry Eddie, but she got hers. When he beat her the last time, she almost died. Look at her; she's lost. She has been to cosmetology school, secretary school, and bookkeeping school. She is so damn confused; she's just a damn embarrassment."

"That's mean Ayanna. Sometimes you can make all of the right decisions and everything can still go wrong. I learned a long time ago we really are not in control. We just think that we are; believe me I know." I see tears forming in her eyes. I have known Ayanna for over five years, and I have never seen her cry.

"Dee has always taken all of the attention. She always has some crazy drama in her life. It is always some outlandish shit that requires both momma and daddy's attention. I'm sick of her. When she moved back home, momma assumed April was going to share my room. But daddy put his foot down and said April had to share a room with her mother." Ayanna and I rarely talk about ourselves. We always talk about other people. I didn't know how much she resented Dee, but it seems to me Dee should have resented Ayanna. Ayanna is obviously her dad's favorite. She has his undivided attention. "Besides, Thandisha, what kind of future does Andreas have? What kind of life can he offer you? Hell, he cuts grass for a living. What kind of life is that?" She is beginning to piss me off.

"So what Ayanna, he makes an honest living. A college degree doesn't mean everything. There are plenty of people who never go to college and manage to earn a good living."

"Yeah but how many people do you know who have good jobs without a degree?" I cannot answer her. I want to remind her that her father has a MBA, but hasn't been able to find a job in his field for years. Yes he still works in an office, but he does not need a MBA to be an insurance adjuster.

I am grateful Ayanna changes the subject and focuses on herself. To be honest, I am mad as hell at her for blatantly insulting Andreas. I listen to Ayanna talk about some new guy name Keith for the next two hours. It is getting late, and I want to get ready to go over to Andreas' house. I keep yawning hoping she will get the hint, but she doesn't. We talk, rather she talks, an hour longer until her cell phone rings. She quickly grabs the phone from her back pocket.

"Girl, I have to go home. This is Darryl. Maybe he will take me out tonight." I want to inquire about Devontae and Keith, her new man, but do not want to delay her departure. I walk her to the door, and we say our goodbyes.

I do not want to shower; I want to wait until I get to Andreas' because it makes me feel as if it is my place too. It feels like we are a couple living together. I go to Khalid's room at 9:00, so he can sleep in my bed. I sit and watch him sleep for a while. He is growing up, and he is so handsome. Khalid is such a good brother. I am surprised at how he adjusted to living without momma. It is easier, for some reason, for Grandma to love him than it is for her to love me.

Before I leave out of the window, I place two pillows next to him. I walk down the street toward Ayanna's house until I see the blinking lights. I jog towards the car, but I really want to run. I am always excited when I see him. I give him my usual kiss and slide in the middle of the seat close to him.

We are quiet the entire drive to his place. We are both tired when we reach the apartment. I want to climb on his back and be carried inside. He is so tired we both probably would have ended up on the ground. When we get inside, we quickly prepare the bed, undress, shower and go to sleep.

A loud, hard knock at the door wakes us; I glance at

the clock. It is 4:00 am. It is Jazmyne, Andreas' younger sister. One of her eyes is swollen shut and her lip is busted and coated with dried blood.

"Damn girl, what happened to you?" Andreas tightly wraps his arms around Jazymyne and escorts her to the chair. I only have on one of Andreas' t-shirts, so I keep the covers pulled close.

"I'm tired of that niggah." Jazmyne is not very attractive, and she looks worse crying.

"Sit down." He helps her into the chair. "Tell me what happened." He goes in the kitchen and gets an ice pack for her face.

"It went like dis." I hate the way Jazmyne talks. Her sentences are always filled with dis niggah dat niggah and the way she sucks her teeth between sentences drives me crazy. "You know Keekee started slangin." He shakes his head in disgust. I don't know what "*slangin*" is. Jazmyne speaks an entirely different language. "Well he just doing it so we can get our own spot. It's a temporary thang. Anyway he was trying to sell a slab. When he looked at his stash, he said some was missing. Since I was the only one in the car, he accused me." He stands, grabs Jazmyne, and pulls her to her feet.

"Girl, I know you ain't smoking that shit!" I have no idea what "*that shit*" is. She does not answer; she continues to talk.

"He made me take off all of my clothes in front of Jerry, Tae, and DeeDee dem and searched me and shit; and when he didn't find it, he jumped on me." She starts crying again.

"Keekee should be tired of me kicking his ass!" Andreas slides into his jeans and grabs a shirt.

"Bro wait; don't go. He packing and shit."

Andreas pushes her out of the way and slams the door. Jazmyne and I have nothing in common; we occasionally look at one another and smile. After sitting in the chair for a few minutes, Jazmyne reaches in her hair and pulls out a white pebble. "Look don't tell my brother; it would kill him." She smokes a cigarette placing the ashes on a pipe she pulls from her back pocket. She breaks off a small piece of the pebble, lights it with a lighter, and inhales the smoke from the pipe. She immediately stops crying and starts talking as if nothing happened. "I hope my brother don't find Keekee. He done beat Keekee so many times; it's a shame. Eventually, somebody is going to get hurt."

"Why does he hit you?"

"He is so crazy. He loves me too much. Don't want me out of his sight." She looks around the apartment nodding her head up and down with approval. "Dis real nice. Dem some real pretty pictures."

"Thank you."

"Thank you? Oh you must live here or sunthin?"

"No I don't live here, but I painted the pictures."

"Oh girl dees are real nice. Um huh." I hate the way this girl talks. I cannot wait until Andreas gets back, so he can take me home and get me away from her.

"So you the reason my brother doesn't come home no more. You putting that thang on him right huh girl." She gyrates her hips. I am speechless. "Me and Keekee trying to get our own spot. Hell I'm tired of getting fucked in the car and on the side of buildings and shit." I sit still and continue to stare at her. I've never had a conversation with anyone like Jazmyne before.

"Do you want some water or something to drink?" She does not respond but continues to talk.

"Dis is real nice. Girl, don't hurt my brother. He a real good dude. He really is um huh. You're only his second girlfriend. Don't you know Katanya Thomas? You know that girl who had the baby a couple of years ago." I do not know her, but I know this will not stop her from telling me whatever it is she is going to tell me about

Katanya Thomas. "Well anyway they went together for a long time. You know like since Jr. High and shit. She got pregnant. My brother thought it was his cause you know he thought she was down with him and shit. Well you know Andreas black as midnight. Her ass is just as black as his. The baby came out light skinned with hazel eyes and shit. He still didn't want to believe it. He was saying something about maybe the genes went way back and shit. The fool didn't believe it until the blood test came back. He was so hurt girl. You know he didn't beat that bitch ass. Shit, but I did. Don't nobody fuck with my brother. Hell." She does this funny movement with her neck, puts the white pebble back in her hair, and sticks the pipe back in her pocket. I am relieved when I hear Andreas place his key in the door.

"You might as well take me home. It's 5:30."

"Oh baby why?" He looks tired.

"I need to get home before Grandma wakes up; plus your sister needs to get some rest."

"I do girl. I'm tired of getting my ass beat, thrown out of moving cars and stripped searched and shit. Damn that fool is crazy." Jazmyne laughs. I do not see the humor. Andreas looks at her and shakes his head in disgust. He looks sad. I change into my clothes. He drives almost in complete silence.

"What's wrong Andreas?" He looks at me and smiles.

"Nothing baby everything is alright as long as I have you." He turns the lights off before reaching the house. I kiss him good-bye. I am tired and sleepy. I crawl back through the window; Khalid is in the same position. I put on my pajamas and go to sleep.

When I wake up, it is 11:30 am. I cannot believe Grandma allowed me sleep this late. I call Andreas.

"Hello." He always sounds so sexy in the morning.

"Hey."

"What's up baby?" I love the way he says *"baby."*

"You."

"I'm sorry about the thing with my sister this morning. She has somewhat of a dramatic life."

"It's okay."

"No it's not. That's one of the reasons I moved. I want to get away from my family and their crazy drama and make a world of my own. I can't seem to escape." He pauses. "Fuck it. I'm going to make it anyway. Hell I got to make it." Although I do not totally understand exactly what he is talking about, I know it is about pain. I have lot of my own; it maintains its place behind every happy, blessed event in my life. Like a dark shadow, it is determined to stay attached to my life. I do not really know how to help him. I cannot verbalize my own pain, but it is there deep inside of me. I cannot touch it, but I know it is there.

School starts next week, and I dread it. How will I see Andreas? When will we have the time? With him doing his lawn business during the day and working at night, it really does not leave very much time for me. I don't know how, but the time will be made. It is essential.

Ayanna is excited, as usual, about school. I walk to her house like I do every year, and she shows me the new clothes she bought for school. She meticulously takes each piece out of the bag as if it is a precious jewel and then cautiously returns it after she admires each piece with me. Of course, she has never asked me about my clothes, which is okay. I am never really into the school-shopping thing. I shop all of the time. Whenever I want to buy clothes, I buy them.

I didn't see Andreas for the first three days of school then Thursday night I couldn't take it. I left a message on his cell while he was at work.

"Hello," it didn't take him long to return my call.

"May I speak to Thandisha?"

"Hey it's me."

"Hey baby I miss you."

"Me too, Pick me up tonight."

"Are you sure? What about school? Won't you be tired in the morning?"

"Yeah, I sure hope so." We both laugh. "I'll call you when I know Grandma is asleep." When Grandma went to sleep, I do not get Khalid. He needs to learn to sleep comfortable in his bed. I push up the window, crawl out and quietly close it. I walk down the street until I see the lights blink on and off. I get in the car; we sit in the car for a minute hugging and kissing. I did not realize how much I missed him.

"I have a present for you."

"Really? I am expecting a present but next week for my birthday." We drive holding and kissing at every red light and every stop sign. When we get to his apartment, I pull out the sofa bed before I shower. I always finish before he does. He has to wash everything three or four times. I lather myself very good one time, and I am done.

He comes to the side of the bed and drops the towel before climbing into bed. He opens the lamp table drawer and pulls out a small, velvet box.

"I wanted to wait and give this to you for your birthday, but I am too excited." Inside of the box is a marquis shaped, diamond ring. "It's only a fourth of a carat, but it's a quality one. It is a nice size for a promise ring." No one has ever given me anything so special. He takes it out of the box and places it on my finger.

We do not look for a condom. I do not care; neither does he. I know Andreas loves me. I know I love him. We are so caught up in the moment we do not care about the consequences.

One Hundred and Thirty-five Degrees

It is October; my period still has not come. Last month, I threw away sanitary napkins splattered with ketchup to conceal my lack of a monthly flow. I am so sick in the mornings I get up early before anyone is awake, go into the bathroom and regurgitate. I am tired all of the time. Most days after school, I go straight to bed and sometimes sleep until the next morning.

Initially, I didn't tell Andreas, but today I am so sick instead of going to school, I call Andreas and confess I have not had a period in a couple of months.

"What? Are you pregnant?"

"I don't know."

"What do you mean you don't know?"

"I don't fucking know!" I am frustrated, so I hang up the phone. He immediately calls back."

"Yeah!"

"Thandisha, don't hang up the damn phone again!" There is a long silence. I am too confused to speak. I guess he is too. "Look, whatever happens we will handle it. I can't believe you didn't tell me. What are you thinking?"

"I am not thinking."

"I am on my way." He picks me up at the bus stop, and we go to the health clinic. The results are positive. The nurse gives us pamphlets and information, so we can make an informed decision. We are silent and do not talk until we are in the car.

"Are you hungry?" The thought of food makes me nauseous. I do not want anything to eat. Andreas stops at a burger stand. Immediately, the smell of food turns my stomach. I regurgitate what seems like everything I have eaten in the last year. He has to eat his burger and onion rings outside of the car. When he finishes eating, he quietly gets in the car, and drives to his apartment.

The apartment is nice and cool. He pulls the bed out of the sofa and covers the mattress with a sheet.

"Baby, lie down." I remove my shoes. He sits next to me and massages my feet.

"I don't want to have a baby. I don't even know how to take care of myself."

"I know; but it's a little too late. Don't you think? Remember I have eight nieces and three nephews. I've changed diapers. I've done it all. All I am asking is that you have the baby. You can still go to school."

School, I have not thought about school. What will Ayanna say? What will she think? Grandma, Aunt Mary, Khalid what will they think of me?

"I can't go to school like this!"

"Yes hell you can!" He stands and quickly sits down again. "I make good money. I have a side business that is growing; by next summer, it should be booming. You graduate in seven months. By then, the baby will be here. We can get married. I know this place is small, but we can stay here until the baby comes."

Marriage! Is he crazy? I am not ready for marriage. I didn't want to be like my momma.

"Andreas, I'm not ready for marriage; my mother was married very young."

"We're having a baby. We need to get married. Okay I'll tell you what, we can live here together until you're ready." I am tired and totally stressed out. Talking to him does not help, so I stretch out and fall asleep. When I wake up, he has prepared chicken soup and crackers. "We're going to have to tell your grandmother." I choke on the soup spraying it in his face.

"Are you crazy?"

"No I'm not crazy. I'm a man, and I'm not hiding behind anything I have done. I love you, and I am willing to take responsibility for you and my baby."

"I'm not telling Grandma anything." I look at him like he is absolutely out of his mind. I cannot believe he is serious about having this baby.

"Now wait a minute Thandisha. Now hold it. No you're right. I'll tell her."

"What?"

"Baby, I have struggled since I was thirteen trying very hard not to be like my father. I'm a man. You're having my baby. I will be responsible for my baby. I will take responsibility for you. I'm not a coward. I'm going to tell your grandmother with or without you." I fall back on the sofa, stretch my body, roll over, and cry into the pillow. I am afraid. What will Grandma do? What will she say? It is 3:00 and time for me to be getting out of school.

"Why haven't you left for work?"

"I called in sick today." Since I have known Andreas, he has never taken a day off work. I cannot believe he is serious about telling Grandma. "I told you I am going to talk to your grandmother."

"No not now." I quickly stand. "I haven't decided what I am going to do yet." I walk back and forth across the living room.

"Thandisha, you're not killing my baby. If you don't want anything to do with it, I'll have to accept that. But it is my baby too. I'm a man, and I will take full responsibility." I sit down on the sofa.

"Are you coming?"

"No, I can never tell Grandma something like this." He leaves. He is gone for over two hours. I cannot sleep. What is Grandma going to say? I anxiously wait for him to return.

Three hours later, he opens the door and comes inside with three suitcases.

"What's that?"

"Your clothes."

"She put me out?"

"Yes and no." He places the suitcase on the floor. "She said she respects me for coming to her like a man. We talked about an hour. She says she loves you, but she cannot deal with your being pregnant. I gave her the address and phone number; she and Khalid will visit this weekend."

"That's all she said?"

"No, she cursed me, talked about my mother and father, and damned me to hell."

"That's it?"

"No she said for you to stay in school, or she will never speak to you again. And she says you can come and get the rest of your things. She also said I could come and get some things that belonged to your mother tonight because you are attached to some of your mother's things."

Andreas unpacks and folds my clothes while I sleep. When I wake up, he is watching the evening news.

"Are you hungry?"

"No, I am still a little nauseous."

"Baby, you need to eat." I don't feel like eating. I don't feel like doing much of anything. Andreas borrowed his mentor's pickup truck and went to Grandma's house to get the rest of my things. My favorite piece of furniture was an antique cedar wood armoire that belonged to my mother. It takes up a lot of space. The apartment is small, but I have to have it near me. I place it on the side of the small foyer that leads to the bathroom and use it to hang my clothes.

I am scared; reality is sinking in. I am 18 years old, pregnant, and my most prized possessions are in my boyfriend's apartment. I enjoyed sneaking over here to be with him but actually living with him is scary. Can Grandma really put me out? Isn't that me and Khalid's house too? I want to call Grandma and apologize. I want to go home. I am crying uncontrollably when Andreas comes back in the room. He is with me, but I feel alone.

I look forward to the weekend. I want to see Grandma, Khalid and Aunt Mary. Surprisingly, I miss Grandma's house. I miss my little brother, who is not little anymore, coming in my room and getting in the bed with me because he is afraid to sleep alone. What is Khalid feeling? Is he feeling abandoned?

Every day is monotonous. Tuesday could have been Friday. Friday could have been Wednesday. The days were all the same until Saturday. I wake up, clean the apartment, and make chicken salad. Andreas goes to the grocery store for lemons, so I can make fresh lemonade and to give Aunt Mary, Khalid, Grandma and me some time alone.

I open the door on the first knock. Khalid speed walks into my arms and hugs me so tight I almost cannot breathe. I am equally happy to see him. Aunt Mary hugs me too. Grandma simply comes inside of the apartment; she does not greet me. She walks in and looks around the apartment.

"This is nice." I thank her. We sit down while Khalid plays with one of Andreas' video games. "You really got yourself in a fine mess Thandie, but I'll tell you like I told that boy."

"His name is Andreas." I know Grandma is going to blow this moment. I really do not need to hear her degrade Andreas.

"Whatever, I ain't taking care of a baby. I've done the best I can for you, but I be damn if I take care of a baby. You grown enough to spread 'em you better be grown enough to take care of it." I can see tears in Grandma's eyes. I know she is hurting. I do not get an attitude with her or give her any rebuttal. I sit quietly and listen.

"Come on now Thelma," Aunt Mary intervenes. "She's a child. She made a mistake; you don't have to be so hard." I want to cry but it is something about Grandma standing in my new home I am now sharing with my man that makes me feel I have to be strong and act like a woman.

"Is anyone hungry? I made chicken salad."

"Did you cook the chicken with that lemon stuff?" Aunt Mary loves my chicken salad. I use lemon pepper and fresh grated lemon zest to season the chicken.

"Lemon zest and lemon pepper? Yeah, Aunt Mary, I know that's how you like it, so I made it with lemon pepper and lemon zest especially for you." We sit at the table talking. To my surprise, Grandma agrees to allow Khalid to spend alternate weekends with me. Before leaving, Grandma gives me an envelope with five hundred dollars.

"I'll send your check when it comes." I am still receiving a death benefit from social security. "I'm sure you won't be going to college. So you'll have to wait until your twentieth birthday before getting the rest of your money. Now take my advice, don't tell that boy all of your business. A woman needs to have something put away for hard times."

One Hundred and Eighty Degrees

I love Thandisha. I have never met anyone who makes me feel this good. She makes me feel like a man or the way I think a man should feel. I don't know many men. Most of the men where I am from have been beaten down for so long by this system or declared personal wars on themselves all they can do is move in with lonely women who can provide guaranteed, government shelter and subsidized food. Thandisha makes me feel strong. She makes me feel like I can accomplish anything. She is pure and untouched. She was a virgin when we met. I feel so special to have been the first man and prayerfully the only man who has touched her. I am going to be a good provider for my baby, and I am going to take good care of my woman.

My mentor has always said no matter what the system has in store for me, I can be a man. His advice to me has always been being a good, black man is cherishing a good, black woman, and no matter what obstacles come my way, I must never abandon my offspring. His advice is I must fight for my children to the end. My mentor always says a man's life is in vain if he is not a father to his children. I intend to be the best daddy in the world to my baby.

Thandisha is a hard nut to crack. She is a good girl. Unlike the last time when I thought I was a father, I know this baby is mine. I can't really explain Thandisha; I know her mother was killed. This is why she and her brother live with their grandmother; but when I really think about it, I really don't know her. It's like she is holding something back. I know she is an excellent artist and a great cook. I know she still has nightmares about her mother. There is something about her eyes. Even when she is smiling, there is a deep sadness in her eyes.

Thandisha is what we call a cookie in the hood, a sweet girl. You never see her at any of the parties. She does not hang with a clique. She has a style of her own. She is gorgeous and sexy as hell. Her beauty is so subtle you can almost miss it. I think she does this on purpose. It's almost as if she doesn't want to be noticed.

I told momma I am going to be a daddy. She advised me to be careful. It was easy telling momma. I knew she wouldn't trip. I understand Thandisha's grandmother's anger. She has high expectations for Thandisha. She wants more for her. It's not that my mother does not have high expectations for me, just different expectations. When you have lived in the projects all of your life, it's different. My mother is okay as long as I am not stealing, using or selling drugs.

"Andreas, baby you know what happened before when you thought you were going to be a daddy." She is talking about Katanya. Yeah that did hurt, but I am over that.

"Momma, I know, but I have no doubt this baby is mine." I still feel special, she chose me. I still have the teeth marks on my shoulder from the first time we made love.

Thandisha is great, but it is a major adjustment living with her. She wakes up every morning before sunrise. She seems to have an internal alarm because she wakes up the same time every day. She showers, spruces herself up then she cleans the apartment from top to bottom. She never allows me to see her unkempt. She makes elegant meals. Her breakfast menu looks like something from a top rate food magazine. I'm just a regular bacon and eggs kind of man, but she has brought an

84

element of elegance and style to my life.

This pregnancy thing has been a trip. The bigger she gets, the more I want her, but she has lost interest in making love. She gives it to me once a week. Although I know it is pity sex, when I get it, I am so damn happy. Sometimes I wish I could be the baby all tightly snuggled inside of her.

She constantly complains she is tired. I understand why she is always tired. She is six months pregnant and still wakes up before sunrise. She will sit on the patio and paint or she may sit on the patio and drink hot tea while reading the newspaper. Even with all of these idiosyncrasies, I love her. Although I am sure my life is going to dramatically change, I can't ask for anything better. I am truly grateful to God she chose me. Even when I have to get up sometimes in the middle of the night, go to the store to get strawberries and whipped cream, and this is after calling home asking if she needs anything before I leave work. I feel as if I am the luckiest person on earth. I am truly on my way to becoming a man.

Khalid comes over every other weekend. I know I am not getting any when he visits. I really do not mind because she loves her brother. They have an attachment that would make an average man feel a little jealousy. Thandisha acts as if she is his mother and at the same time his best friend. She is very catering to her brother. Khalid gives his sister respect I have never seen in a typical sibling relationship. When Khalid visits, the apartment is crowded. I really have to get on the ball and look for a bigger place. The baby will be here soon, and this place is too small.

I have gone to all of her doctor visits. I was excited when I saw the baby during her first ultra sound. Though I could not see the detail Thandisha claimed she saw, the shadowy outline brought tears to my eyes. Thandisha claims she can see full detail. She and the nurse point to different features; all I can see is a round moving blob, but it was beautiful.

Thandisha will graduate in three weeks. The classroom setting became too stressful for her, so she completed her requirements in the Outbound Program for Pregnant Teens. I am very proud of her. It's been very hard for her. She lost her best friend, Ayanna. Ayanna quickly cut ties with Thandisha when she learned she was pregnant. She kept the pregnancy a secret from Ayanna as long as she could. When her pregnancy became obvious, their friendship was over. Every time Thandisha called Ayanna, Ayanna was always busy or on the other line. It took Thandisha a while to get the message. I understand her pain from losing Ayanna. After all, they were best friends for years. I really didn't care for her; I found Ayanna bossy and overbearing. I encourage her to find other friends, but she basically stays in the house cooking and painting.

I am anxious searching for a larger place, as that big moment is fast approaching. It is hard trying to find a place that satisfies Thandisha. She is determined we will live in West End. We look at different apartments, but she does not want it if it does not have hardwood floors. If it has hardwood floors, then something would be wrong with the ceiling. She does not seem to realize price is a consideration. It makes no sense to pay a grand a month for rent; I want to save money, so we can buy a home. Thandisha is clueless about money and has no concept of saving money.

When she gets her social security check, I ask her to save something. I pay all of the bills and buy all of the groceries, but she does not want to save. I put her name on my savings account and have to drag her to the bank and literally take $200.00 from her monthly check. She will not speak to me for a couple of days afterwards. She spends the remaining $300.00 in a week. She buys art supplies and clothes she cannot wear because she is too big and then gets depressed because she can't wear them. But I notice she rarely bought the baby anything.

It is the beginning of summer, the peak season for lawn care. I have saved $13,000 dollars. Not a lot of money for three years of working two jobs, but I am proud. Very proud because I know where I come from. I have a good momma, but she barely made the ends meet. I want to give Thandisha and my baby all of the things I dreamed of having when I was a child like a spacious home with pretty, clean, new furniture and soft, thick, clean carpet. I accept the hardwood floors because that's what Thandisha likes, but I really like carpet. I walked on tile covered with a throw rug here and there all of my life. They do not allow wall to wall carpet in the projects.

After several weeks of looking at almost every vacant apartment in West End, we finally find an apartment we both agree on. It is a two bedroom duplex in the West End. Although Thandisha does not like the ceilings, she compromises because she loves the hardwood floors. The bedrooms are humongous. Thandisha loves antiques, and the pieces she has collected fit perfectly in the new apartment. Her decorative taste reminds me of the colorful home decorating magazines at the checkout counter in the grocery store.

I love her so much. I am very proud of her too. I really want to give her my best. I want to take care of her. I mean really take care of her the way I would have wanted my pops to take care of momma. Momma had to worry about too many basic things while raising me and my siblings, and it took a toll on her.

Al, my cousin, helps me move into our new apartment. What should have taken all of three hours, took all damn day. Al and I move the same piece of furniture about five times before she is satisfied.

I am in the living room hanging pictures when I hear Thandisha scream. I run into the bedroom and find her kneeling forward holding her stomach. The front of her pants is wet. She looks down at the wet spot on her pants, then looks up at me, and starts crying.

"I peed on myself."

"No you didn't baby; your water broke. We're ready to have the baby." I hug her so tightly I can feel the wetness on my thigh.

"Oh God it hurts!" She holds the lower half of her stomach. I am trying to remain calm. I am only a man. I begin to panic. I call the doctor; he advises me to bring her to the hospital when the contractions are five minutes apart. I cannot sit still listening to her scream, and I am too damn anxious to sit and time contractions. I grab her bag and proceed to the door.

"Come on baby; let's go."

"Where are we going?

"To the hospital."

"I can't go like this." She looks down at the big wet spot in front of her pants.

"Thandisha, sit down." I support her as she walks kneeled over to the chair by the door. I pull her pants down; her panties are wet. I go to the bathroom, get a wash towel, and wipe her off.

"Oh God hurry, it hurts! It hurts!" She is crying still holding her stomach. I pull her top over her head and replace it with a thin pullover dress.

"Come on; let's go."

"What about underwear?"

"Damn, you're getting ready to have a baby; you don't need any."

"I can't go without underwear." She screams again. I look in the boxes and find a pair of her underwear. She steps in them, and I pull them up to her stomach. The contractions are about eight minutes apart; I think. When we get to the hospital, I call her grandmother. Ms. Thelma advises me to call her after the baby is born. I thought this is kind of cold; but she said she is coming.

The doctors are getting on my nerves. They are taking their time and acting as if this is not an emergency. Thandisha is screaming so loud I want to leave. I mean literally run out of the door. The nurse finally comes in and checks her.

"You're not quite ready sweetie."

"What do you mean she's not ready? Don't you see she is in pain?" I am perspiring as if I am the one in labor getting ready to push a baby out.

"Well Sir, you don't want her to rupture her uterus do you?" I do not know what she was talking about. I just want to stop my baby from hurting. I hold her hand, as she tries to do the breathing exercises. She starts off breathing exactly like the video instructed but ends up screaming and cursing me out.

"Look what you did! Damn you!"

"Just breathe baby just breathe. Don't push yet. You're almost ready." She screams again calling her mother and father. I never knew she had a father. Well I knew she had a father, but I assumed he wasn't in her life that maybe she didn't know him.

The nurse comes back in the room and checks her cervix again. "Honey," She gently touches my hand. "I think we are ready for this baby."

"You're ready baby." I change into doc wear and get ready to watch my baby enter the world. They wheel her into the delivery room. I stand at the top, but I can see. I hold her up to push. She pushes hard. Tiny beads of perspiration cover her face.

"Push," I lift her back and push her head toward her knees. Her face is tight; her veins protrude on each side of her temple. She pushes hard. I see the baby's head. Dr. Martin gives the command to push again. I am mesmerized; I forget to lift her back. Thandisha grabs her knees and pushes again at the doctor's command. I see the baby's small shoulders. The next push, the baby enters the world.

"It's a girl." Dr. Martin suctions her nose and mouth. The loudest wail I have ever heard comes from her tiny mouth. He gives the baby to the nurse who passes her on to me. Tears of joy flood my eyes. She is beautiful. I know I will do whatever I need to do to take care of my baby. I wash the baby and carry her to her mother. She lifts her head and meets my mouth with a long, passionate kiss.

The nurse takes the baby to the nursery while Thandisha rests. I call her grandmother; she says she will come to the hospital in the morning. She is cold, but nothing can take away my joy today. All of my family is at the hospital. My brothers, sisters, aunts, uncles and cousins fill the waiting area. Thandisha is overwhelmed by the abundance of relatives.

"Boy, that's a pretty baby. She gonna have good hair just like her mother. When they bald as an eagle that's how it turns out." My Aunt Annie is so into *"good hair"* she only had children with men that could produce light-skinned children with wavy hair. This is strange because she is dark skinned with tight, course hair. She passed this self-hate to her children. All of her children married Caucasians, Mexicans, or Puerto Ricans to produce kids with the *"good hair"* Aunt Annie worships.

I place the baby's bed in our room. I have everything in order when I bring my family home. Thandisha is still sore from the stitches, so my mother stayed with us for two weeks. I guess I did not have the opportunity to observe Thandisha's social skills. Most of the time, we were alone except when her brother visits. I notice she is very standoffish around my mother. She really doesn't relate to my mother. I am accustomed to everyone trying to create a good bond with my mother, as she has a very welcoming spirit. My mother tries conversing with her, but Thandisha's conversation consists of providing answers to my mother's questions. She does not initiate conversation nor does she sustain conversation with my mother. She is obviously uncomfortable, but I know eventually they will get along. Everyone likes my mother.

It takes a month for Thandisha to start getting around normally. She lost all of the weight. Her stomach is flat as a pancake. She looks good. I come home today before going to the second gig expecting to get some. Thandisha is on the pill and is more in the mood these days. I am pissed off when I see Jazmyne lying on the floor. Jazmyne is my sister who I truly love, but I honestly do not want Thandisha hanging out with her. I stopped fighting Keekee, her boyfriend. I have my own family now and cannot afford the trouble, and Jazmyne is trouble.

I know people blame the parents, but I can tell you my mother is not the blame for my trifling sister. I have three sisters and four brothers. We all worked our way out of the projects, but Jazmyne never understood that nothing is free; everything has a price. My mother did everything she could. I have a lot of siblings. But no one can call my momma a whore. We all have the same father. When my father left us, my momma did not have skills to support us, so we had to live in the projects. Momma always told us we made our own futures. She would often say, "We may live in the projects, but the projects are not in us." We didn't have money. My mother never owned a car, but once a month when her welfare check came, we would get on the train and travel to the upscale parts of town to see how other people live.

My mother was very structured. After school, we immediately completed our homework. She would sit at the table with us and look over our homework. She was so good I didn't realize she could not read until I was almost out of junior high school. Dinner was always ready when we came home from school, and we ate a good, hot breakfast every morning.

Unlike most of the kids in the neighborhood, we

were not allowed to go outside to play every day. Sometimes we had to sit still. When I say sit still, I literally mean sit still no television or radio just quiet time. My mother called this weekly two hour time period reflection. Jazmyne was never satisfied, and she could not reflect. She was more interested in the happenings going on in the street. She had to have name brand clothes and shoes. She wasn't bold enough to steal them, so she dated older men who bought her things. My momma did not look the other way. She beat her and punished her, but none of this did any good. Jazmyne is Jazmyne, and she does what she wants to do.

Jazmyne has lost a lot of weight. Dark circles surround her once beautiful, almond shaped eyes. Her skin is darker and blotchy. She and Keekee have their own place now, so I wonder why she is here. Thandisha is lying down with Kyia on her stomach. I hate when she holds the baby lying down; it is unsafe. What if she accidentally rolls over on the baby or mistakenly allows her to fall? Her hormones are still unstable, so I don't say anything.

I go into the bathroom and shower. When I come out, she is awake and arranging her perfumes on the dresser. I walk behind her, wrap my arms around her waist, slide my hand inside of her panties and massage her hardened clit.

"Did I tell you I love you today?"

"No," she turns around. "I don't think you did." I kiss her. We close the door. I enjoy making love with Thandisha. She is very passionate and there is a freedom in knowing I am the one and only.

"You take the pill today?" I hate to interrupt the mood, but as much as I love Kyia, I am not ready to have another baby.

"Hell yeah, I don't ever want to go through that shit again." I hate when she curses. It does not sound right when she curses. It may be okay for someone else but not

Thandisha.

I sit on the bed and watch her undress admiring the fullness of her breasts and the curve of her behind. She comes to the bed, straddles me and places a passionate, moist kiss on my lips. I use my tongue to part her lips and explore her warm mouth. I slide down and lay flat on my back. She crawls up and plants her neatly shaven mound on my mouth. I open the lips of her vagina and find the brown berry that always brings her pleasure. I lick and suck. She rocks back and forth to the rhythm of my tongue. The whimpers and moans follow pleas for me not to stop are music to my ears. I lift her hips and slide her down to my throbbing rod. She isn't ready. She takes my rod in her hand, strokes it, and places it in her mouth. She sucks and pulls until I am ready to explode. She crawls up towards the headboard, straddles me and places my erect manhood inside. She rapidly rocks back and forth and bounces up and down. She squeezes my chest tight. Her eyes are closed. Soft whispers escape her slightly open mouth. Her rhythm slows and she collapses on my stomach shaking as if she is having a mild seizure. I roll her on her back and go to work. Her body feels so damn good. Every time is always like the first time, good. I grab her legs and place them around my shoulders. I give it to her deep and hard. It is so damn good I am almost screaming. She places her hand over my mouth to muffle the sound, so Jazmyne cannot hear. After I climax, I lay quietly holding her in deep thought. I have never known her to go for what she wanted like this before. Usually I am the one who initiates and sets the tone to our lovemaking. Our eyes meet. We both have wide satisfying smiles. I kiss her and quickly get up, take a quick shower, and get ready for work.

"Are you going to your second job today?"

"Of course, I have three mouths to feed."

"Andreas come on, you work too much; we never have fun anymore." She looks sad and disappointed.

"Baby, I'm trying to put something together for us. It won't be long." I kiss her and leave. I pass Jazmyne who is now asleep on the sofa. I wake her up and tell her to put a sheet on the sofa. I do not like her with Thandisha and the baby.

I am happy. Things are going good. Thandisha, on the other hand, is not. She professes restlessness and boredom and no longer wants to stay home with the baby. Instead, she wants to work. I am reluctant about Thandisha getting a job, but it may be a good idea after all. A job will reduce the time she spends with Jazmyne. Her social security check ends next month; she really needs to start selling her art instead of working a job. She has painted six beautiful pictures since having Kyia, but she is determined to find a job. I try to explain to her she should work for herself, so Kyia will not have to go to daycare. I am not ready for Kyia to start day care. I try to convince her to sell her art at private showings. But she complains daily about being in the house with Kyia. My mother volunteered to keep Kyia, as she agrees with me that she is too young for daycare. Thandisha found a part- time job working from 8:00 am until noon at the library.

The job brought on arguments. I fill the car with gas every Sunday night. I give her lunch money. The problem is not what I do for her; the problem is she does not like to save. She cashes her check on Friday, and she is broke by Monday. She does buy diapers for the baby, and she buys an outfit every week for herself and Kyia. She and Kyia have so many clothes; it is pathetic. I had planned on quitting the night job; but then decided if we are going to buy a house, I had best continue working. I cannot depend on Thandisha to help with anything financial. Nor can I depend on her as a partner in purchasing a home for our family. When I attempt to include her in the savings plan for our future, her response is always, *"Whatever you want."* Although my business is doing well, I am still afraid to let the job go. I am afraid of not having enough money to provide for my family. That's one of the effects of growing up poor; there is always the fear you will not have enough.

Thandisha constantly complains about working and then keeping Kyia every day. I have to remind her that I suggested she find friends, so she could have a social life. She has not had another friend since Ayanna. Jazymne cannot be considered a friend. I hope she will end her relationship with my sister. I love my sister, but she is manipulative and untrustworthy. After constantly complaining of no social life, Momma agreed to keep Kyia until 8:00 p.m. on Fridays to give Thandisha time to herself. I am truly okay with this arrangement because I feel Thandisha should get out more.

I am focused on my work when I hear my name on the intercom. I have an emergency phone call. The boss came and got me off the floor; it is momma. I panic because she has never called me on the job. She is worried; it is 10:30 and Thandisha has not come for the baby. Kyia has a fever and is very irritable. Momma tried to take her to the emergency room, but they wouldn't see Kyia because she is not a parent or legal guardian. I panic. My first instinct is Thandisha has had an accident with the car. I clock out and go to momma's to get Kyia. When I get there, Thandisha still has not come for Kyia nor has she called.

By the time Kyia and I reach the hospital emergency room, her temperature has climbed to 104. She is immediately given liquids and antibiotics. Momma is right; she has a bad ear infection. We stay at the hospital until her temperature stabilizes. While I wait, I call around to several hospitals to see if she has been admitted. There is no Thandisha Riley Glaze checked in at any hospital in Atlanta, Georgia. We sit at the hospital for more than three hours. I have left several messages on her voicemail. Thandisha has not returned my calls nor has anyone heard from her.

When I get home, I call momma. She still has not heard from Thandisha. I thank her for calling me when Kyia was ill and let her know that everything is okay.

Every time I attempt to place her in her crib, Kyia screams. So I wait until she is sound to sleep before attempting to put her to bed. I wake up around 3:00 am to the sound of Thandisha trying to get her key in the door.

"Hey!" She jumps. She is surprised. Jazmyne is with her. I ask Jazmyne to leave.

"Bro, I need to spend the night; Keekee gone kill me." She walks through the door assuming it is okay for her to stay.

"Sounds personal sis."

"Come on now bro, Keekee gone beat the hell out of me. Look at the time."

"Well you obviously like it. Go Jazmyne. Get out!" I open the door and push her out of it. Thandisha is anxious. Her hair was loosely curled, thick, and beautiful. I can tell she has been to the hair salon. She is sexy as hell. The black halter dress she wears drapes her thin, shapely body. I am turned on but too pissed off to touch her.

"Where in the hell have you been?"

"I was out with Jazmyne."

"Until 3:00 in the fucking morning? Doing what?"

"We were just hanging out." She has the nerve to act as if my questions are getting on her nerves.

"What about Kyia? Did you know I had to take her to the emergency room?"

"You are her father; you are supposed to take her to the doctor if she is sick." Her nonchalant attitude makes me furious. We yell and argue until we wake the baby. She goes in the bedroom. I follow her, and before she can reach Kyia, I push her out of the way. She trips and lands on the floor. I pick up the baby, go in the living room, and watch television.

I hear water running in the bathtub, which makes me suspicious. My mind takes me places I really don't need to go. She stays in the bathroom a long time. When she comes out, I am in bed. She lets the towel fall, put on one of my t-shirts, and comes to bed. I am mad as hell, but I have a hard on out of this world; plus I want to make sure she isn't fucking around. She wraps her arm around my waist. My back is turned to her. She slowly slides her hand across my side and then down to my manhood. That's all it takes. I turn over.

"Oh Andreas baby I'm sorry. I'm so sorry baby." She covers my face with passionate kisses. I don't return the passion; I just want a good nut. She is on top of me holding on to the headboard giving it to me like she really wants to cum. I am pushing it to her strong and hard. I relish the disappointment on her face when I climax. She falls on my stomach, snatches the covers away from me, and rolls to her side of the bed.

Thandisha and Kyia are sound to sleep when I leave for work. I have to cut ten yards; thank God I finally purchase quality, landscape equipment. I have a good commercial lawn mower that can cut a two-acre yard in less than thirty minutes. I love doing lawn work. It's like play time for me. The smell of fresh, cut grass almost gets me high. The personal satisfaction of planting and seeing the seeds grow is indescribable. It's amazing how a seed grows into a little stump of greenery and then into a beautiful flower. Landscaping is like therapy for me. I feel so good I let that shit Thandisha did yesterday roll off my back.

I finish early. When I come home, the car is gone. I figure she and Kyia are at the mall, Thandisha's favorite hangout. I fall on the sofa, grab the remote and start flipping channels. My body is tired. Just as I doze off, I hear what sounds like a baby crying. I roll over onto my back and go back to sleep. I wake up when I hear the sound of a baby wailing. At first, I think I am dreaming surely she didn't. I know she wouldn't. I go into the bedroom. The smell is awful. Kyia stands in her crib holding on to the rails. Her diaper hangs off her behind showing the crack of her bottom. Fecal matter is stuck on her legs. The bed is soaked with urine. It takes a second before I can pick her up. I cannot move. Kyia and I stand still looking at one another. Finally, I take her out of the bed, remove the dirty diaper, bathe her, and powder her down. I give her a bottle. She literally gulps it down in what seems like three swallows. She sucks air and immediately begins to wail. I give her a jar of mixed veggies and a jar of fruit.

After feeding her, I play with her for over an hour before Thandisha walks in the door. I place Kyia in her walker. Thandisha stands still as if she is deciding whether or not to come inside. I grab her and pull her inside of the apartment and slam the door. I don't know what came over me, but I follow my first instinct. I slap her so hard a stinging sensation vibrates from my hand up to my shoulder. I totally lose control. I know I am hitting her with a closed fist, but I can't stop myself. I hear a mixture of crying from Kyia and screaming from Thandisha. When I pull myself together, she is covering her face trying to block the blows. Although she deserves it, I can't believe I allowed myself to go this low. I have seen my father hit my mother more times than I care to remember. I vowed I would never hit a woman no matter what. Thandisha whimpers and is cowering on the floor. Part of me wants to apologize and beg her forgiveness. The other part of me wants to kick her ass again and then throw her out in the street.

I go to my daughter and take her in the bedroom and hold her. I hold her so close it seems as if our heartbeats are synchronized. I am confused. I know I am doing what I am supposed to do. I am trying hard to be a man. I have nothing but my imagination as well as the advice of my mentor to guide me into manhood, but I am determined I am going to be a good man. I feel remorse and anger towards Thandisha at the same time. I am ashamed. I still can't believe I actually hit her. I vow to myself I would leave her before I allow myself to go this low with her again.

I go all kind of places in my head. I start noticing strange things like she stopped getting her brother every other week. She never has money although she is not buying anything for herself or the baby anymore. And worst of all she was hanging out with my sister.

Maybe she found someone and does not know how to leave or how to tell me. This shit is getting wicked. I could not have imagined in my wildest dreams she would behave this way. Kyia and I leave the apartment to visit my mentor. I have to get out of the apartment. I feel so many different emotions. I am suffocating. I told him I hit Thandisha. I told him I lost control when I came home and found the baby alone. He advised me to never hit her again to leave first. That positive, therapeutic, mentor shit sounds good, but damn, did he realize my baby was left home alone? I don't know how long she was alone. Kyia and I stayed away from the apartment for several hours.

When we return home, I see cigarette butts in the ashtray and smell smoke. Thandisha is asleep on the sofa. I hate cigarette smoke, and she knows I would never allow anyone to smoke in the house. What would make her want to smoke anyway? I didn't wake her. Her eye is swollen. She has on a t-shirt and underwear. She is bruised all over her arms and thighs. I do not want to wake her because I do not want to face her. Regardless of what she did, I had no right to hit her. My mentor is right; I should have left.

I take Kyia with me to rent movies. She is asleep, but I wake her up. I do not trust leaving her in the house alone with her mother. When we get back, Thandisha is awake. She has taken a shower; her hair is wet and stuck to her head. Her face is swollen. Her eyes are puffy and developing a black ring around them. I put Kyia on the floor. She immediately crawls to her mother. Thandisha picks her up and holds her. I really do not want her to touch Kyia, but she is still her mother.

"I bought Chinese takeout. You want some?"

"Yeah thanks." I really didn't want to give her ass nothing, but that would have been a little too rude not to mention somewhat immature. I brought two plates and two sodas in the living room. I prepare her plate while she plays with Kyia. We eat the Chinese food and watch the movies in silence.

I am enjoying this moment with my family until Jazmyne knocks on the door. She looks at Thandisha. "Damn girl you got a good ass kicking didn't you?" She laughs. Neither Thandisha nor I feel the humor. "What are you doing tonight? Do you want to go to the 24 kt tonight? Big Mac and the EZ's are performing tonight."

"Hell no, she don't want to go nowhere!"

"No Jazmyne not tonight."

"Nor any other night!" I step close to Jazmyne invading her personal space. "Look, don't come around here anymore. I don't know what's going on. You're my sister, and I know you ain't nothing but trouble."

"You think you're so damn much!" She stands back with her arms folded across her chest. "But you ain't no better than me! We come from the same damned sorry ass place! You ain't no damn better than the rest of us!" She rolls her eyes and jerks her neck. I push her out of the door and slam it in her face. I walk back to the sofa. We continue to watch our movie. Actually we are really just looking at the screen. I am waiting for her to say something, and she is doing the same.

"I'm sorry about today. I went to get something to eat and stopped by the store. I didn't think I would be gone that long."

"Thandisha, Kyia is a baby. You can never leave her alone. Don't you know this? She could choke; anything could happen."

"I am so sorry." She is crying uncontrollably. She is so different. Earlier it was as if she did not have emotions. She acted as if she was totally disconnected from her emotions.

"What's the matter with you baby? You been acting strange every since you been hanging with Jazmyne." She simply looks at me. She does not respond. I feel guilty. She comes to me. I hold her close. She cries; I mean really snotting. I wipe her face with one of Kyia's cloth diapers. She kisses me with a strong and yearning passion. Kyia is on the floor looking. She puts her hands down my pants. "Come on, baby wait; Kyia is watching." Where is she getting this shit? I am confused, but I like it. I give Kyia her medicine and a bottle; she finally dozes off on the blanket.

I never work on Sunday. Sunday is my day of rest; I am truly exhausted from working the job and running my business to go anywhere. Thandisha constantly complains I need to spend more time at home. She is right. I really do need to spend more time with my family, but I am consumed with making enough money to provide security for my family. She is lying on the bed flipping channels. Even after the baby, she still looks good. A lot of women let themselves go after they have children and believe me I understand. Taking care of a baby is not a joke. But Thandisha still has it. She still puts herself together very nicely. She is happy when I offer to take her and Kyia out for the day. We get dressed and go to Thandisha's grandmother's house.

I can't say Ms. Thelma is a model grandmother. To be honest, she is a horrible grandmother. She has seen Kyia three times. Ms. Thelma fusses over Kyia. She tries to hold Kyia, but Kyia isn't having it. She clings to me and screams every time Ms. Thelma tries to take her out of my arms. Ms. Thelma gives up on holding her, and admires her while I hold her.

"Thandisha was the same way. She didn't want to be bothered with anyone but her daddy." I find this strange; Thandisha never mentioned she had a relationship with her father. She never talks about him; I have never seen pictures of her with her mother or her father. I assume she was like many people I know who did not know their father, or the father was not part of their life.

I notice Thandisha and Mrs. Thelma really do not have very much to say to one another. They greet one another like distant friends unlike granddaughter and grandmother. It is strange; however, as always, Thandisha is very responsive to Khalid. She makes French toast, Khalid's favorite. We eat while Ms. Thelma tries to get Kyia's attention. Kyia continues to ignore her.

Khalid wants to go to the mall, and as usual, Thandisha obliges him. I spent all of the cash I had. I never write checks except on Friday to pay myself and pay my help. Reluctantly, I drive to the bank and use my ATM card to get money from my savings. I look at the balance. It is short by $2300. I take the money and walk back to the car.

"I don't believe this shit."

"What?" I look in my workbag and pull out my account register.

"Something's wrong."

"What?" Thandisha is occupied with filing her nails. Although she is responsive, her eyes are glued to her nails.

"They have shortened me over two grand. You haven't taken any money out have you?" I cannot see why she would need to. She works every day. Though it's only part time, she doesn't have to pay bills. She does not pay childcare, and sometimes I give her lunch money.

"No. Why would I do that?" She looks as if I have

insulted her. I feel guilty for asking.

"It must be a mistake with the bank. I will straighten it out on Monday."

Khalid wants to go to an electronic store. He is fifteen, but not a street-smart fifteen. There is no sign of a girlfriend. Maybe he does not have time because he is active in a lot after school activities. The disturbing thing is it seems to me their Aunt Mary, who is not really an aunt, is his best friend. Thandisha says Aunt Mary is the closest thing to a male role model Khalid will ever have. I think this strange. I mean he is fifteen years old, and she is an elderly woman. Why didn't he hang out with other fifteen year old guys in the neighborhood? I didn't understand what Khalid would have in common with an elderly woman. Khalid spent the entire $200 I withdrew from my account. It must be in their blood. He is like his sister. Neither of them understands the value of money.

On Monday morning, Thandisha wakes up feeling ill. I think she may have gotten a stomach virus because she is sweating and constantly in the bathroom. We ate a lot of junk food yesterday while hanging out with Khalid. I do not want to leave her, but I have six yards to cut. I call momma, but she does not answer the phone. I reluctantly leave Kyia with Thandisha and give her instructions on Kyia's medicine schedule.

I drive to the storage building and load my equipment. I drive back to my old neighborhood to get Jerome, my helper; he is drunk as hell. I don't feel like being bothered with him. I drive off, as he staggers towards the truck. It is 9:30 and still cool outside. It takes two hours to cut my first yard. I cut MRH's yard every two weeks. I am so proud of this yard I would almost service it for free.

When I first started my business, I had a walk behind lawn mower I transported in the trunk of my car. MRH is a small manufacturing plant. John Murray owns it. I drove by one day and saw the yard was getting out of hand and offered my services. Initially, Mr. Murray thought I was crazy when he saw my mower. He could not believe I would attempt to cut two acres with a cheap, walk behind, mower. He gave me the contract, and the rest is history. I go into the office and give him my invoice. As usual, he comes out of his office and talks with me about local news, politics, and the stock market. I respect Mr. Murray, and he respects me. Through him, I have gotten four other commercial accounts. He is a good businessman; what really impresses me most is he takes good care of his family. It seems the Mrs. is always on vacation or expensive shopping sprees.

Initially, Mr. Murray intimidated me. He is no-nonsense and very straightforward, but he is one of the few white men I have known who shows true friendship. It's just like my mentor always told me, "*If you conduct yourself like a man then you will be respected as a man by any man no matter if he is black, white, or green.*"

"How's the baby?"

"Mr. Murray, she is getting so big. She's wonderful."

"Son," he places one heavy arm over my shoulder. He reaches to shake my hand with the other. "When are you going to bring Ms. Wonderful by the office?"

"Soon I've been so busy; I haven't had time. I promise; I will bring her."

"My brother with the realty company mentioned how much he likes your work." He pulls out a piece of paper and gives me a phone number. "When you get a chance, call him. He has some business for you." We shake hands again, and I leave for the bank in hopes of straightening out the $2300 discrepancy.

As usual, the line is long. The line is never this long when I transact business in the predominately white neighborhoods. Luckily, they have a line for commercial accounts. I talk to one of the bank officers and ask for a print out of my account. I cannot believe my eyes. Thandisha has taken over $2300 dollars within the last two months.

We are saving to buy a house. She put money in the account but nothing close to $2300 dollars. Besides, we agreed not to touch the money without telling each other. I am puzzled because she hasn't bought anything for herself or Kyia lately. What is she doing with the money? I am certain it has to be another man. My mind goes back to the night she came home and took a bath, something she never does. Thandisha is a five minute shower woman. I am about to really nut up but decide to put this on hold. I have five more yards to service. Hell, no matter what was going on with Thandisha, I have to take care of Kyia.

It is two o'clock and time to take a break. The temperature can get painfully hot in Atlanta, Georgia. Today is one of those hot and humid days. I put my key in the door looking forward to the cold air from the air conditioner, but the safety latch hinders me from opening it. I hear several footsteps steps hustling around the apartment.

"Thandisha, open the door!" She does not come to the door. "Thandisha, open the fucking door!" I wait a few more seconds for her to open the door then I kick it in breaking the safety latch.

The apartment is smoky, but it is not a cigarette smoke. It is a thick, cloudy and stubborn smoke that does not move. It is not a marijuana smoke. But a subtle smoke that is kind of sweet but pungent at the same time. Keekee and Jazmyne look odd. Jazmyne has lost a lot of weight and looks like pure hell. I pick up the lamp and swing it at Keekee and push Jazmyne out of the door knocking her ass on the floor. Keekee leaves Jazmyne on the floor almost tripping over her as he runs outside.

I walk into the bedroom. Kyia is asleep; a bottle of cold medicine clumsily lies next to her. I feel as if I am trapped in a horrible nightmare. I walk back to the living room. She is sitting on the sofa; I stand behind her staring at the back of her head in total disbelief. I walk in front of her. Her face is an ashen, gray color, and she looks bad. There are no words to describe how bad she looks.

"Did you give her this?" She looks at the bottle of cold medicine and does not respond. She acts kind of antsy but not nervous just antsy. Her not answering is an indication I am right; she gave Kyia the cold medicine. "How much did you give her?"

"Not a lot, not even a full teaspoon." I walk out of the living room and back into our bedroom with the baby. I examine Kyia again. She is drowsy but seems okay. I am shocked and in total disbelief. I don't know how to deal with this. I place Kyia back in her crib and walk back in the living room with Thandisha.

"Why did you take the money?"

"What fucking money?" I am speechless. I am surprised. She is bold as hell. I do not know who the hell this is. The face and body are the same. But who or what occupying it is a stranger.

"I went to the bank; why did you take over $2300 dollars out in less than two months?" I look around for evidence of something she spent the money on, but there is nothing.

"I didn't take your damn money!"

"Don't lie to me!"

"What the hell is wrong with you anyway?" She clings tightly to her purse. I snatch the purse out her hand; she lunges at me like a wild animal. It is like she jumps off the sofa and into my chest without putting her feet on the floor. I push her back on the sofa and open the bag. When I see it, I almost collapse. My heart falls. It is a lipstick top with a broken ballpoint pen burned into the side. The top of the tube is covered with aluminum foil. It is still warm. Why in the hell would she have a crack pipe? I want to believe it is Jazmyne's pipe. My baby would never risk what we have for this, but no matter how hard I try, I can no longer ignore the signs. I go into the bedroom and pack a bag for Kyia.

There are so many women in my neighborhood on that shit. I have seen it drag down some of the people I grew up with; many were once honest, hard working and respectful people. It seems to drag women worse because when they run out of money, they can turn a trick for a hit. Not only does it fuck up the user, but it devastates the entire family. I do not know what to do. I just know I have to get my baby away from this scene. She sits on the sofa with her knees tightly pulled to her chest. I can't tell if she is crying because she is hurting or crying because her secret has been revealed. I walk from the living room back to the bedroom about five times before I can speak.

"Who gave this to you?" She doesn't answer; she holds her face in her hands; she is crying. It is not a loud, free flowing cry. It is the kind of cry you want to keep to yourself. I push her head out of her hands. "Did you hear me? Who gave you this?"

"I saw Jazmyne doing it, and I tried it."

"How long? How long have you been doing this?"

"About six months."

"Six fucking months! How? How could I not have known? Give me the keys to the fucking car!" She does not move, so I snatch open the purse again, throw the pipe on the floor, and crush it with my foot.

"No! No!" She is crying and screaming at the same time. She is on her knees trying to put the pipe back together. I knock it out of her hand and push her away from it. I go through her purse and take the car keys. I go back in the bedroom, grab Kyia, change her diaper, and leave. "Where are you going with Kyia?" She is crying uncontrollably; I can barely understand what she is saying.

"You need to decide what you are going to do by

the time I get back. You can either get some help or get out. I mean it!" God knows I don't want her to leave. I love her so much. I don't want Kyia to have the life I had. I want her to have her mother and her father in the same home. I don't want Kyia to ever question the love of either of her parents. I drive around for two hours trying to decide if I want to go to my mother's house. I really do not want to burden her. But I cannot think of anywhere to go.

The screen door is latched, but the wooden door is open. She comes to the door, unlatches the screen, and holds it open for Kyia and me. I step inside and stand in the middle of the living room. I am speechless. I look at momma; she looks at me, and I break down.

"Andreas, what's wrong?" I can't talk. "Arnell, come and get the baby!" Momma takes Kyia from my arms and calls for my sister. I sit on the sofa crying for what seems like an eternity.

"Baby, tell momma what's wrong." She places my head on her chest like she used to when I was ten years old and rocks me back and forth.

"Momma, she's on drugs. She's using crack."

"Who? Who's on drugs baby?"

"Thandisha."

"Thandisha?"

"What's wrong with Andreas?" Arnell comes back in the living room obviously eavesdropping. Kyia reaches for me trying to wiggle out of her arms.

"Thandisha is smoking that shit. She is on crack." Arnell does not look surprised.

"I told you momma; you know Jazmyne is on that shit too. And since they are together all of the time, I knew Thandisha had to be doing it too. Tell him momma that's why you won't allow Jazmyne in the house."

"Why didn't someone tell me?"

"I had to give Jazmyne to the Lord. I just couldn't continue seeing her so messed up or hear about all of those dirty things she is doing." Momma holds her head down and wipes the tears from her eyes. "Lord knows I did the best I could. If I didn't do right it was because I didn't know."

"What am I suppose to do momma?" I hope she will have a magic answer. I need something definitive. Something tangible that will work for sure like when I was a child, and I was afraid of the boogey man and she would come into the room and turn on all of the lights in my room, and we would look under the bed and in the closet and see nothing was there and then I could go back to sleep.

"Pray and give it to the good Lord. Take care of yourself and my grandbaby." I think, *is that all? Surely she has a more tangible suggestion than this.*

"But I love her momma."

"I love Jazmyne too, but I did all I could then gave it to God. Son, you are a hard worker. You are doing a good job. You have come a long way. Don't stop now; take care of yourself first and everything will fall into place." At this moment, the concept of powerlessness is very real to me. I would do anything to erase this shit. We sit quietly and do that reflection thing she had us do when we were kids.

"All of this crying is making me hungry. Want some dinner?" I follow her into the kitchen. Momma cooks Sunday dinner Monday through Friday and not that canned stuff either. She cooks fresh greens, candy yams, ham and corn bread. I sit at the table, as she prepares my plate with man size portions of everything. She takes Kyia from my arms and sits her on her knee. She then smashes up corn bread with the greens and feeds it to her.

"Momma, I have baby food. I don't think she supposed to be eating that yet."

"You ate it; look at you." Kyia gobbles the food down barely swallowing one mouthful before opening her mouth for more.

"Momma, I have to go back to work. I don't want to take Kyia…"

"Don't you even ask boy. You know I will watch my grandbaby anytime."

I leave Kyia with momma and finish the rest of my lawns. There is no way I can make it to my second job tonight. I am drained not physically but emotionally. I call in and take the night off. I know momma will keep Kyia, but there is no way I can work. Besides Kyia is not momma's responsibility; she is my responsibility.

I go home for a quick break before cutting the last yard; Thandisha sits on the sofa. She cannot look at me. I really don't have anything to say to her. We cordially greet one another.

"Where's Kyia?" She stands and pulls up her jeans. I notice she has lost a lot weight.

"I took her to my mother's."

"Why did you do that?" I cannot believe the nerve of this woman or whatever this is.

"I have more lawns to cut. Oh you didn't think I would leave her with you did you?"

"Why not? I am her mother." I want to slap her ass around again, but it wasn't worth the guilt I know I will feel later.

"Yeah you are her mother, but a sorry ass excuse for one."

"I am not a bad parent."

"You're an awful parent. You left her in the house alone. You allowed drugs to be used in the house while she was here and to make sure she didn't interrupt your party, you gave her fucking cold medicine. I guess you want to make her a druggie too. And to top it all off, you're a damn thief."

"Fuck you Andreas!"

"Fuck you bitch!" I leave on that note. I feel

horrible for talking to her so harshly, but she is really getting under my skin. I have to get out and away from her before I hurt her. By the time I reach the car, I am filled with anger. I can't leave. I turn over the engine three times, but I cannot manage to place the transmission in drive to leave. When I come back into the apartment, she is still sitting on the sofa. I walk to the sofa and stand in front of her. She does not move. "What the hell did I do to deserve this from you? Is there anything you wanted I didn't provide for you?" She does not respond. Her nonchalance is working my nerves. Without thinking, I grab her and pull her off of the sofa. We are screaming at each other neither of us hearing what the other says. Then she says it, and I cannot believe it.

"I had a mother and a father." She speaks like a confession as if she has done something wrong. She describes her father as a very successful businessman, something I am striving to become. She tells me about That Day. *That Day when her father killed her mother.* She can't give details. Though I am inquisitive, I know I should simply listen. She says she and Khalid were there. She says she was a happy little girl who loved her mother, but adored her father. She talks about Friday presents. She talks about the guilt she feels for still loving her father, guilt for still wanting to see him, and anger for not knowing where he is. She is crying sitting on the sofa holding herself with her knees bent and pulled tight to her chest. I am too angry to touch her. I try but can't touch her. "Please Andreas help me. Please don't leave me." I have seen Thandisha cry a few times, and it touches something so deep inside of me I can almost feel her pain. How can I help her? I am trying to build one man from several images. I have no personal example to follow only the advice of my mentor, a minister here and there, or a boss I try to emulate. She is still crying. I am powerless because I know there is nothing I can do, so I finally put my arms around her and hold her close. I kiss her and try to reassure her everything will be okay. I don't know how, but I know it will be okay. "I am going to quit the job at the plant and work my business. Maybe if I am home more often, it will take some pressure off of you." I take three days of vacation from work to spend with Thandisha. It turns out to be a good decision. My body actually needs the rest. I have been working two jobs for so long I almost forgot what it is to rest. We don't leave the house the entire three days.

On Thursday morning, I get up, shower, and cut my scheduled lawns. When I come home, Thandisha is deep in sleep. I kiss her and leave for the second gig at the plant. I speak with Mr. Duncan before going to the work line. Without going into detail, I tell him I am having family problems and offer to give a two-week notice.

"Son, I will accept your resignation; but I thought you were saving for a home for your family."

"Yes Mr. Duncan, that was definitely the plan, but something has kind of come up making that next to impossible right now."

"You have worked here for a while now. You're a damn good worker. There is a supervisor position coming open. Management has their eye on you. Why don't you just take some time off and work out whatever is going on? Don't quit now. You have your woman and a baby to think about."

"Yes sir, I know. To tell the truth, my family is the reason I need to quit. My girl is having some problems, and she needs my support. If I get a home or promotion and she is not with me, what's the point?" He doesn't like my answer, but he reluctantly accepts my resignation with a two-week notice. I am relieved. I know I will eventually be able to purchase a home. It may take a little longer, but it will happen.

After work, I go home; not knowing what to expect, so I don't expect anything. She is in the bed lying on her stomach asleep. I go in the bathroom and take a shower. I am hungry; I warm leftovers. I am laying on the sofa watching television when she comes in the living room. I greet her, and continue to watch television.

"Where is Kyia?"

"She is with my mother. I'm tired. I let her stay with momma." She lies on the sofa with me. Initially I don't touch her. I am angry, scared and hurt. I thought I had everything a man could want. I have a beautiful baby; I make decent money. I thought Thandisha and I were solid. This latest revelation has turned my world upside down, but I still love her. I eventually wrap my arms around her. I hold her very close to me. I hold her so close I can feel her heartbeat. I want to protect her and take all of her pain away. I want to make everything okay. I am tired. Thandisha is tired; we go to sleep.

When the alarm goes off, I don't want to get up. I am exhausted. Not a physical tired but a mental tired. She is cradled in my arms holding me tight. I try to slide from under her without waking her but to no avail.

"Good morning," I place a soft kiss in the center of her forehead.

"Good morning." We lay still in the bed holding one another.

"Are you hungry? Do you want breakfast before you go?"

"No that's okay; get some rest."

"Are you bringing Kyia home?"

"I don't know."

"What do you mean?" Surely she understands. Surely she knows after this latest revelation, I would not trust her with Kyia alone.

"I have to work tonight." Before I leave, I remind her Jazmyne and Keekee are not welcome in the house. She does not respond, but I know she gets the message.

TWO HUNDRED AND TWENTY-FIVE DEGREES

He thinks it is easy. He doesn't understand. I am trying. I have not used in a few weeks. I am trying, but it is hard. When I heard a knock on the door, I did not answer. I was afraid it was Jazmyne or Keekee. I didn't want to get high. I am too afraid to start. Because once you get that first hit, it's over. Everything goes downhill from the first hit. I never intended for it to get like this. I never, in my wildest dreams, thought I would get hooked. I thought I could control it. But I couldn't. I would have never allowed it to get out of control if it were in my power. I fought hard for the control, but each time I was defeated. Each time I was defeated, I felt more and more like a loser. The more I felt like a loser the more I needed to use.

I cook chicken manicotti smothered in marinara sauce and clean the apartment from top to bottom then start on a picture of Andreas and Kyia. I hope he will bring her home tonight. I love my baby. But when I am smoking, it blocks everything. The only thing I can feel is the urge to use more drugs and fear I will run out. I wish like hell I never tried it. Sometimes just thinking about it, oh God even now, when I am thinking about it, I get so anxious I have to clear my bowels.

I saw Jazmyne smoke crack a while back. I didn't try it for a long time, but I remember the look on her face. She had gotten into a fight with Keekee. She was upset and crying. But after she inhaled the smoke from the pipe, the anger and hurt on her face was replaced by a peaceful, euphoric glow.

I tried it for the first time after Kyia was born. I felt a lot of pressure. My whole life had changed. Although Andreas was with me and totally supported me, I still felt alone. He was gone all day and half of the night. On the outside, I looked okay. I dressed myself up, but even that was a copycat style of some chick I saw in a magazine. On the inside, I was empty and still haunted by the memory of *That Day*. It is as if my past is stalking me.

I used crack to stop thinking about the memories. It allowed me to pretend I never had a mother or father as if that life never existed. I went several years with the memories of momma and daddy locked safely away from my conscious mind. But after Kyia was born, I couldn't stop thinking about them. I felt the pain over and over again. I was always thinking about momma, remembering her smile, and all of her unique facial expressions. My fond and beautiful memories of my momma were replaced by a deep and empty longing to see her. I would have given anything just to touch her. I felt so much guilt for still loving daddy, longing to see him, and still thinking he could make everything okay. I could not think about momma and daddy and not think about That Day; the two went hand in hand. My own mind was attacking me; I declared war on myself. My weapon of choice was crack, a weapon of assured destruction. From the first hit, I was doomed. I could not control the compulsive obsessive nature of the drug. Sometimes I wouldn't want to do it, but I couldn't help myself. I couldn't stop myself at will. Using made me feel okay; it allowed moments to escape the horrible, fixed images and thoughts that were constantly occupying space in my mind.

He thinks it is easy. Andreas has a foundation; he knows what he wants. I don't have a foundation. Grandma provided for my physical needs, but my emotional needs were totally neglected. We never talked about That Day. We never talked about momma or daddy. We really didn't live together; we lived amongst each other. There were so many times I wanted to write daddy. Although he did what he did, he was the only parent I had left. I don't know how many years he was sentenced to prison. I don't know what the actual charges were. Grandma may have known, but I knew better than to ask.

Andreas is a good man. He is strong. He is a good father, but unlike Andreas, I have no purpose. I am simply occupying space. I know God placed him in my life for a reason. It feels good having someone love me, but I really don't love myself. I am empty, so I can't reap the rewards of his love. The only thing I feel good about is my art and cooking. I put a lot of feeling into my art and a lot of love into my cooking, just like momma. When momma gave away her recipes, she would write down the ingredients and the last ingredient was always "two cups of love."

People love my art. They love my cooking, especially my pastries, so I put a lot of energy into them and became a great artist and a great cook. When I paint, I have total control. I can create my world any way I want with the stroke of a paintbrush, charcoal, or pencil. I have been painting all day. Well at least since Andreas left. I am tired of painting, so I make lunch and turn on the television. As usual, there is nothing on the television. I have never watched a lot of television anyway. When I was a kid, momma rarely allowed Khalid and me to watch television; instead, we played games and read books. Television was a treat like going to the movies.

My life is so different now. I have been exposed to all kinds of people. Most of these people are not really people but demons that have taken on human form. The evil, sick behavior associated with drugs is a nightmare. It is worst than any boogey man I could have ever imagined. It's like carrying the boogey man with you all of the time.

I knew I would never be the same. Evil has a way of permanently changing you. When I smoke, I would usually go to Terri's house. Jazmyne introduced me to Terri when I first started smoking crack. Terri lives in run down apartments owned by a rundown slumlord. She has four children with three baby daddies. She doesn't work, but she does *"favors"* for people to keep her rent paid. We would sit in her apartment all day smoking and drinking. Even when her children came home from school, the party would continue. Her children would walk in and speak to her as if having bugged eyed, crack smokers throughout their home is normal. She may place the pipe down and nonchalantly ask about homework but then quickly continue the party. I sometimes felt guilty for smoking crack when her children were in the home; however, my guilt did not stop me.

We would start off buying a gram. It would be gone in an hour. Terri never has money, but she allows people to sit in her home to use, so she can smoke for free. At the beginning of the month she allows drug dealers to set up camp in her apartment to cash in on the welfare moms. Jazmyne never has money either, but she steals from Keekee or turns tricks.

Addicts, the broke ones, play a trap game. It took me a while to get hip to it. Jazmyne would give me a small hit, and that's all it would take. Once I started, I couldn't stop. I would go to the bank and withdraw $200 at a time. I went through this vicious cycle all day sometimes. Andreas thought I was working. In fact, I only worked a few months, and when I did work, I spent my entire check in the crack house with Jazmyne. This is how I spent over $2300 of Andreas' money. I didn't mean to do it. I was somewhat conscious of what I was doing. I know Andreas is very meticulous about his money; his checking and savings account registers are balanced to the penny. He can even project his quarterly interest to the penny. I knew he would eventually find out I was taking money from the account, but my cravings were so strong, I didn't care about the consequences. I was only concerned with getting high.

Initially, I would share everything, but the drug made me selfish; it became all about me. I wanted it all to myself. I would buy two grams, share one, and smoke the last gram by myself. Everyone would get mad sometimes to the point they would want to fight. I was oblivious to the danger of getting high in the presence of drug craving addicts. As long as I had my rock, I really didn't give a damn about anything. I knew it was a use game, but I was getting something out of it. I didn't care. It is a crazy game.

I have some morals about myself. I do not sleep with drug dealers for it. Jazmyne once told me she slept with D380 for a gram and tried to convince me to sleep with him too. D380 is a supplier to the street peddlers in Jazmyne's neighborhood. Sleeping with a supplier can bring celebrity status in this game. When I look as Jazmyne, I see myself if I don't stop. Right now I want one. I want one bad. Keekee, Jazmyne's boyfriend, is always propositioning me. He tells me to keep my money and rubs the inside of my palm when he places the rock in my hand. Andreas would kill me. I guess I would kill myself.

I hear Andreas place his key in the door, and Kyia's familiar whine. I stand in the threshold waiting to greet them, as he opens the door. Kyia reaches for me; I gladly take her out Andreas' arms.

"Does she need her diaper changed?" I check. She is wet. Andreas goes to bathroom. I hear the shower. I clean the kitchen sink, so I can bathe Kyia without Andreas looking over my shoulder. I pour baby bath oil in the sink and allow her playtime in the water. I wash her hair, dry her, and powder her down. It feels good holding her in my arms. Andreas comes back into the kitchen. His back is still wet.

"Did you have a nice day?"

"Yeah," his tone is dry. I wait for him to say something about me bathing Kyia in the sink; he does not.

"What about you?"

"I kept busy. I did a lot of cleaning."

"I see; everything looks nice." He smiles as he looks around our small but very clean apartment.

"Are you hungry?"

"Yeah," he acts as if he is bipolar; his answer is cold and pompous. He is trying to piss me off so we can argue, but I am determined not to argue. I prepare a plate filled with chicken manicotti and buttered garlic bread on the side and place it on the table in front of him. He doesn't thank me. He immediately eats the meal by the spoonful. It always amazes me how much Andreas eats and still maintains his sleek physique. The food must have been good. He ate without saying a word. Everything is going good until he opens his mouth.

"You okay? You didn't do any of that shit today did you?"

"No, I fought it; Jazmyne knocked on the door two times, but I didn't open it." He smiles; I am happy he finally gives me a genuine smile.

"That's good. That's real good."

"My stomach has been cramping all day, but I made it." He smiles a little easier this time.

"That's good baby; that's real good." Kyia is fussy. I give her to her father while I wash dishes and warm her bottle. "Thandisha, you don't have to warm it; she is old enough to drink it cold. In fact, she is too old for a bottle any way. She is almost a year old." I hate when he does that. He acts as if he knows everything and as if I don't know anything. He seems to forget when he worked all day and night; I was the one who took care of her.

"Yeah I know, but it is better on her stomach if it's warmed. My mother gave me and Khalid warm milk until we were five years old."

I cradle Kyia in my arms, and give her the warmed bottle. She looks deeply into my eyes. I stare deeply into hers. If not for myself then I have to stay clean for my daughter. I love my baby. It may seem as if I don't, but I do. Andreas is reclined on the sofa with the remote flipping channels. His constant changing of the channels is annoying. I am tired. Kyia and I go to bed. I place her on the bed close to me. She is snuggled tightly in my arms.

"Thandisha, she is not supposed to sleep in our bed. She has her own bed." Before I can respond, he takes Kyia out of the bed and places her in her crib. After placing Kyia in her crib, he walks to his side of the bed and jumps in the bed. I can't say he is trying to disturb me on purpose, but it seems to me he could have gotten in bed much gentler. I bounce up and down at least three times before the mattress finally settles. He reaches for me; I am not in the mood.

"I'm a tired tonight." The truth is I am angry and hurt. He acts as if I don't know anything. I messed up. I messed up bad, but I am not stupid. Kyia wakes up as usual at 3:00 am. I change her. Before I can finish, he is standing next to me inspecting a fucking diaper change, something I have done a thousand times.

"What?" I roll my eyes. He acts as if he doesn't understand. He makes me so fucking sick always acting as if he is so damn perfect. "I am changing her diaper and getting her a bottle. Do you have to watch everything I do?"

"Maybe I do."

"When she was born, I was here not you! I took care of her all day and night! So I messed up, but I am still her mother!" I reach to get her. He pushes me out of the way. He picks her up, goes in the kitchen, and gives her a bottle of cold milk.

He sleeps on the sofa with Kyia the rest of the night; I sleep in the bed. Actually, I don't sleep. I lay in the bed listening to music. At sunrise, I get out of bed and shower. It is cool outside. The air smells good. I make an omelet, hot tea, sit on the patio, and read the newspaper. He walks into the living room and places Kyia on the sofa. She is still asleep. I continue reading the paper. I figure he is going to shower and leave for work. I look forward to him leaving, so I can spend time with Kyia alone. I am very uncomfortable with Kyia when Andreas is around. I feel as if I am under surveillance.

I am livid when he comes back into the living room fully dressed with Kyia's bag in his hand. We make eye contact. I don't say anything neither does Andreas. He leaves. I am angry and frustrated; I have no money or transportation. The walls are closing in on me. I don't want to be home. I know Jazmyne will come, and the way I feel, I probably will open the door. To keep my mind occupied, I clean a spotless kitchen, mop a clean floor, and dust dustless furniture.

I feel a sudden and almost urgent need to leave the house. I know he has an extra car key. I go to the closet and check the pockets of all of his clothes throwing each piece in a pile on the floor, as I finish. I cannot find the car key. I pull the backs out of all of the pictures. I still cannot find the key. I am frustrated. My stomach begins to cramp, and I have an urgent sensation to empty my bowels. I run into the bathroom barely making it to the commode. When I finish, I continue to search the house for the key. I find it under the corn plant in the bathroom. I grab the key and contemplate my next move. I begin to feel guilt, so I rearrange the pots in the kitchen, clean the refrigerator and mop the kitchen again.

I grow tired of cleaning the house. I feel claustrophobic again. I have to get out of the house. My heart tells me to stay home, but the obsession quickly takes over. It's like I really don't want to go. I know I am harming myself and causing a great deal of pain to my family. I am cognitively aware of the pain I am inflicting on the people who love me most, but my feelings are shut off. I cannot respond to their pain. I walk towards the door.

I open it and close it again. The key without money is useless. I can't go to the bank anymore because he closed our joint accounts and opened new checking and savings accounts. I know not to call Andreas and ask for money. He will want to know what I need and purchase it for me.

I call Aunt Mary. I act as if I called to chat. She brings me up to date on some happenings I could have cared less about, but I pretend to be interested waiting for the opportunity to slip in a request for a $50.00 loan. I know she will give it to me. I lie and tell her I need the money to buy diapers and milk for the baby.

Aunt Mary's house is very feminine with pretty, pastel colors. It is the complete opposite of her masculine persona. She greets me with a genuine, welcoming embrace. As always, I enjoy talking to her. My initial plan is to get the money and leave, but her presence is calming and peaceful; I almost forget my motive for the visit.

"Where is the baby?"

"She is with her grandmother. I need to take diapers and milk over because she is running out. Andreas must not have looked in the diaper bag before he left." I didn't want to tell her everything. She knows I am not working and probably wonders why I don't have my own baby.

We talk about *That Day*. I can't believe I actually initiate the conversation.

"If I tell you something, will you please try very hard not to tell Grandma?" She does not respond which means I will have to take my chances. "I've been thinking about *That Day*." She looks at me. I continue. "You know when momma was killed." Tears begin to fill my eyes. "The day daddy did what he did. Aunt Mary I try so hard, but lately I can't get it off my mind. I can't stop thinking about it. I don't even know what happened to daddy. This may sound awful, but I want to find daddy. I want to see him. I know what he did was wrong. I know what he did left me and my brother orphaned, but I also know he loved my mother."

"I know he did. I know he loved your mother too." I am surprised to hear Aunt Mary say this. "I don't know what made him lose it like that. I just know Riley was Thelma's only child, and Thelma was devastated." I look down and away from Aunt Mary. I feel guilty because it occurs to me I have never considered my grandmother's pain.

"You are so much like your mother. I know your grandmother may have not been what you wanted." She pauses for a second and ponders what to say next. "Really no one could be your mother but Riley. Every time she sees you, you remind her of her loss. You look almost identical to your mother. Can you imagine having to relive your daughter's death every time you see your daughter's child?" I really couldn't imagine that. Grandma and I never talked about momma or That Day. We acted as if it never happened. Actually, we never talked about anything. I never felt Grandma took care of me out of love. I felt she cared for me out of an obligation to my mother. I know she adored my mother, but I didn't feel she loved me. Even before *That Day*, Grandma and I were always at odds. She really didn't like my daddy or anyone else who occupied momma's attention.

The urge to release my bowels returns. I want to take the money and leave. But I know she would think that strange. Aunt Mary and I sip tea and talk for a while longer. I excuse myself to the bathroom. When I come out of the bathroom, I thank her for the loan and drive to the mall. I attempt to do something to distract myself from the crack house. I am trying very hard not to use, but the cravings are strong.

I take advantage of the ten-minute reprieve, when the cravings disappear, and walk around inside of the mall. I used to love to shop, but fifty dollars will buy me the kind of stuff I like. I don't feel like trying on clothes because I know I would not be able to afford my taste in clothing with fifty dollars. I go to the gallery next to the mall and look at work of other artists.

My stomach begins to turns when I think about the fifty dollars in my pocket. I try to walk it off. I try to talk myself out of it, but my body is in pain. My stomach feels as if it has turned inside out. I quickly exit the mall and walk to the car. My stomach cramps and a sharp, piercing pain permeates the left side of my head. I turn off the road and into the parking lot of a corner gas station and run into the bathroom to empty my bowels.

I am in route to Keekee's and Jazmyne's house still trying to talk myself out of it. I turn around three times and was almost home, but the compulsion takes over. I turn into a fast food restaurant. I barely make it to the bathroom. I run back to the car and drive to Jazmyne and Keekee's apartment. I want relief. I drive into their driveway. A loud squeal from under the car startles me. I mistakenly shifted the transmission in park before the car completely stopped.

Jazmyne and Keekee meet me at the door. Keekee pushes Jazymyne behind him. He stands in front of me licking his lips and looking at me from head to toe.

"Girl, my brother let you out of the house and gave you the car too?"

"No, I found the extra key. Give me a dub." I give Keekee twenty dollars. I smoke it in less than thirty minutes. It wasn't enough. So I buy another dub and then a dime. It isn't enough.

"You need anything else?" Keekee stands behind Jazmyne rubbing his crotch. The scene is eerie, so I grab my bag and leave. I am so high; I can hardly drive. I look at my watch. It is 7:00; I pray Andreas will not be home before I get there, but as Rev. Deal used to say, *"God always answers prayer, but sometimes the answer is no."*

I start to drive off, but he opens the door before I can shift the transmission in reverse. I place the transmission in park, turn off the engine, and get out of the car.

"Where have you been?" I close the car door and walk through the patio door without answering him. His voice becomes louder. He is oblivious to the neighbors who stop in their tracks to see the sideshow. He grabs my chin and looks in my eyes. "You high, ain't you?"

"No."

"Then where were you?"

"I went to the mall, and I spent some time with Aunt Mary."

"I thought I took the car key."

"You did." I place the key in his hand, as I walk pass him. "I found your extra key." I walk to the bedroom. I don't have to look back to know that he is following me. I can feel the heat from his breath on my neck. "Where is Kyia?'

"She is asleep." He is still waiting for an explanation. I keep walking. I go in the bathroom and fill the tub with hot water. He sits on the bed, so I stay in the bathroom to undress. He comes into the bathroom while I soak.

"What is up with you and this bathing thing? You usually shower. When did you start this?"

"Since today about three minutes ago." He picks up my panties, looks at the crotch area, and puts it to his nose.

"When you finish doing whatever you are doing, please be so kind and close the door." I roll my eyes and sink down in the bathtub. He stares at me hard and long then walks out of the bathroom slamming the door behind him.

I soak for half an hour trying to bring myself down from the high. I begin to feel remorseful. Andreas is a good guy and really does not deserve this. My baby does not deserve this shit either, but I honestly didn't start out with the intention of getting high. If he had left the baby, I wouldn't have done it. I would have stayed in the house and taken care of my baby. I get out of the tub, slowly dry my body, put on a t-shirt, and get into bed. He comes into the room and turns on the light. I pull the covers over my head. He slams the nightstand drawers. Then he goes to the dresser and to the closet slamming the doors as hard as he can. I know he is trying to get on my nerves, but I ignore him.

I wake up at 3:00 in the morning and cannot not go back to sleep. I look over my shoulder; Andreas is sound asleep. I go into the kitchen to get a glass of milk. We are out of milk. I make a mental note to tell him to pick up a gallon on his way home from work. I go back to bed and try to go back to sleep. I am not sleepy. A pungent, sweet, smell slowly enters my nostrils. Initially, the smell is faint but keeps getting stronger. My stomach starts to turn. I run to the bathroom and empty my bowels. I go back to bed but still cannot sleep.

I try to wake Andreas. He mumbles something, turns over, and goes back to sleep. I run back into the bathroom to empty my bowels again. My stomach cramps hard. I slip on my jeans and a sweatshirt, creep in the living room, and call Terri. I ask her to meet me at the corner. I feel so sick I should have called an ambulance. I quietly walk to the dresser and get his wallet. He has thirty dollars. Initially, I was only going to take the money, but I saw his checkbook. I flip to the back of the checkbook and pull out the last two checks. He is so meticulous; he would have remembered the last check number he used. The cravings are strong and painful. I grab my jacket and walk to the corner. I wait five minutes before Terri arrives.

"Girl, what's wrong with you?"

"Let's go to Jazmyne's and Keekee's house."

"You sure you want to go there? You know they are cheap as hell." I know what she says makes sense. I heard Keekee and Jazmyne are both using, and nothing is worse than a dealer who is his best client. I know I can get more for my money elsewhere, but they live closer than anyone I know.

"No Terri I really don't want to, but I am craving so bad; I'm sick. Let's just go and get a hit from them and then we can go somewhere else."

It's almost 4:00 in the morning, and their lights are still on. People are walking out of the house looking like zombies. The drug is so evil and powerful after a few hits you quickly begin to look like the walking dead. Almost immediately after the first hit, an ashen layer coats the skin. It's the kind of ash you can't get rid of with lotion or even petroleum jelly. Karolyn, one of Jazmyne's friends, answers the door. Her eyes are bulging, and she looks as if she has been up for a week.

"Is Keekee and Jazmyne here?" She stands in the door blocking the entrance.

"What you want to see Keekee for?" He comes to the door and gives Karolyn a long, wet, and sloppy kiss. He steps outside closing the door behind him.

"What's up?" He props himself on the door while slowly rubbing his crotch.

"Give me a dub." I anxiously count twenty, one, dollar bills.

"You know baby you don't have to pay for anything. Anything I got is yours. All you have to do is ask, and it will be given." I know exactly what that means. I find it hard to believe someone so unattractive can think this much of himself.

"Look I have money; you going to sell to me or what?"

"Who the hell you getting smart with crack head, stank, bitch?" His name-calling doesn't bother me. All I want is a good hit.

"Are you going to sell to me? If not, I'll go elsewhere." He steps close to me, grabs me, pushes me against the door, and fondles my breast. I scream. "I've wanted you for a long time." "Bitch, what you doing with my old man?" Jazmyne comes outside and pulls him away from me. I am speechless. I may be a crack head, but I still have taste. I want to tell her what happened and reiterate to her that she is probably the only woman on earth who wants Keekee. Jazmyne is obviously stoned out of her mind, and I don't think she will understand. She looks like pure hell. Her teeth are decaying, and the fact they are outlined in gold make them a focal point. She curses me, but I really don't understand what she is saying because all I want is a hit. "I know you been wanting to get with Keekee bitch. If you weren't my niece's mother, I would kick your ass bitch." Although bitch is a one-syllable word, Jazmyne rolls it out of her mouth and manages to make it two syllables. I don't respond. I get back in the car with Terri, and we leave.

I want to curse Terri out because she didn't try to help me. I really am not surprised because you have no friends in this game. It is truly everyone for themselves, and the name of the game is, "*I am gonna get me me.*" I want to drop her, but I need her to get around. We drive ten minutes to D380 and buy a gram for the $30.00. He gives us a $20.00 credit. It is not that he trusts us or even likes us; this is the way they reel you in. It's kind of like holding you hostage. You are free to roam, but when that craving hits; you come back to the dealer who cut you a little slack in hopes of getting something extra, but that rarely happens.

We go into one of his rooms in the back of the house. I am so anxious I cannot not hold the pipe steady long enough to place the rock on the ashes. My legs are shaking and my stomach is turning so bad that I need to clear my bowels again, but I have to get this first hit. My muscles immediately relaxed. The sensation to release my bowel disappears. My hands instantly stop shaking. I am calm. The first hit feels good; it's a set up. The first one starts the chase, and you will never catch it again.

Everything is okay, and then paranoia sets in. I feel as if something is going down as if someone is plotting to harm me. What or who is out to hurt me, I don't know, but it is a strong feeling.

"Come on Terri; let's go." She looks at me as if I am crazy.

"Where are we going?"

"Hell I don't know, but something is going down. We have to get out of here. They're watching us." I stare at the closet door. I quickly walk to the door and snatch it open. Of course, there is no one inside. Although I don't see anyone; my mind tells me someone is there. I look through the clothes that clumsily hang on shapeless wire hangers. I look under old shoes that obviously have not been worn this decade. My mind tells me someone is in the closet, and I believe it.

"Aw girl ain't nobody messing with us; we are the only people here. Sit down and relax." Terri has the pipe in her hand getting ready for another hit. I quickly grab my jacket and dart for the door. She reluctantly follows behind me; I have the money. We get in the car and start driving. It is nine o'clock. The bank is open. I remove one of the checks and write it to myself for $500.00. I sign Andreas' name and cash it.

"You are dead. Don't go back home Thandisha; Andreas is going to kill you." Though she is laughing, I take her comment seriously. I know he will be angry and would probably try to kill me if he finds me. We drive past Keekee's house and decide against going inside; instead, we drive to Norris' house.

Norris lives a block east of Keekee and Jazmyne. It seems as if everyone in this neighborhood is drug affiliated. It is a shame because the houses on this street are well maintained. Most of the lawns are perfectly manicured. The neighborhood is old, but the homes are sturdy. Original owners, elderly people, who have lived here since the establishment of the neighborhood, occupy most of the homes. The drug dealer are usually the grandchildren, or in some cases the homeowner's children, who for whatever reason got attracted to quick money and decided that a minimum wage job wasn't going to get it. Why work forty hours a week for $200.00 when you can make $500.00 in two hours?

Norris inherited his house from his grandparents. They raised him after his mother died. Norris is not as harsh as some of the other dealers in the neighborhood. I used to think he and Terri had a relationship, but then I found Terri doesn't have relationships with anyone. With Terri, everything is about getting high, and she only socializes with people who can provide the means for her to get high.

Terri knocks on the door. It is 9:30 a.m.; everyone in this game is usually asleep. It's a nocturnal game. You play all night and sleep all day. It takes a couple of minutes for Norris to come to the door. Terri briefly speaks with him and walks back to the car.

"He's still working. What do you want to do? He says we can stay here and hang out."

"Okay, that'll work. I give her $150.00 to buy three grams." I get out of the car and walk into the house behind her. We walk into the living room, step over sleeping bodies that are probably crashed out for the day after smoking all night. We walk down a dark hall, that reeks of urine, into a back bedroom. I immediately lock the door and pull out my pipe. I am calm and still coming down from my first high. When I think about it, it really is a waste of time. I get high for hours, but after the first hit, you don't get high anymore. You are simply blowing smoke and chasing after the first high you will never get again. I constantly pace the floor. I know I am getting on Terri's nerves.

"Girl, will you sit down?" I sit down. I am actually tired. My body is exhausted, but my mind is going a hundred miles per hour. I sit on the floor and smoke some more; we must have smoked for five hours straight. When I look in my pocket, I only have $60.00 left.

"Terri, give me my money! I know you got my fucking money!" She is baffled.

"Thandisha, you are really tripping. You bought nine grams instead of three. Look in your pocket. She is right. I look in my pocket, and I have five grams left.

"Girl, I'm tripping." We sit down and smoke and smoke and smoke. I am so tired I fall asleep. Usually it's hard to fall asleep when you still have drugs. Even when you have smoked all of your dope, your heart is beating so fast it is hard to calm down and actually sleep. I don't know how long I slept, but when I wake up, it is dark. I look over my shoulder to find Terri deep in sleep. I am too tired to wake her, so I go back to sleep.

The sun, shining through dark green, water stained curtains, wakes me. I don't know the time, but I do remember going to sleep in the daytime and waking up in the middle of the night and now it is light outside again. I sit up and look at the walls. I am not sure how long I have been here, but I know it is too long. I place my hands in my pockets only to find them empty. I don't have drugs or money. I place my hands in my bra and find the other check.

"Terri, wake up." Terri is still deep in sleep. She does not move.

"Terri! Terri!" I slide closer to her and push her shoulder back and forth in an attempt to wake her. She grumbles but still does not wake up. I had money in my pockets earlier. I thought I had sixty dollars left. I am almost certain, but not quite sure, I had more money. If I did have money, I am sure Terri stole it. She is the only person who knew I had money.

I nudge her again. She rolls over on her side.

"What?"

"Let's go."

"Where? Where do you want to go now?"

"I don't know; I just want to go." I sit for a second contemplating the next move. "Let's go to your apartment."

"I thought you were afraid Andreas would find you."

"I am sure Jazymne has already brought him to your place by now." We stand still half-asleep. We step over the same bodies we stepped over when we came in.

"Thandisha, I am tired. I need another hit. You have anything?"

"No, I'm all out."

"Let's go cash another one of those checks." I think to myself, *how does she know I have another check*? She probably took my damn money, but the excitement of chasing a high again is overwhelming. I don't have time to spend interrogating Terry.

"Okay let's go." I keep looking at her out of the corner of my eye, as Terri is very cunning and cannot be trusted. We drive to the first Asset Capital Bank we see. I am nervous. I think to myself: *What if he knows I took money out of his account? What if he has already reported the checks stolen?* I am afraid of getting arrested, but the desire to get high is overwhelming, eradicating any fear of going to jail.

I stand in line and cash the check. I know I must have an offensive body odor. I have not been home in at least two or maybe three days. I really can't remember if it was two days or three, and I have not bathed in as many days. I am self-conscious about my appearance. My hair is frizzy and in an unraveling, long, thick plait that hangs down my back; it is obvious I have not combed my hair. I look at other women in the bank. They are neatly dressed with well-groomed hairstyles. In comparison, I look a mess. My body odor is pungent, and my clothes are dingy and wrinkled. Dark circles surround my puffy eyes. It is obvious I am in need of sleep.

I place my identification on the counter and present the check to the teller. I am nervous as hell on the inside, but I am able to hold a trivial conversation. She enters the check numbers into her computer. I am relieved when I see her place the check in the stamp machine. She counts five, crisp, one hundred dollar bills and places them in my hand. I place the money in my bra and exit the bank. I want to run to the car. My mind keeps telling me it is a trick, but I am relieved when I leave the bank's parking lot without being followed by policemen or bank security.

We go to Keekee and Jazmyne's house and buy a slab then drive to the liquor store and purchase a bottle of cognac. By the time we get to Terri's house, we are both craving like crazy. We are shaking so badly we can hardly walk. My stomach cramps; the pain permeates the entire lower half of my body. I have emptied my bowels so much I doubt if there is anything left in my intestines. The first hit immediately calms both of us down. It takes a lot of hits before we can talk again. We were hitting back to back on a hopeless chase for our first high. We are so engulfed in getting high that it takes a while for us to respond to the knock on the door. Terri and I are looking at one another hoping the other will stop smoking and answer the door.

Terri finally places her pipe down and answers the door. It is Jazmyne with Keekee standing close behind her licking his lips and eyeballing me as if I am a tasty lollipop.

"Well ain't you going to invite us in?" Jazmyne stands in the door with her hands resting on what used to be wide, voluptuous hips.

"No, I'm not."

"What you mean you ain't going to invite us in? Hell I could put an end to this damn party. I hear Thandisha is spending money like water. I'll call my brother. I'm sure she stole the money from him because I know neither one of ya'll whores could have sold enough pussy to be buying like everybody say ya'll is."

"Jazmyne, you can stay if you want, but Keekee ain't bringing his stank ass in my house, and I don't care who you call."

"Terri, why come he can't stay?" Jazmyne's eyes bulge from her head. She looks as if she has not slept in weeks. What I thought were gold teeth were not gold after all but tarnished, gold colored metal.

"Fuck you bitch, we ain't gotta stay here in this rat trap. Come on Thandisha; girl, let's go."

"I'm going to stay here." I agree with Terri. Keekee is bad news. I am in a catch twenty-two. I do not want Jazmyne and Keekee's company, nor do I want Jazmyne to tell Andreas where I am. She is right I stole the money from Andreas, and I am not ready for him to find me and end my party. I walk Jazmyne to the door and place a dub in her hand.

"You my girl Thandisha. Don't worry I won't tell Andreas where you at. You got a couple of dollars I can hold?" I pull out a twenty and give it to her. "This the best you can do?"

"Girl, I am busted."

"Cool, we will hook up later." She looks at Terri, turns her nose upward, and rolls her eyes.

"Cool." With Jazmyne and Keekee gone, Terri and I are free to continue our party, but the guilt is setting in. I have not been home in two or three or maybe four days. I continue to smoke to keep from coming down. I don't want to feel the guilt. When I smoke crack, I know I will not feel anything, but no matter how much I smoke, I am no longer getting high. I am simply blowing smoke.

I gather my things and walk to the first bus stop I see. Terri comes out of the house calling my name begging me not to leave. It is not that she enjoys my company; I have money. I don't look back; I continue my route to the bus stop. When the bus comes, I don't bother to ask the driver his destination. As long as the bus goes to a train station, I know I can get home. That's one of the advantages of living in Atlanta; all of the buses eventually stop at a train station. The high quickly wears off. Remorse sets in. I cannot remember how long I have been gone.

I smell myself. Although it is not hot outside, I am drenched with perspiration. A strong stench is attached to my skin. I am in desperate need of a shower. I don't know exactly what I am going to say to Andreas. I know I can't say I was at the mall; besides, he already knows. I have broken many promises to him. I know he loves me, but I honestly can't help myself. If I could do better, I believe I would. At this point, I am totally powerless to this drug. Crack cocaine knows my name, my social security number, and my DNA pattern. It has all of the control. Even when I say I am not going to use, when it calls my name, I am totally helpless. I don't want to be at its mercy, but I am helpless. I can't seem to fight it. It starts with a smell that slowly creeps into my nostrils. Initially, it is a subtle aroma that increases to a strong pungent but sweet aroma. I can be simply washing the dishes, and it comes after me; no matter how hard I fight, it always wins.

The train is crowded. It must be the morning rush hour. I am self-conscious about my appearance. I can smell myself, so I know the passenger next to me can smell me too. I try to keep my arms down and keep still in an attempt to keep my odor subdued. I am scared but relieved when I arrive at my stop.

The apartment is around the corner from the bus stop. I walk as slowly as I can. I ponder what I will say when I see him. I decide I will simply tell the truth, and we can take it from there. The apartment is quiet. The only noise comes from the television in our bedroom. I walk down the hall. The door is slightly open; I slowly enter.

Andreas is asleep. I walk closer to the bed. A slim, curvaceous body is snuggled next to him. I pull the covers back. Dee briefly holds her head up, looks at me, and lays her head back down. I am too upset to cry. Of all of the women in the Atlanta Georgia, he has to fuck my ex-best friend's sister. I walk out of the room and close the door. I walk back to the bus stop. Just as the bus arrives, I see Andreas standing on the patio in his robe. I board the bus. I didn't start out with the intention of going back to Terri's, but somehow that is where my feet take me. She opens the door, as I am getting ready to knock.

"Hey girl, you back?"

"Yeah, I'm back."

"Well come on in. I have a run to make, but I will be right back."

The apartment is quiet. It actually has the potential to be a nice apartment. It looks old and run down on the outside, with abandoned cars, old furniture and remnants of household trash scattered about. It is obvious the landlord's only interest is the monthly rent check. On the inside, the apartment has potential. It is clean and decorated with thrift store furniture. If it weren't for the half dressed dolls and a couple of children's books, I could easily forget Terri has children. The oldest two now live with her grandmother. Although the youngest two have different fathers, Derrick, Terri's last boyfriend, took them both. She was in the process of losing the children to child protective services, so she gave them to relatives. It is rumored she persuaded her oldest, the nine year old, to perform oral sex on D380 for a twenty dollar rock. She shows no remorse. Nothing has changed; Terri's routine remains the same. Her daily agenda is finding the ways and means to get high.

I am almost asleep when she reyurns. She was gone for a couple of hours. She comes back with Keekee, Ron, Cedric and Jazmyne. I am uneasy when I see them. Terri always acts as if she hates Keekee. I understand her bringing Ron and Cedric. Ron is a drug dealer and Cedric is his sidekick, but I do not understand why Keekee is here. "Hey man, let's fire up some Yay." I know Keekee is smoking now, but I thought he and Jazmyne are still trying to keep that on the down low. It is almost shocking to see him jumping for a hit like a regular dope fiend. "Wait a minute man. Hell chill out! You already owe Ron $200; you need to make good on that." "I told you man; I'll have your money tomorrow." "Yeah you need to have my money, and I want cash. Jazmyne's pussy done got old." Ron and Cedric are laughing giving each other high fives. Keekee is laughing but his laughter does not appear genuine. He is smiling, but his facial affect is flat and expressionless.

"Ron, you so crazy." Jazmyne is laughing so hard her body trembles as is she is having convulsions. I find it hard to believe she finds this funny.

"Thandisha, don't you have some money?" Terri knows I had money earlier.

"I got a couple of dollars." Actually, I have $100 in my pocket, but I am not going to tell Terri how much money I have. This scene makes me nervous.

"I got $25 on a gram." This is a surprise since Terri never has money. I go in with Terri to buy a gram. Of course, we have to share with Keekee and Jazmyne. I can't get high looking at Keekee. He acts as if he has been smoking crack all of his life. A gram is a decent amount of dope for one person, but it is not enough for four crack smokers. We finish the gram in no time. I am focused on Keekee. His behavior is strange. He is in the corner with Ron almost begging for another hit. Jazmyne is on Cedric treating him as if he is God. It does not seem to bother her that Keekee is in the room. When I see Ron with his pants down standing in front of Keekee who is on his knees, I almost throw up. I have to leave. I have to go. I grab my bag and head for the door.

"Hey little momma, where you going?" Cedric pushes Jazmye out of his way and walks towards me.

"Excuse me!" I try to look tough. "You talking to me?"

"Yeah I am talking to you. You smoked some of my dope too. You need to pay one way or another." I know what this means.

"Look motherfucker, I paid for my dope! I don't owe you shit!" I attempt leave again. He slaps me so hard I hear bells ringing in my ear.

"Bitch, you ain't leaving till I say you are." I start to panic. I want to scream, but in this neighborhood I doubt if anyone would care. I scream for Terri to help, but she is in the kitchen getting high and totally oblivious to me. Cedric slaps me again knocking me onto the floor. He grabs a hand full of my hair and pulls me back to my feet.

"Look Ron; she is kind of pretty." Ron walks towards me pulling up his pants looking straight in my face.

"Oh this that bitch Jazmyne's uppity ass brother been looking for."

"Hell it sure is. Damn, she looks good."

"Come on man let's take her ass for a ride." They give each other a high five laughing while pulling me out of Terri's apartment. To no avail, I kick and scream and fight with everything I have. I have never been this frightened before. I cry, plead, and beg them to let me go. We are almost to the car when I hear a loud bang

"What the fuck?" Cedric and Ron immediately let me go.

"Leave her alone!" I cannot believe Keekee is actually helping me.

"Boy is you crazy? Get your whimp ass over here and suck my di…" I hear two consecutive, rapid gunshots and then Ron falls to the ground. Blood pours out of both of his knees.

"Look who on their knees now." Keekee laughs like a mad man. His eyes are sad, but he laughs so hard I can actually see his tonsils.

"Wait a minute now Keekee, man, don't take this shit so seriously." Cedric walks towards Keekee pleading with his hands up. Keekee points the gun straight at Cedric.

"Go on Thandisha!" The gun is pointed at Cedric. Keekee's hand trembles like an addict feigning for a hit. "Get out of here!" He motions for me leave. I turn around and run down the street away from Terri's apartment. I hear a third gun shot. I stop, but I don't look back. I keep running. I do not know where I am going. I run to the first bus stop I see. I sit on the bench, catch my breath, and try to grasp what happened at Terri's. I pray Keekee hadn't killed anyone, but grateful he didn't allow Ron and Cedric to hurt me.

My heart is pounding so hard it feels as if my heart will jump out of my chest. I am too afraid to stay at the bus stop. I sprint to the phone booth across the street. I do not know who I am calling; I dial the first numbers that enter my head. I am relieved when I hear Grandma's voice.

"Thandisha, is this you?"

"Yes Grandma, it is me, Thandisha. I am in a situation. Can you come and get me?"

"Where are you?"

"Grandma, I don't know. I don't know where I am."

"What do you mean you don't know? What is wrong with you? Are you high on that stuff? Andreas told me you are using that crack stuff. He said you stole his money." I do not respond.

"Grandma, someone tried to hurt me. Please can you come and get me?"

"Where are you?"

I look up and see the name of the street. "I am on Caitlyn Avenue Grandma. I am on Caitlyn."

"Well Caitlyn Avenue is a long street, and it's too

late for me to come there. I don't go out at night. Call me in the morning, and I will meet you somewhere." Grandma hangs up the phone. My heart sank. The little to no traffic on the four lane street makes the normally busy street appear desolate. The silence is chilling. I've slept in unfamiliar places before but never outside in the open elements. I am cold and scared. I sit with my back against the building jumping at every unfamiliar sound. I must have sat behind the dumpster for four or five hours before the sun began to slowly rise above the Capital Building. I feel more at ease as the street slowly comes alive with moving automobiles on the street, and pedestrians walking the sidewalks.

I am relieved when the first bus arrives. I dodge oncoming traffic, as I run across the street to the bus stop. The bus driver slows down, looks at me, and keeps driving. I am sure I look a mess. I walk to the gas station at the corner of the street and sneak into the bathroom. I am right; I am a mess. My hair is all over the place. My eyes are bulging and surrounded by dark, puffy circles. My face has a grayish undertone; it is so sunken, it looks like I am sucking the inside of my cheeks. I pull my hair back with my hands, walk back to the bus stop, and wait for the next bus.

I ride the bus to the train station, transfer to another bus, and go to Grandma's. I wait down the street outside of the subdivision until Khalid leaves for school before I knock on the door. I do not want him to see me like this. I am hesitant, but I find the courage to knock on the door.

"Hi Grandma," she is speechless. Her eyes scan me from head to toe. She does not invite me in. I have to lightly push the door open and walk around her to get inside of the house. "Grandma, I know I'm a mess." She stands with both hands on her hips unable to take her eyes off of me.

"Thandisha," She raises her shoulders and throws

her hands in the air.

"Grandma, I've been sick. Andreas is right. I am addicted to cocaine." I want to say crack, but if I admit to using crack, I have no hope of her helping me. People react worse to crack though it is a derivative of cocaine. I want to cry to persuade her to take me serious, but the tears will not flow. I still cannot feel all of my emotions. She stands in the doorway still speechless. "I would like to get some help. Maybe I can go to a treatment facility or something. I've heard people go to those places when they are sick."

"With what?" She laughs. "Thandisha, I don't have insurance on you anymore. Remember you refused to go to college, so your insurance benefits stopped when you turned nineteen."

"Grandma, I need help. Someone tried to kill me. I have been on the streets for three maybe four or five days. I don't even know exactly how long."

"Well what happened between you and Andre'?"

"You mean Andreas."

"Whatever, he said you have been gone for over two weeks."

"We had a difference of opinion." I do not want to address how long I had been gone because the truth is I do not remember.

"He said you were on drugs, and you left the baby."

"That's almost true."

"What part is true?"

"I guess all of it Grandma. Only I didn't intend to leave my baby." She continues to stare. I can't read her expression. "Grandma, I want to be honest. I am sick. I need help." I try to control my sporadic movements. "Can I please stay here until I figure something out?"

"I don't know Thandie; you have to be able to follow my rules. You and I both know that is not possible. You do things the way you want to do them." She stops speaking and stares as I compulsively scratch my arms.

"Why do you keep scratching? You don't have anything. Do you?"

"No, it's just a nervous habit." I pause to read her mood. "Grandma, will you please just give me a chance? I mean just long enough for me to get a job and a place to live." She never said I could stay, but she didn't tell me to leave.

I cautiously walk to my old room praying she will let me stay. I am so tired; I can barely walk. I go through the closet. Grandma has not changed. She never throws anything away. I find an old shirt. I tip toe to the bathroom and shower. The water is purifying. I feel cleansed. I sit in the tub for several minutes before drying myself. I go back into my old room, fall on top of the bed and instantly fall asleep.

Two Hundred and Seventy Degrees

I feel a soft, warmness brush across my cheek. The touch, light as a feather, stimulates the surface of my skin.

"Thandie," the voice is familiar. It is soft and raspy as if it is plagued with laryngitis. I am not afraid. I do not feel threatened because I know this voice. I have heard it many times many years ago.

"Momma, is that you?" I sit up in the bed and search for more detail, but all I can see is a cloud-like form.

"Hi baby; it's me. I came to tell you it is okay now. You don't have to hurt yourself anymore." I begin to think I am dead or dying. I touch my face, and it still feels the same. I place my hand on my heart; I can still feel its rhythm. I reach out to her, but I cannot feel her; there is only the cloudy form.

"Why are you hurting yourself? Do you think this is what I want for you?" She used the same matter of fact tone she used when reprimanding me when I was younger. "I was taken away, but it was not your fault. It was my time. I want you to forgive yourself for whatever you feel you have done that would cause you to bring this pain in your life. I have forgiven you. God will forgive you. All you have to do is ask. Ask him Thandie, and he will forgive you."

Tears flow from my eyes like a gushing river. I know this is my momma. I cannot see her, but I can feel the comfort, the same comfort I felt before *That Day*. I long to feel her arms wrapped around me. I want to touch her soft, pecan, brown flesh. I want more than this cloudy form.

"Momma, it's you. Momma, oh God, you're back. I prayed for a long time for God to bring you back to me.

You're here." I move closer to the form. "Momma, I have been so bad. I have done so many bad things." I sob so profusely I can barely talk. I whisper, "I am addicted to crack cocaine. I have neglected my family. I have brought shame to my brother."

"I know. I saw. I feel your pain, and that's why I am here to tell you it's okay now. Let go. You can go on. You don't have to hurt yourself anymore. My spirit is at peace. Everything happened for a reason." There is a familiar calmness in her voice. "Your brother loves you; you can never bring shame to Khalid." The form slowly begins to disintegrate. "Thandie, I have seen you grow into a beautiful young woman and fall in love with a great guy. I have seen my beautiful grandbaby. I know you love her, but you have to stop hurting yourself. It was not your fault." The hand that is not actually a hand but a cloudy outline of a hand moves closer and slides across my face. It is warm and soothing. The form comes closer and lay on the bed next to me the way momma used to. She had a way of lying on her side with her body slightly curved like a model or movie star. "Remember I am still here with you; it's okay." The form is gone, but the feeling of peace is still present.

"Momma," I call out to her, but the soft, raspy voice does not answer. I look at the clock; it is 7:30 a.m. I am not tired. I am relaxed. I know I am not dreaming. My momma was here, and she told me everything is okay. I feel a sense or peace I have not felt in a long time. At least at this moment, I do not have the desire to use; my addiction does not have control of me. I feel good and strong enough to look at my life and go back three hundred and sixty degrees to *That Day* when my daddy shot and killed my momma. I can face it now. I have to forgive myself and ask God to forgive me. I drop to my knees and pray. I ask God for forgiveness for having anger towards him. I ask for forgiveness for having no faith, and I pray for the strength to face my fears and my pain.

I sit still and bask in my new peace. Something surreal has taken place. I am ready to face the world. My hair and clothes are drenched with perspiration. I go to the bathroom and shower, wash my hair, and twist it in a tight bun. I go back to my old room and rummage through the closet. I find a pair of old jeans and borrow one of Khalid's sweaters. The jeans are baggy. I was always petite, but I lost a lot of weight. I sit on the edge of the bed engulfed in this new aura of peace. I know God heard my prayer. There is no battle within me. I feel a sense of peace for the first time since my daddy killed my momma.

I tiptoe to the kitchen and make toast. I know Grandma does not mind, but I am uncomfortable eating her food. I don't want to wear out my fragile welcome. I sit at the table and read one of Grandma's magazines. Everyone in the pages appear happy. I want happiness again. I want to smile again; not a superficial smile but a smile that comes from my soul.

So far Grandma has not asked me to leave, but I know this is not a long term living arrangement. I need a job, so I can take care of myself. Someone has always taken care of me. Although my inheritance will be coming soon, I need to support myself until my twentieth birthday. I want my own place to live and feel comfortable living alone. The house is big enough to accommodate me, but I know my healing process will be better if I live on my own.

Khalid is awake lying in his bed watching television, as I walk pass his room. Grandma finally allowed Khalid a voice in decorating his room. He finally has age-appropriate furniture. I do not like that he sleeps on a futon mattress; he needs more support. I like the flashing lights in the ceiling as well as the framed posters of pretty girls and hip-hop stars that adorn his bedroom walls.

"Hey Sis, what's up?" I stand in the doorway of his room. "Have you eaten breakfast?"

"Yeah I made toast."

"I am kind of hungry myself." Not only do I enjoy talking to him, I enjoy looking at him and admiring his maturity. He has a very gentle spirit unlike the young men I grew accustomed to interacting with when copping drugs. I follow close behind him, as he goes into the kitchen. He opens the refrigerator, reaches for the gallon of milk, and places it on the table. A sudden sadness comes over me. I missed a lot quality time with him, but he acts as if nothing has happened. He still shows me respect and love. When he first saw me after coming back to Grandma's house, he was speechless. I was a mess. I had lost a lot of weight. My once perfect complexion was gray and blotchy, but he acted as if he did not notice.

"Are you going to drink the whole gallon?"

"No, just half of it." He laughs. I know momma would be proud. Khalid is not only handsome, but he is smart. He still makes all A's, and he is involved in many extracurricular activities at his school.

"Khalid, I am so sorry. I am sorry for not taking care of you. I know you have heard bad things about me; some of them are probably true. I am truly sorry." My eyes are slowly filling with tears.

"Thandisha, you don't have anything to be sorry about. I feel bad I wasn't old enough to protect you and take care of you; I don't care what anyone says or said about you. You are a star to me, and I am not talking about a rock star." We both laugh. Rock star is one of the many street synonyms for crack addict because the drug looks like rocks. "But seriously Thandie, it has been a long time. I made peace with momma's death a long time ago. Don't get me wrong. I still have bad dreams. I still have bad days, and I still miss her. For a long time, I didn't allow myself to like girls because of what happened."

"Yeah right as handsome as you are Khalid, I have a hard time believing that."

"No seriously Thandisha for a long time I was afraid I was like daddy. I was afraid I could kill. I didn't allow anyone to get close to me like maybe there was a gene that could cause someone to kill, but then I realized I want a fine honey to take to the movies and hang out with. I realized daddy's behavior was his and not mine. I don't have to carry his issues. I am only responsible for my own. Momma came to me in a dream; I guess it was a dream. It seemed so real." He looks up toward the ceiling and quickly shakes his head as if he is trying to jog his memory. "She told me she was okay. She told me I was okay that I didn't have to worry." I couldn't believe it. I didn't tell Khalid about my experience. But it is comforting to know I am not crazy, and she was actually here with me. "Thandie, I don't know if you can handle this, but daddy writes me."

"What?" I am shocked. I didn't think he would have the desire to communicate with daddy. He was a momma's boy, and I was a daddy's girl.

"Grandma doesn't know, and I understand it may upset her, so I don't tell her."

"Where is daddy?" I am not interested in Grandma. I want to hear more about daddy.

"He's still in prison, but he gets out in three years."

"Do you write each other often?"

"Yeah, at least once per week." I want to ask for the address, but I do not have to. He goes in his room, comes out with a box of letters, and gives them to me. "Thandie, if you want to read them, you can; I understand if you don't want to read them. I want to tell you one more thing."

"What's that?"

"I want you to know I love you more than anything on earth. I remember how brave you were the night momma was killed; I understand if life has been too much for you, but I want you to make peace with yourself." His eyes are filling with tears. I punch him in the arm. He pours a glass of milk, stands, hugs me, and returns to his room.

Khalid has a contagious calmness. I enjoyed the family reunion with Khalid, but I have to start looking for a job. I go back into my old room, put on my shoes, and leave for the store. I pass Ayanna's house. I want to stop and see her parents, but I am ashamed. Ayanna is in college, and she is probably doing very well. I would love to see Mrs. Williams, but I don't want her to see me like this. I walk to the store and purchase a newspaper. I take my time walking back. I am truly enjoying myself. It is as if this is the first time I have ever walked these streets. I can smell the taste of freedom. Although I am still sick, the chains of my addiction feel lighter.

Grandma and I return to the house at the same time. She gets out of the car with bags in both hands. A strange, accusatory look covers her face. I am not trying to make myself at home here. I know she will not allow that to happen. She has placed dead bolt locks on all of the bedroom doors except for the one I sleep in. I cannot get offended. Just because I have not stolen from her does not mean I won't. When you are on drugs, anything is possible.

"Where have you been?" Although she asks this question accusingly, I am so happy I do not get offended. No one is going to steal my joy today.

"I just came back from the store to get a newspaper. I am going to look for a job today. Let me get your bags." She is reluctant. She holds tight to the bags, as I take them out of her hands. I carry the bags into the house and place them on the kitchen counter. I go to the den, sit down, and read the newspaper. I circle jobs of interest. Grandma stands in the threshold of the door that connects the kitchen to the den; she watches me as if she is waiting for me to do something crazy. I ignore her and continue to read. Khalid leaves the table shaking his head in disgust. We make eye contact and give one another a reassuring smile.

Grandma quietly stares at me, as I make phone calls. It is obvious she is eavesdropping, but I don't care. I am on a mission. Finally, after several *"No we are not hiring"* responses, I am given an appointment for an immediate interview at CNR Bookstore. I do not have anything modern and up to date to wear, but I find old suit in the closet. I shower and apply some of Grandma's makeup to my face. Although my color is coming back, I still have a light ashy coating on my skin.

"Grandma!" I knock hard; it takes a couple of minutes for her to come to the door.

"Where do you think you are going?" Her accusing tone catches me off guard, but I do not allow her to get next to me.

"Grandma, I have a job interview today. I am going to CNR Bookstore. I'll be back later."

"Wait a minute." She closes the door, leaves me outside for several minutes then comes out of her bedroom fully dressed with her purse on her shoulder and her car keys in her hand. "Khalid, I'll be back. I am taking Thandisha to her job interview." I am grateful for the ride. I really do not feel like walking to the bus stop and waiting on the bus anyway. We drive in complete silence. The only noise in the car comes from her favorite gospel station. There is a lot I want to say to her, but with Grandma there is always a shield. She never lets you totally in.

Grandma parks the car while I go into the bookstore for my interview. The bookstore is humongous. A small coffee shop occupies one side of the building and several shelves filled with books occupy the remaining space. I know this is my job. I can feel it. I check in with one of the sales clerks at the counter.

"Hello, my name is Thandisha Glaze. I have an interview with Cersi Hunter." A young, trendy, dressed woman comes from behind the counter.

"Hello, I am Cersi." She extends her hand and embraces mine with a firm, confident handshake. I give a firm handshake in return and follow her to an office in the back of the store. She interviews me for thirty minutes. She and I have the some of the same interests. I am surprised when she offers me the Purchasing Coordinator position instead of the Sales Clerk position. Ten dollars an hour is not a lot of money, but it is a start. It is Thursday; we agree I will start on Monday. When I walk out of her office, Grandma is entering the bookstore. She gives me an *I know you did some fucked up shit, and I ain't forgot it* look. I greet her with a wide smile and a tight hug; she is initially resistant, but she reluctantly embraces me.

"Grandma, I got the job!"

"Well that's good, but don't get too excited; a sales clerk is not going to take care of you and a baby you know."

"I didn't get the Sales Clerk position. She hired me as a Purchasing Coordinator."

"Do you have to deal with money?" I know where she is going.

"Actually, I don't. I will be ordering books and arranging book signings." She appears slightly impressed. I really do not care one way or the other. I know it is going to be okay. I am on my way.

I need to get my clothes from Andreas' apartment. I have not talked to him in a couple of weeks. I know he is disappointed in me. He really did not deserve this, but it was not personal. He has to know I did not do this intentionally. I fucked up. I am human. Although Andreas is a great guy, he is not as perfect as he would like to believe. I messed up, but I don't think that gave him a right to have Dee in our bed.

I feel bad about the way I behaved with Andreas but
I am totally guilt ridden about Kyia. I have not seen my
daughter since I left. He decided I was not good enough for
Kyia. I guess I decided the same. I was tired of Kyia
seeing me high. She may not have known I was high, but I
knew. The guilt I feel is overwhelming. I can't believe
some of the stuff I did like leaving her home alone. I told
Andreas I was gone for only a couple of hours. Actually, I
was gone all day. I initially planned on getting a hit then
coming home, but after that first one, I could not leave. It
was as if my feet were glued to the floor. I didn't leave
until I spent all of my money. It's amazing; I am just now
feeling guilty about it. The image of Kyia alone in the
house constantly flashes in my mind. I hope she has no
memory of my neglect; and if she does, I pray she will
forgive me.

"Hello." I don't feel like dealing with Andreas, but I
need my clothes.

"Andreas?"

"Yeah, what do you want?" He is nasty, but I expect
it. I am sure I deserve it. Khalid is the only person who
loves me enough to feel my pain and hold me accountable
for my actions without constantly trying to make me feel
bad.

"How are you?" I am nervous.

"If you are calling to see Kyia, don't bother to ask.
The answer is no! Hell fucking no!" Everyone is trying my
patience, but thank God for this new shield because it is not
working.

"Actually Andreas, I need to get my clothes. I start
a job Monday." He is silent. I know he does not believe I
am capable of getting a job again. I am sure as I felt
doomed to a life of using drugs, he probably felt the same.

"I don't have any of your clothes."

"What do you mean? I have clothes in the closet,
the dresser, and the armoire. You didn't throw my armoire

151

out did you?" I pray he didn't throw it out because that would drive me over the edge. It belonged to my mother, and it is very special to me.

"No, the armoire is still here. I gave it to Kyia." I hear a soft feminine voice in the background. It sounds like Dee, Ayanna's sister.

"Where are my clothes?"

"I don't know and really don't give a damn! Call the fucking landfill!" He hangs up the phone. I begin to panic. I cannot believe he threw away my clothes. I had a nice wardrobe with many classy pieces. I pick up the phone and dial again.

"Andreas," he does not say anything, but I know he is on the phone. "I need my clothes! If you have them, please allow me to come over and get them, or bring them to me if you don't want me in the apartment."

"Didn't I just tell you? I don't have any of your shit!"

"I know what you said. I heard you loud and clear."

"Well is there anything else you want?"

"Actually there is, I would like to see Kyia."

"Well that ain't going to happen!"

"Andreas, I want to let you know I am okay now. It may not be today, but I will see Kyia because I am her mother."

"Please don't fucking remind me Thandisha; I would rather forget!" He hangs up the phone.

I panic. Monday is only three days away. I do not have clothes. I do not have money. I can feel the depression setting in. The pungent odor is forcing its way into my nostrils. It is faint but growing in intensity. I go to my room and lay on the bed. The smell gets stronger. My stomach begins to cramp. I go to the bathroom to empty my bowels. Khalid's door is slightly open when I come out of the bathroom. I lightly knock on the door.

"Come in," he is lying on his futon and throwing a small basketball into a miniature basketball goal that is nailed to his closet door.

"Hey guy, what's up?"

"Are you okay Thandie? Why are you so pale?"

"It must be something I ate." I sit next to him. "Guess what?" I do not allow him time to respond. "I have a job."

"Great, what kind of job?" He is genuinely excited for me.

"I am the new Purchasing Coordinator for CNR Bookstore. Well that's if I can find some clothes to wear."

"That's great Thandisha. That's really good. But you don't look very excited."

"Didn't you hear me? I don't have clothes. Andreas threw my clothes away."

"We can go to the mall. I have money in the bank. I'll take you shopping; be happy and enjoy your good news." The cravings are slowly leaving me. It's just as momma said, "It's okay now."

"What are you doing in here?" She looks at me as if I am ready to put the house in my pocket and walk out with it.

"I am talking to Khalid."

"Come here; I need to talk to you." I follow her into the den. "I don't think it is a good idea for you to be all over the house and in everyone's room. You have your room, and that's where you need to stay." I want to give her a piece of my mind. I think to myself *why allow me in the house to treat me so bad?* She could have left me in the street and allowed strangers to do the job for her. This is Grandma's house; I agree to stay in my room and go no further than the kitchen and the bathroom.

After my talk with Grandma, Khalid comes into my room; we are getting ready to leave for the mall to shop for clothes. We meet Grandma in the foyer.

"Where do you think you are going?"

"Khalid and I are going to the mall. Andreas threw my clothes away. Khalid agreed to loan me money to buy a few pieces until I get my first check."

"Khalid, go to your room!" Grandma's reaction is almost violent and shocking.

"Why? What is wrong with you Grandma?"

"You are not going to buy her a damn thing! No one told her to get on drugs. She will get some clothes when she buys some." Khalid grabs his keys and leaves the house slamming the door behind him. My heart drops to my feet, but I am not going to give up. If I have to go door to door asking for clothes, then that is what I will have to do.

"And you," I look around. There is nobody present but me. "You are walking a fine line, and don't forget it."

I go into my room and write out my plan. Getting the hell out of this house is my first priority. I am not angry with Grandma. After using drugs and socializing with addicts, I can understand why Grandma feels uneasy around me. I understand her lack of trust in me, but I am human and at this point, very fragile. If I save my money, I can move within a month. I do not need a big place. I just need something big enough to accommodate Kyia and myself. I do not know what Andreas is thinking, but I hope he knows Kyia is going to be in my life. I hope he knows I am going to see my child. I understand I hurt him, and I hurt the baby. No one can make me feel worse than I already do, but I will do it right this time.

I hear Khalid's car enter the garage after being gone for several hours, but I stay in my room. I know Grandma made him angry. What she doesn't understand is regardless of what I have done, Khalid is my brother. We share the same pain, and nothing and no one can come between us.

"Thandie?" He softly knocks on the door.

"Come in," He enters the room carrying several bags.

"Thandie, try these on, and see if you like them." I can't believe Khalid has such good taste. The black suit is a good choice for the first day of work. I really didn't like the Khaki skirt, but I am grateful to have clothes for work. "Thank you so much Khalid." I give him a big hug. My little brother has grown into a tall, muscular young man. I am proud of him. I am determined I will also make him proud of me. It is awkward we feel the need to whisper, but that will eventually be okay. I accept the fact Grandma also needs time to heal.

With the exception of quick kitchen runs and brisk bathroom breaks, I stay in my room all day Saturday and Sunday. I am bored, but I do not want more confrontation with Grandma. I do not have anywhere to go. I don't have friends. The relationships you form in active addiction are superficial, based solely on one's ability to get drugs. It would be nice to have someone to talk to. Sitting in my room brings back memories of Ayanna, but I honestly have no time for friends. My number one priority is to heal the relationship with my daughter.

I pray Andreas will forgive me. I know I have caused him a lot of pain and disappointment. He acts as if he hates me. I take responsibility for my role in our break up, but it is not totally my fault. It is very hard for me to talk to Andreas. He is holding on to my recent past. What he does not understand is I was not capable, but I have a desire to right all of my wrongs, mainly the wrong I did to myself.

Three Hundred and Fifteen Degrees

I am awake, as usual, at sunrise. I immediately jump out of bed, fall to my knees, and give thanks to the creator. I turn on the radio, go to the bathroom and shower. The hot water is purifying. I stay in the shower my usual five minutes and quickly dry off to keep the moisture in my skin. I could stay under the hot water forever, but today is my first day on the job. I don't want to be late. I stand in the mirror and observe my entire body as I dress for work. My stomach is flat as a pan cake no stretch marks and no signs of my pregnancy with Kyia. I am thin and could stand to gain ten to fifteen pounds, but I look good. I turn the television off, grab my bag and leave for work. Grandma is sitting at the table with a coffee mug in her hand. She follows my every move from the kitchen to the door. She makes me feel uneasy, but I walk to the bus stop with a confidence I have not had in a long time.

At 6:45, I am at the bus stop. The black suit Khalid purchased for me looks great. The shoes are sharp as hell. I arrive at the bookstore thirty minutes early; I walk to a nearby Deli, buy a cup of coffee, and read the paper to kill time. I am at the bookstore ten minutes before 9:00. Cersi greets me, finds a place for my things, and gives me a more detailed tour of the store.

Cersi and I share the same office space, but we each have our own desk; our desks are about five feet apart separated by an Asian room divider. There is a stack of folders two feet high on my desk. We immediately get to work. Initially, I am overwhelmed when I discover I have to learn to use the computer. I can type, but I do not have software skills.

"Cersi, I don't know if you knew this when you hired me, but I have never used this software before. To be honest, I have never turned on a computer." I wait for her to thank me for coming and escort me out of the door.

"Don't worry about that; you will catch on. I didn't know how to use a computer either, but you quickly get the hang of it the more you use it. Besides, for the next two weeks, we will train." I am relieved. I really need this job. I guess I really don't need the money. I can basically flip burgers and live with Grandma until my inheritance kicks in. But the job is a boost to my damaged self-esteem. It gives me a purpose. It is a catalyst for my transition back into mainstream society.

By lunchtime, I am tired; I can barely keep my eyes open. I am hungry as hell, but I don't eat lunch. I want to make sure I have enough money to survive until payday. Instead of eating, I take a walk hoping to get some energy from the sun. Midtown is absolutely beautiful. I have been here before but never seen it with these eyes. I know all of the buildings were here probably before I was born, but I have never paid attention to them. I continue to walk with no particular destination in mind. As I pass the library, I see Andreas' truck. I walk to the truck. I am hesitant, as I really don't want or need his negative vibes. He is concentrating on trimming hedges and initially does not see me.

"Hi," I tap him on the shoulder.

"Hey, what are you doing down here?" He is surprised to see me. He turns the hedge trimmer off and removes his eye protecting glasses.

"I told you; I am working now. How is Kyia?"

"She is doing well. She is in daycare now. She needs to be amongst other kids. Since there aren't kids at momma's house, I decided to put her in a childcare program."

"I am coming over Saturday to see her. I don't have to take her with me, but I am coming to see her."

"Who in the hell do you think you are?" His demeanor instantly changes. "You are not going to tell me when you are coming to see her! You have been hanging out off and on with your druggie friends, and now you want to play mommy! I don't think so. If you will excuse me, I have to go back to work. I have a child to take care of." I grab his arm, as he walks away.

"Andreas, you know what I did; everyone and their momma probably know, but I am coming to see Kyia Saturday morning. I will be there by 9:00." I didn't give him a chance to respond; I walk away. It is 12:45, and my lunch break is almost over. I quickly walk back to the bookstore.

"Did you have a nice lunch?" Cersi sits at her desk and flips through a magazine while eating a salad.

"Actually, I did; thanks for asking." I am eager to get back to work. There are books left on my desk that need entering into the database. Cersi gave me a list of soon to be released books to order from the distributor. One of my responsibilities is to read the reviews of books by new authors and decide if they will sell with our clientele. If a book is chosen as a good seller, it is my responsibility to order the book, the promotional materials, and contact the author for book signings.

At 5:20, I am still working. Cersi reminds me we are off the clock at 5:00. I am so into my work I forget to look at the clock. I read the instructions I wrote down earlier, so I can properly shut down the computer. I grab my things and walk to the bus stop. I had a great day today. I looked strangers in the eye and felt no shame. When I smoked crack, I could not look anyone in the eye because I had become an empty shell willing to do almost anything, including steal from Andreas, for a hit. I did not care who was hurt in the process. I am so happy; at this moment, I feel good enough. I feel worthy enough and feel very much part of the mainstream.

When I walk in the house, Grandma is in the den. Her bifocals hang low at the tip of her nose; her eyes are glued to the newspaper. I greet her, go into the kitchen, and make a sandwich. For some strange reason, I feel uncomfortable. Though I am in the kitchen, and she is in the den, I can still feel the negative vibes. I quickly eat my sandwich, go into my room, and undress. I am lethargic and can hardly wait to throw my body across my bed. I am still withdrawing. It almost feels like I am coming down from a high. I take an aspirin, shower, and go to bed. When I wake up, it is 6:00 in the morning. I quickly shower, dress for work, and walk to the bus stop. I do not feel as pretty as I felt yesterday. I wear the khaki pants and a white, cotton shirt. I thank God Khalid knew to buy basic black shoes. I look forward to my first check, so I can add more basics to my wardrobe, take myself to a nice restaurant, and buy gifts for Kyia.

I arrive thirty minutes early again. Cersi's car is parked in its usual reserved parking space. I walk around to the back of the store and knock on the door. She greets me with a welcoming smile.

"Wow you're such an early bird. I'm going to give you a key, so you don't have to wait around outside if no one is here." Initially, I am afraid to take the key. It has been a minute since anyone trusted me. In fact, it has been a minute since I trusted myself. I reluctantly take the key and place it in my bag. It is not like I can say, *"hey I can't take the key because I may get a craving and steal."* I go to my desk, turn on my computer, and start my workday. The work is interesting. Cersi is a very good trainer. In just one day, I develop a working knowledge of book promoting.

"Cersi, have you ever thought of decorating the office with art?" I love my workspace, but it is bland.

"Yes, actually there was art in here." She points to the small holes in the walls. "But when I bought my ex-husband out, he took the art with him. I have not had time to look for more."

"I have several pieces of art in my collection. I can bring them and if you like any of the pieces, I can donate them to the office."

"That won't be necessary. I can just give you what you paid for them."

"Actually, I didn't pay anything for them; I paint in my spare time. I've been told I am a very good artist." She is excited about seeing my work. Now that I offered, I have no idea how I will get the pieces to work. I can ask Khalid, but Grandma would probably die if she sees me in his car. I call Andreas on my break to see if he will consider giving me a ride to work and bring some of the art I left behind the armoire at his apartment.

"Hello," I didn't expect to hear a female voice.

"Hello, may I speak with Andreas?"

"Who's calling?" It is Dee, Ayanna's sister.

"Can you tell him it's Thandisha?" I hear arguing in the background. The voices are muffled as if someone placed their hand over the phone's mouthpiece.

"Yeah?"

"Hi Andreas, this is Thandisha."

"What do you want?" I hate when he attempts to make me feel like a microbe. Can't he see I am making progress?

"I have finished art pieces in your apartment. Hopefully you didn't throw them away. I need it to decorate my office. I was wondering if you could bring the pieces to the bookstore or maybe give me a ride to work in the morning because I have pieces at home I would like to bring." He is silent. If it were not for the female cursing and screaming in the background, I would have thought he hung up the phone.

"What time?"

"I have to be at work at 9:00. Can you pick me up at 8:00?"

"Yeah," he hangs up the phone without a good-bye. I don't care. I have a ride to work. I go back to work, finish entering the monthly sales data in the spreadsheet, and work on a book promotion. Cersi is right; once you work with the computer, it becomes easy. The more you use it; the more comfortable you become with it. I don't have money to buy lunch, so I window-shop during lunch. The first thing I want to buy for myself is a purse. I am tired of carrying one of Khalid's bulky book bags. I am slowly beginning to feel cute, sexy and feminine again. I want a soft, feminine bag to carry my things. Cersi is my fashion inspiration. She makes a fashion statement even when she wears jeans.

After lunch, the day goes very fast. I am glad to see 5:00. I miss the first bus, so I wait thirty minutes for the next bus. I am an hour late getting home. Grandma meets me at the door, as I enter the house.

"Where have you been?"

"I was at work. I missed the first bus." She snatches the book bag out of my hand, opens it, and drops all of its content on the floor.

"I am not going to have drugs in this house!" She bends down on the floor and goes through all of my belongings. When she does not find anything, she leaves everything on the floor and walks away mumbling to herself. I am too angry to hear what she is saying. I sit on the floor, put my things back in the bag, and go to my room. I shower and prepare for tomorrow's work day. I am so mad; I skip dinner.

I wake up at 2:00 in the morning hungry as hell. I go into the kitchen to get something to eat. Khalid is in the den talking on the phone.

"Hey sis, what's up?" It is obvious; he is talking to a girl. He sits on the sofa leaning deep into the back cushion, talking low, and smiling from ear to ear. He reminds me of Andreas. Andreas and I would sometime talk on the phone all night.

"What's up guy?" I make a sandwich and go back to my room. I am uncomfortable in this house. To be honest, I was never comfortable living with Grandma. It was never a home. It was simply shelter. I look forward to getting my own place. I look forward to feeling totally free. Everything in my life is working out. I enjoy my job at the bookstore. A stranger trusts me with a key to her business, but I am living like a convict at Grandma's house. It is imperative I get a place so my baby can visit. I would not feel comfortable bringing Kyia here. Grandma did not take to her. I don't feel welcomed, and I am sure Kyia will feel the tension here. I miss Kyia. I may not have been a good mother, but God knows I love my baby. I want to mend the relationship with my daughter. Her father is trying to prevent it, but I know when Andreas realizes I am clean and making a change in my life, he will allow visits with Kyia.

It's sunrise; I am not as eager to get out of bed. That 2:00 a.m. snack made me sluggish. I immediately fall to my knees and ask the creator to give me this day. That faint, pungent smell is in my nose. Initially, I thought of calling Cersi and requesting the day off, but the thought quickly left my mind. Last night, I dreamed I was using. The dream was vivid. It was so real I woke up with a strong urge to clear my bowels. My body does not feel right. I don't immediately get out of bed for fear my feet will take me some place I really didn't want to go. Andreas will be picking me up, so I sit at the end of the bed and watch television before getting dressed. Grandma walks pass my room. I can feel her intense stare, but I do not look at her. She walks toward the kitchen and then comes back.

"It's 7:15. Are you going to work? You need to get ready. You are not going to lay your ass up in here all day." She is really pissing me off. I really want to curse her too, but she is my grandmother. Besides, I am determined I am going to stay and endure whatever she dishes out until I have the finances to leave.

"I am going to work. Andreas is giving me a ride. I am taking some of my art to decorate my office." She stands in the threshold of my bedroom door. I guess she cannot think of anything insulting to say, so she leaves. I quickly shower and dress for work. I gather some of my art from the garage, sit in the living room where I have a good view of the driveway. Andreas arrives at exactly 8:00. He gets out and opens the trunk of his new SUV. I have to give it to him; he looks good. I meet him at the door with my things before he presses the doorbell. I glance at the window while getting in the car. Grandma stands in the window; the famous disapproving look covers her face.

"Good morning."

"Good morning, did you bring Kyia?"

"I took her to school."

I hoped I would get to see her, but I did tell him I was coming to see her this weekend.

"Thanks for the ride. I would have never made it with all of this on the bus."

"You look better than you did the last time I saw you. You are getting it together, and you are looking good." He is right. I know I look much better. The ashen coating that covered my skin is now replaced with a soft glow.

"Thanks, I am trying. It gets hard at times, but this time I am going to make it. I am a little stressed right now, but when I get my first check, I can at least buy clothes for work."

"I shouldn't have thrown your clothes away, but I was angry as hell."

"It would have been nice if you hadn't, but I am not going to cry over spilled milk."

"If you like, I can take you shopping this weekend." I want to tell him to go to hell, but I need clothes.

"Are you sure your girlfriend won't mind? Wasn't that Dee who answered the phone?"

"I don't have a girlfriend. I have a friend. Besides, what difference does it make who it is?" He is right; besides I really don't give a damn. I have too much work ahead of me trying to stay clean.

"I don't want to cause any problems for you. How is Kyia? I can't wait until Saturday. I don't have money to buy her a present. All I have is bus fare until I get paid, but when I get my first check, I would like to take her shopping." I stare straight ahead, but I can tell he is looking at me. I know he wants to exert control, but he has to give me my props. I am doing okay; at least, I am putting up a fight.

We arrive at the bookstore at 8:20. I do not have to be at work for another forty minutes. I am happy when he offers to buy breakfast. We leave the bookstore and stop at a fast food joint down the street. We order biscuits and juice, but for me it is like a sit down, wine and dine meal at a five star restaurant.

"Damn Thandisha, you must have been hungry. I can remember on our first date at the Taco Stand you pretended like you wasn't hungry and your stomach made hunger sounds like crazy." He is reminiscing about our first date at the mall.

"Yeah well I was shy then, but I'm not shy anymore."

"Yeah I see." He looks at his watch. "I have a lot of work to do today."

"Yeah, me too. I better get back to the store. I don't want to be late."

We clean off the table and exit the restaurant. It takes all of five minutes to get back to the bookstore. I take the key out of my bag, as he parks his truck. "You're moving up; they gave you a key. I am impressed." He takes the paintings out of his truck, brings them inside, and sits them down next to my desk. "What time do you get off work?"

"5:00."

"If you want to wait about fifteen minutes, I can give you a ride home. I am over this way today."

"Sure I would appreciate that." I smile and walk him to the door. I spend the entire day on the phone making phone calls planning for next month's book signings. I confirm times, dates, and make hotel arrangements. Reynolds Jordan is making her debut. She obviously has a big advertising budget. The Renaissance is a very prestigious hotel, but she is requesting a five star hotel. I spend the day faxing brochures from different hotels to her assistant. At the end of the day, she is not satisfied with any of the accommodations. The only thing confirmed is CNR's commission for the publicity and the forty percent discount on the books.

"Are you still looking for suitable Lodging for RJ?"

"I'm trying, but she is very particular." Cersi looks disappointed as if I am not doing my job.

"Well what about the Renaissance?"

"I faxed the Renaissance brochure. She wants something more upscale."

"Wow how much is her marketing budget a million dollars?" We both laugh. Her laughter restores my comfort zone. I like this job, and I want to do a good job. I have not gotten to the place where my self-esteem is self-sufficient. I am still trying to please people. I want Cersi to like me and feel confident with my job performance. She comes back to my desk.

"Oh I forgot to tell you; I love the art. You are a great artist! Why don't you try and sell some of your work?"

"I have thought about it. I need to find a place to sell it."

"If you like, you can sell it by the coffee counter. Make some space for yourself, bring in one piece at a time, and see what happens."

"Wow, Cersi I'd love to do that!" I cannot believe Cersi is giving me an opportunity to sell my art. Andreas was always trying to get me to sell my art on consignment.

I fax a copy of the brochure from the VIP Elite Hotel to Reynolds Jordan. Finally, she is pleased. I am surprised because the Renaissance is more convenient. It is close to the bookstore and is walking distance to a few hot spots in town.

The day went by very fast. I look forward to going home. I worked hard, and I am tired. I expected to have to wait on Andreas, but when I walk outside, Andreas is waiting.

"What's up?" I return his greeting with a slight wave, but I am more interested in the little head in the backseat of the truck. I run to the truck and open her door. "Kyia!" She is so beautiful. Her hair is all over the place. Mix match hair clips hang at the end of half braided hair. I can tell Andreas tried to comb it; the parts in her hair are not uniform. She isn't as excited to see me as I would have liked. I unfasten her car seat and give her a big hug. I do not want to let her go. "How have you been baby?" She is not looking at me. She looks at her father.

"Kyia, daddy is going to take you to McDonalds. Do you want to see Ronald?" She easily gives her daddy a big smile. I get in the truck and sit in the back seat with her. "Kyia, do you want momma to go to McDonalds with us?" She moves her head up and down. I am excited and nervous being with my child again. I cannot think of anything or anyone you could love more than a child. Seeing Kyia reiterates to me I was once loved and I am still loved. Only a God who loves me could allow me to produce a child as beautiful as Kyia. We stay at McDonalds for two hours playing with Kyia. The longer I am with Kyia, the more she interacts with me. I know she can't verbalize her feelings, but I know it is painful to have a mother one day and be motherless the next day. I vow to make it up to her.

"Thandisha, this has been fun, but I need to get Kyia home, so she can go to bed." I know he is right, but I want to spend more time with her. I am in tears when he fastens her in the car seat. I sit in the front seat with Andreas. I don't want Kyia to see me cry. Andreas touches my shoulder reassuring me everything will be okay. I would have felt better; however, if he would allow more time with my daughter.

I continue to sit in the car for several minutes after we arrive at Grandma's. I don't want to say good-bye to Kyia. He doesn't turn the engine off, so I know he is ready to leave. I walk around to the back of the car, open the door, and kiss her. At Andreas' command she gives me what feels like is a genuine hug and waves good-bye.

"Thanks Andreas, I had a great time." I turn away and walk towards the house. Before I can enter the house, Grandma meets me at the door and blocks my entrance. Aunt Mary stands close behind her.

"I told you once; I was not putting up with anymore of your shit. Where have you been?" I look at the clock. It is 7:30. I usually get home by 6:00.

"I was spending time with my daughter."

"I know what kind of car Andreas drives. You got out of a truck."

"Andreas has a new truck. It's the same truck he was in this morning when he came for me."

"I doubt very seriously he would allow you around Kyia." I am trying to stay at Grandma's for three more weeks, but I can tell it is not going to work. Grandma thinks she is tired of me, but I am equally tired of her. "Grandma, everyone is not like you. Some people are forgiving." She stands in the door as if she is not going to allow me in the house. Aunt Mary stands like a military commando behind Grandma. Her facial expression confirms this is the plan.

"I think it is best you go on and move."

"How can I move Grandma? You know I won't have money until I get paid on Friday."

"Not having money or a job never stopped you from finding a place to lay your head." I am hurt and angry at the same time. I don't know which emotion to act on; both are equally as strong.

"Can I come in and get my things?" She has my things packed in a black, plastic garbage bag. She passes them to me through the door. "Can I say good-bye to my brother?" I make an attempt to walk in the house. She steps in front of me and blocks the entrance.

"He is not here." It is useless, so I take my belongings and leave. I do not know where I am going. It is dark. I am scared. I didn't want my feet to take me somewhere detrimental to my shaky foundation. The bus ends its last route in this neighborhood at 7:00. Wherever I am going, my feet will have to get me there.

I turn around and contemplate knocking on the door again to ask one more time if I can stay for the night, but the thought of looking into Grandma's face makes me ill. I creep around to the back of the house to the laundry room and use my driver's license to open the door. I make a makeshift bed by placing my clothes on top of the washer and dryer. It is an uncomfortable sleep but better than walking all night.

Three Hundred and Sixty Degrees

I was never alarm clock dependent. I always wake up at sunrise. I turn on the washing machine and use hot water and a pinch of laundry detergent to wash up. I quietly gather my things and creep out of the laundry room. I catch the earliest bus destined for downtown. It is Thursday, one day before payday. I am officially homeless.

I get off the bus and walk to the women's shelter on the corner of Ponce and Avondale Avenue. Addicts are very resourceful. You hear so many stories in the crack house. It seems that homelessness is part of every addict's reality at some point during the cycle of addiction. The shelter has a gloomy, doomed look. It is a pretty, historic, antebellum home, but it has a gloomy ambience. An aura of hopelessness and despair permeates the atmosphere. It may be the look of desperation and depravity that covers the faces of the women in the long line requesting services. It may be the look on the young children's faces, as they stand in the long line holding tight to hands that have nothing to hold on to. I don't know what it is, but the pretty building surrounded by a nicely landscaped lawn looks doomed. After waiting in line for almost two hours, I receive the expected news; *the shelter does not have an available bed for a single woman.* But the counselor advises me to call back after 12:00. I really didn't want to bother calling back. As many homeless people as there are in this city, I doubt if they would ever have an opening. The counselors are trained to leave you hopeful.

I board the next bus and go to work. I do not want Cersi to know I am homeless, so I hide my things behind the file cabinet out of view. I go about work as usual. I don't have extra money to buy lunch, so I eat some of the crackers in the basket Cersi keeps on top of a small, dorm size, refrigerator on the side of her desk. I call the women's shelter at noon. I know it will be useless, but I call anyway. They do not have an available bed but gave me a list of referrals. It's like I said, they don't like leaving the homeless hopeless.

I call Andreas. He does not answer the phone, so I leave a message. I didn't want to be in a situation and not have a place to go for the night.

"Did anyone call Andreas from this number?" Two hours later, he responds to my call.

"Yes, it's Thandisha; I need a favor. Grandma put me out of the house."

"Why did she do that?" I can tell he is going to be judgmental, but this is no time to have pride.

"She didn't believe I was with you and Kyia."

"Why wouldn't she believe you? You must have done something to make her not trust you."

"No shit I have done a lot for her not to trust me, but not lately and definitely not yesterday. Remember, I was with you and Kyia."

"I know your grandmother would not put you..." I hang up the phone. I cannot take Andreas' shit. I don't know where I am going after work, but I am not going to a dope trap, nor am I going to live on the street. I have come too far. I am nervous as hell dialing Grandma's phone number. I pray Khalid will answer the phone.

"Hello," God does answer prayer and sometimes the answer is yes.

"Khalid, I am so happy to hear your voice! I know you may not believe me, but I have not been using drugs. Last night, I was out with Kyia and Andreas. Grandma does not believe me because..."

"Thandie stop. I believe you. Where are you?"

"I am at work. The problem is I don't have anywhere to go after work. I don't have money, and I will not have money until tomorrow. Can you loan me money for a hotel until tomorrow?"

"No Thandie, I will not loan you money. I will give you the money for a hotel. I'm also going to help you find a place to live." I give him the address and directions to the bookstore. I am relieved. I go about my workday as if all is well. The urge to use drugs crosses my mind, but it is definitely a passing thought. The day started out scary and filled with uncertainty but ends calmly and filled with hope. I am so happy and relieved that I lose track of time.

"Thandisha, are you spending the night?" She points to the clock; it is 5:30.

"Oh no Cersi, I am finishing up some work." I do not want her to know my situation. I am embarrassed and feel a lot of guilt. I must have been awful. Andreas knows I was with him and Kyia. For Andreas to believe I was getting high amazes me.

"Make sure you lock up when you leave."

"Oh sure Cersi see you tomorrow." I am relieved when she leaves. I finish working on the plans for the next book signing. I can't very well say I was working on a project and have nothing to show her tomorrow.

It seems as if it is taking Khalid forever to get here. I begin to panic. What if Grandma does not allow him to leave the house? I really should not have involved him in my mess, but I am desperate. I need to hold on to this job. It would have been almost impossible to work and not have a place to live. I am fighting hard to stay clean. I knew it wasn't going to be easy, but I didn't expect this. I expected my family to be happy for me. I didn't want a free ride just a chance. I want the people who profess to love me to believe in me especially when I am telling the truth. I don't remember asking Grandma for anything. In fact, I stayed as far away from her, Khalid, and Aunt Mary as I could. I didn't want them to see me when I was using crack. I looked a mess. I don't care how well I attempted to dress up; I was still a crack addict. There is something repulsive about the aura of a crack addict that no one wants to be around them.

I am relieved when I see bright lights shining in the parking lot. I want to eat, take a hot shower, and sleep on a soft, firm mattress. I am so hungry I feel as if I am at the stage where my body will soon begin digesting itself. I open the door and wave at him, so he knows I am still inside. I grab the garbage bag with my clothes from behind the file cabinet, activate the alarm, and lock the door behind me.

"Hey Sis."

"What's up

"Do you want to get something to eat first?"

"Please, I am starving." fast food is exactly what I need.

Although there are only three cars in the drive thru, it seems as if it is taking forever to place my order. I am hungry; I order a double burger and fries. I practically gobble the burger down in three bites after leaving the restaurant. Khalid gives me a ride around the corner from my job to a residential area. I saw a garage apartment for rent two days ago while walking. This is not exactly what I had in mind, but I am desperate. He drives into the driveway so I can get the number before taking me to a hotel.

"Where do you want to stay tonight?" I really had not thought about it. I simply want a place to lay my head.

"Pull over there Khalid." The hotel looks kind of sleazy, but I don't care.

"Here?" He does not like it. I don't either; it really does not matter because all I want is to watch television, take a hot shower, and relax. Khalid gives me the money to pay the room rate for one night. After I pay for the room, he gets out of the car and walks with me inside of the hotel. "Thandisha, I want you to know I believe in you. I know you are handling yourself, and I have a lot of respect for you." He reaches in his pocket and pulls out three hundred and fifty dollars.

"Where did you get all of that money?"

"Look at me. Do I look like I wear the latest fashions to you?" I stare straight in his eyes and wait for an answer. "I save my money Thandie. Where do you think I got it?"

"I don't know that's why I asked." Many of the drug dealers I used to cop from, were my brother's age. I definitely don't want my brother getting caught in the street game. "Khalid, I will have to pay you back in a week." Although, tomorrow is payday, I have to get a place to live with my first check.

"You don't have to pay me back. Just get a stable place to live and take care of yourself." Khalid leaves. I make myself comfortable. I call the front desk to get a wakeup call so I can get to work on time not that I need it. I am very much in tune with the sun. I lie across the bed and flip channels. I cannot find anything on television. I am bored, so I call Andreas to remind him I am coming for Kyia Saturday morning.

"Hello."

"May I speak to Andreas?"

"Who is calling?" I know it is Dee, and I know she knows it is me. I remember feeling sorry for her when I was younger. Her sister, Ayanna, was very hard on her. I now agree with Ayanna; Dee is a trifling bitch.

"Can you tell him it's Thandisha?"

"Yeah, whatever." She slams the phone down so hard it hurts my ear.

"Hello," his voice is deep and still sexy as hell.

"I am calling to remind you; I am coming for Kyia Saturday morning." He is silent.

"I'll be there around 9:00 am."

"I thought you said your grandmother put you out."

"She did, but we don't need to talk about that. Do we? I will be there at 9:00." I hang up the phone and go to bed. I look forward to tomorrow. Khalid agreed to pick me up at lunch to look for other places close to my job in case the garage apartment is no longer vacant, or for some reason the landlord will not rent it to me.

As usual, the sun serves as my alarm; besides, I did not receive the wakeup call I requested from the hotel desk. I shower and listen to the morning news while getting dressed. My clothes are slightly wrinkled, but they will pass. I stuff my belongings in my book bag, grab my garbage bag, and walk to the bus stop.

Cersi is at work when I arrive.

"Good morning." I quickly place my things under my desk.

"Good morning, Thandisha. You never did get back with me about selling your art." A big smile stretches across her face. "Guess what?" I don' feel like listening, but as long as she is not telling me I am fired, I can take any news. "My friend, Ron, wants to buy that painting behind my desk."

"Are you serious?"

"Yes, I am very serious. I didn't know how much you wanted for it, but I said $300.00. Is that okay?"

"When does he want to pick it up?"

"He will be here after lunch and before five."

"Great!"

"You know Thandisha, this could be another avenue for the bookstore. I was thinking I can provide a small space for your art behind the dining area and in return the bookstore receives thirty five percent of what you sale." This is a wonderful idea. I have several paintings in the garage at Grandma's house, plus I have a vision of a charcoal piece in my head. Of course, Cersi typed a contract, had me sign it, and had it notarized. And of course, the contract was retroactive. She is always about business. I will have an extra $195.00. It feels good having money again. One of the problems Andreas and I had is I didn't save money. That will change; I will open a savings account and put money in it every payday. I hope to never be in this predicament again.

I sit at my desk, complete the work on three book orders, and make contact with the authors' publicists. I also make contact with a Michelle Harvey, a new self-publisher. CNR is a unique bookstore; it has a section in the store for self-published writers. To my surprise, many of the self-published titles are good sellers. I really like the way some of the self-published writers conduct business, and they are much easier to work with.

Khalid is always on time. At 12:00 noon, just as I grab my jacket, Khalid enters the bookstore. Cersi meets him at the door. I do not like the way she looks at him. She throws her sewn in hair all over the place. She moves her body so seductively it is as if she is performing a mating dance.

"Hello Khalid, I see you have met Cersi, my boss." He extends his hand to her. She softly embraces his hand. She is behaving as if Khalid is a man instead of a boy. To my surprise, Khalid appears to be flirting with her also. "Come on little brother, let's go." Khalid and I leave for lunch. The first thing we do is drive to the garage apartment. It is still available. I cash my check then go back to the adjacent house and knock on the door. A petite, middle-aged, African American woman answers the door. For some reason, I expected the owner to be white. The neighborhood used to be predominantly black; but in the last five years, most of the African Americans sold their homes to young white singles and couples who wanted to return to the city. Many of the black residents who didn't sale their homes lost them because their meager earnings could not keep up with the rapid increase in property taxes. Ms. Manley introduces herself while scanning me up and down, front and center.

"How many people will be occupying the unit?"

"Just me, but my daughter will visit on the weekends." The rent is four hundred dollars per month. I thought this was steep for a one bedroom over a garage, but I do not have time to look for another apartment. The good thing is it is walking distance to my job, and it has hardwood floors. I complete a short application and give Mrs. Manly the application fee; she instructs me to call back after two o'clock.

While I was out to lunch, Mrs. Manly called and left a message on my voicemail. My application is approved. I return her call and make arrangements to bring the money, sign the lease, and get the keys. I called the utility companies and found they would bill the deposits, but the electricity will not be connected until Monday. I am ecstatic about moving into my own place even if I do not have electricity. It will be an easy move. The only thing I have is what I carry in my garbage bag. I still have some things at Andreas'. He couldn't have thrown everything away.

I feel good. I am grateful, but this life is challenging. Cravings for crack cocaine have plagued me all day. I don't know what triggers it, but for no apparent reason, I am plagued with a pungent odor. It starts out subtle then increases to a strong almost forceful sweet, yet pungent, aroma. Thank God the obsession is gone. I now know I don't have to use just because that smell seeps into my nostrils.

Cersi's friend, Ron, arrives at 3:00 to pick up the painting. He is handsome. It appears as if Ron and Cersi are dating or at least have more than a platonic relationship. He stands comfortably in her personal space, and she appears to enjoy it. He gives me three, crisp one hundred dollar bills. I give Cersi $105.00, her share of the sale. I think thirty-five percent is a bit much. When I factor in my time, the cost of the canvas, paint, framing, and matting, I really wasn't making a big profit. Ron wants to see more of my work. I cannot tell him the other paintings are at my grandmother's home, and I am not allowed in her home. I am very embarrassed about my situation.

"I am flattered you like my work. I'll bring a couple of paintings to work on Monday." He is pushy, but I convince him to wait until Monday. I emphasize I am going to be busy all weekend. It isn't actually a lie because I plan on cleaning and decorating my new home and spending time with my baby.

After work, I pay the rent, deposit, and get the keys from Ms. Manly. The apartment reeks of mildew and musk. I buy bleach to disinfect and pine cleaner to give the apartment a fresh smell. I do not have lights, so I purchase candles. The silence is uncomfortable, but I am not afraid. Although there is no electricity, I have a phone. I established phone service with a simple phone call. I sit by the candle and write out a list of things I need. I have plenty of linen. I kept my expensive linen in the bottom of the armoire. I have a couple of nice Egyptian cotton sheet sets that I assume are still inside of the armoire. The crazy thing about Andreas is although he constantly complained about my spending habits, he liked the things I purchased. I blow out the candle and go to sleep on a makeshift bed I made from a piling my clothes on top of each other.

As usual, the sun serves as my alarm clock. I don't have soap, so I walk to McDonalds and wash up with the rough paper towels and hand soap in the bathrooms. I change my clothes in one of the stalls, walk back to my apartment, put my clothes away, and catch the next bus to Andreas'. When I get off the bus, I call him from the silver, graffiti covered pay phone at the corner across the street from his apartment. He does not answer the phone. I take my chances and walk to his apartment. Both of his vehicles are parked side by side.

I knock on the door. Initially, there is no answer. I knock again. This time I use both fist.

"Who is it?" He sounds as if he is just getting out of bed.

"It's me, Thandisha." I hear a lot of movement inside of the apartment. I am not concerned about the female voice. I didn't come for trouble. I simply came to see my daughter.

"Hold on," he comes to the door and slightly opens it; only half of his face is visible. "What time is it?"

"It's 9:00. I told you I was coming at 9:00. I came to see Kyia. What you are doing and who you are doing it with is totally insignificant to me."

"Well come back a little later." I know this fool does not think this is going to fly with me. He attempts to close the door. I place my foot in the door to prevent it from closing.

"Hell no I came to see my daughter. I don't give a damn about what you have going on. In fact, you can tell Dee I said hello, but I am not leaving until I see Kyia." He turns his head and mumbles to Dee. He really is not what one can call a ladies' man. He's very good looking, but he is not one to date different women at the same time. Although I cannot see inside, I know it is Dee on the other side of the door. "Open the damn door Andreas, or bring my baby outside!" I am getting angry and ready to kick the damn door down if I have to. I am not leaving without spending time with Kyia. I hear a loud shouting match inside of Andreas' apartment.

Initially, I am afraid when I see the blue lights flashing and the police car speeding down the street towards me, but then I realize I am not doing anything wrong. He must have forgotten we were never married, and there is no court order granting him custody of Kyia.

That's another thing about the crack house; it's filled with street lawyers. It wasn't that I abandoned Kyia, I simply backed away because I didn't want to cause more harm. I did not want Kyia to see me messed up anymore.

"What is the problem ma'am?" The balding, six feet, two hundred plus pound, police officer has his hand on his gun approaching my small, five feet and four inch, 115 pound frame as if I am a threatening criminal. I remain calm and keep my hands visible.

"Sir, I really don't know. I am here to see my daughter. My ex-boyfriend has company and will not allow me to see my baby. I told him I was coming to see her at 9:00. I think he is uncomfortable because he has a woman in what used to be our home, but I am not the least upset about that. I would simply like a visit with my daughter." Andreas stands in the door with a blank look on his face.

"Sir, is there a reason she can't visit the child?"

"No, she can visit; I simply wanted her to come back later."

"Officer, he and I were never married. He has not taken me to court for custody. Can you explain to him I can come for my child anytime because I am still her legal custodian?"

"She is right if that is the case. Do you have custody of the child?"

"Yes sir, she has always lived with me." Andreas is confused but quickly recognizes he is outdone. Dee comes to the door and snatches it open like a wild woman.

"The reason he will not allow her to see the baby is because she is a crack head."

"Ma'am, are you using illegal drugs?" The police officer positions his weight on one leg, looks at me and then at Andreas and Dee then back at me again.

"Officer, do I look like I am on drugs?" A bewildered look is plastered on my face. "I work every day. I have my own place, and I simply came to get my daughter for a visit." Dee is ranting, raving, and cursing like a sailor. The officer threatens her with arrest before she finally calms down.

"Andreas, all I want is a visit with Kyia." I give him a nasty look. "I told you I was coming at 9:00. If you had company or other plans, you should have come by my job or called, so we could work something out."

"Sir, she is right. Unless you can show legal papers stating you have custody, she can take the baby." Andreas stands speechless; actually he looks damn stupid.

"I don't have that. Thandisha, can you stay here with Kyia while I take Dee home? I'll come right back, and we can talk."

"That's fine with me." This gives me the opportunity to look for some of my things, and he said he would take me shopping for clothes today. I am a winner all around.

"Is that okay with you ma'am?"

"Sure I have no problem with that." I wait outside while Andreas and Dee get dressed. I hear Dee screaming at Andreas, but when they come outside, she is smiling and acting like the confident girlfriend.

"I will be back in twenty minutes."

"Sure, where are her clothes? I'll get her dressed while you are gone."

"They're in her room. I'll be right back."

"Okay, ya'll drive safe." The apartment is still nice. It is decorated the same as it was before I left. My armoire is still in the hall. The bed is covered in the same coverlet. I look in my armoire. Thank God my coverlets and linen are still inside. I go into Kyia's room; she is still asleep. I decide not to wake her. I find her clothes and lay them on the rocking chair in her room. I sit down and wait for Andreas to return.

He enters the apartment; initially, he is speechless. It is as if he wants to say something but does not have the verbiage to express it.

"Thandisha, I am sorry about that. I had no idea she would call the police."

"Andreas, I really don't give a damn about all of that. I told you I was coming for Kyia today. I don't know why your girlfriend got so upset."

"She's not my girlfriend."

"Well I can't tell, and we really do not have to discuss that because I really don't care. As I told you, I have too much to do to go there."

"Okay, let's not argue." He does not want to argue; neither do I. I would prefer to snatch his face off, but I want to focus on spending time with my daughter. "Where did you want to go?"

"What do you mean? I came, as I told the officer, to spend time with Kyia. I have a place now, and I figure Kyia and I will go to flea markets and find a few things for my place."

"Why can't I drive you around? I really don't mind, and I would really enjoy spending time with the both of you." I hope he does not think I believe that. He wants to chaperone my visit with Kyia. "Remember, I am supposed to take you shopping to buy clothes for work." I am glad he remembers.

"By the way, I would like some of the things you have here that belong to me like my pots and my armoire; while you were gone, I looked inside of the armoire and found some of my linen."

"Okay that's fine."

"So where is your place?"

"It's around the street from my job."

"You found a place fast huh?"

"I was put out of the house; I had to find a place fast or live on the street. I had planned on living with Grandma for six weeks, but of course, that didn't work out."

"Thandisha, I am sorry. I guess I still have some stuff to get over." As if he is the only person who has shit to get over. Hell, life has been pretty rocky for me too.

"That's cool believe me I didn't take it personal. After going through the hell I have been through, the only thing anyone can do to me now is kill me."

"Where do you want to go first? Mall? Out to eat?"

"First, I would like to move my armoire into my apartment. I see you didn't throw away my Le Creuset cookware. If you don't mind, I would like to take my cookware with me." He looks crazy as if he can't believe I am asking for my things. I do not care. I paid good money for the cookware.

He loads my things into his truck, and we take them to my place. He gives me the antique chair and ottoman I picked out from the thrift store for his first apartment. He never really liked the chair anyway. My place is small and over a garage, but it is nice and cozy. The yard is well manicured with pretty flowers and green shrubbery. I am proud to call it home. There is no electricity, so the apartment is warm but still comfortable. Andreas appears impressed with the apartment. There is a small foyer at the entrance. The floors are walnut stained, which I prefer because it is easier to match furniture. He puts the armoire in my bedroom; he places the chair in the living room. I have a couple of pictures in Grandma's garage I want to put in the living room. My apartment may not be much, but it means a lot to me. This is the first time I have felt at home since the day my father killed my mother.

After placing the furniture in my apartment, we go to the mall for my promised shopping trip. He picks out a straight black dress that subtly fit my body. The dress came just above my knees, and it is classy as hell. He buys a pair of up to date, high-heeled black shoes to match. I pick out four pair of dress slacks with matching tops. The clothes are basic colors, so I can mix and match them. I still do not understand why he threw my clothes away.

"I see you still have expensive taste."

"Yes I do especially when I am spending your money." He laughs. We are actually having a good time. Even Kyia is comfortable with me. She even called me momma. After we leave the mall, we go to the thrift store. Andreas does not want to go, but I need a bed.

"I can't believe you are going to buy a used mattress." He turns up his nose. Initially, I think about forgetting the mattress. Then I think if he wants me to have a better mattress, he can buy me one. As long as it is clean, there is nothing wrong with a used mattress. Besides, Mr. Smart Ass obviously hasn't heard that bleach kills 99% of germs and bacteria.

"You can tie the mattress and box spring onto the top of the truck." He looks as if he didn't want it on is new SUV, but I really don't care. I know his vehicle is new, but a mattress and box spring will not hurt it. The salesclerk appears confused as if he does not know if he should place the mattress and box spring on top of the SUV or leave them in the store.

"Okay put them on, but carefully." Kyia and I continue to pick up a few items at the thrift store. I still have over $200.00. I find a small radio for three dollars and a used colored television for fifty dollars. The television does not have a remote, but that does not matter. I can change the channels manually. Andreas places the other items in the back of his SUV.

"Andreas, thanks a million. I could have never put my place together this fast without your help."

"You are welcome. I am happy you are getting yourself together." He smiles. "Thandisha, since you don't have utilities you can come home with me and Kyia."

"What about Dee? What is your girlfriend going to think about that?" He is uncomfortable talking about Dee.

"She is not my girlfriend. She is a nice girl, but I don't have a girlfriend." I want to curse him out; I don't think the bitch is nice at all.

"She obviously thinks she is your girlfriend. I mean she called the police on me for trying to see my own child."

"I am sorry about that. I really didn't mean for that to happen." He appears sincere. "You don't need to stay in your apartment without electricity." He is right. Besides if I go home with him, I can spend time with Kyia. We leave the thrift store and go back to my apartment to put the bed and the other items I purchased inside. I pack a bag for the weekend and include work clothes for Monday morning. When we arrived at his apartment, the first thing he does is go to the phone and turn off the ringer. I put my things down in Kyia's room while he orders pizza. I am glad he orders pizza because I am too tired to cook. I would have felt uncomfortable cooking at his apartment; this was now another woman's kitchen.

"Momma!" Kyia yells for me pointing at the refrigerator.

"Now what do you want in there?" It makes me happy when she calls me momma. I pick her up and carry her to the refrigerator. I open the refrigerator door, and she points to the milk carton. I pour milk in her sippie cup, take her to the bathroom, and undress her for her bath.

"Momma," Kyia's speech is delayed. It does not seem to be as developed as it should be. She uses one-word and her finger to point to what she wants. I am sure it is my fault. I should have been talking to my kid rather than chasing a high. I pour bubble bath in the water and place her in the tub. There are bubbles in her hair and all over her face. Kyia has a beautiful head of kinky, thick, jet black, hair. Her hair is long and thick like mine and momma's. Andreas really does his best to manage it, but she really needs a woman's touch. After bathing her, I allow her to play in the water and then dry her off and put on her pajamas. I sit on the sofa, place her between my knees, part her hair in small sections, and apply oil to her scalp. I braid her hair and place barrettes at the ends to keep the braids from unraveling the way momma used to comb my hair.

I shower after putting Kyia to bed. When I come out of the bathroom, Andreas is sitting on the sofa watching television. I sit at the opposite end of the sofa and join him.

"You know you still look nice. Am I really that bad? Did you have to leave like that?" He knows as well as I do it wasn't him. He knows I was the problem. I am beginning to think he enjoys hearing me put myself down.

"Andreas, you know I was on drugs. It's like your girlfriend said: I was a crack head. I couldn't enjoy you. You are a good man. I think you know that." He slides close to me and tries to kiss me. I push him away. I know he is involved with someone. Although I still love him, I am not playing second fiddle. Besides, I am not emotionally ready for a relationship with anyone. "I don't think that is a good idea. I think we should keep this on a friendly level and parent our child." I can tell by the bulge forming in his boxers he does not agree. I do us both a favor and go to Kyia's room, climb in bed with her, and go to sleep.

The hard knock at the door wakes me. It sounds as if someone is trying to beat the door down. Andreas is still asleep. I go into his room to wake him up, but I forget my jeans. I walk back to Kyia's room to get them. By the time I reach his door again, he is awake. He sits on the bed and acts as if he is oblivious to the knock on the door. He appears reluctant to answer the door, but whoever is at the door is persistent. I go to the bathroom and turn on the shower. The bathroom door is closed, but I can hear every word of their conversation.

"Why didn't you answer your phone last night?"

"I was busy."

"Doing fucking what?"

"Look my daughter is asleep and watch your language."

"Well who the hell is in the shower?" I know he is thinking he should have kept his mouth shut, but Andreas has always been an honest guy.

"Dee, I don't have to explain my life to you. We agreed; we are just friends. We are not committed. If you have to know, Thandisha is spending the weekend here until her electricity is turned on Monday."

"And your ass is worried about my language, but you are not worried about a crack head around your daughter?"

"Dee, I think you better leave."

"I ain't going no damn where!" The front door closes so hard I can feel the vibration in the bathroom. I finish my shower and dry off as slowly as I can. I am getting tired of people referring to me as a crack head. I know for sure I hurt myself more than I could have ever hurt anyone else. Thank God I am getting clean for me. I am so thankful I no longer need the approval of others.

I come out of the shower wrapped in Andreas' robe. Our eyes meet. He appears remorseful. My face is blank and expressionless.

"I am sorry about that."

"You know Andreas. I will be glad when everyone gets over my past because I am slowly but surely getting over it. I really don't care what Dee says about me. After all I've been through, I am too grateful to be alive to care about you or anyone else who sums me up in two words, crack head." I don't give him time to respond. I go into Kyia's room and put on my clothes. I am making breakfast when I hear rapid, hard knocks at the door again.

"Hello Dee," I snatch the door open. "How are you?" She is speechless. I want to give her the opportunity to talk to the crack head face to face. "It's as Andreas said. I am here spending the weekend until Monday morning when my utilities are turned on. You called the police on me because I was trying to visit my child. You referred to me as a crack head in hearing range of my baby. I am not going to waste my time attempting to convince you I am not a crack head. You are too insignificant to my life, but I will tell you this." I pause and scan her unflattering, maturing body up and down. "You can say anything you want to say about me. Who cares? But you will not disrespect me in the presence of my child. Remember I am still her mother. I don't care how much or how good you fuck Andreas that will never change." I look at her; she looks at me. I open the door as wide as it will go and yell as loud as I can, "Andreas, you have a guest!"

He reluctantly comes to the door. I leave the living room. He does not invite her inside. Instead, they go outside. He is outside for several minutes before coming back inside. He is speechless, and so am I. We sit down, eat breakfast and watch television. I know he is embarrassed. Regardless of what I've done, he knows me. He has a great deal of information on me, as I have a great deal of information on him. I know he still loves me. There are some loves that just don't go away. I am not saying I am so great, but he remembers. He remembers when I was innocent. Don't get me wrong. He knows the other side of me too. I know no matter how he tries he can't sum me up as a crack head; he knows there is much more to me than that. Active addiction was not my life. It was a moment in my life. He knew me before I became an active addict. He knows the trauma I experienced when my father killed my mother. Andreas understands my pain, and he knows the progress I have made. He may have a sexual relationship with another woman, but he will always love me. My only advice to Dee is she not get attached.

I would have made Sunday dinner but decide I will cook for Kyia when she visits. I do not want Andreas to think I am trying to come back into his life at this point. I want to grow and get to know myself, so I can get the strength to truly face my trauma. I am determined; it will no longer hold me hostage. Whatever happens, I will be okay.

Monday morning came fast. I enjoyed my weekend stay with Andreas and Kyia. I had the opportunity to spend time with my daughter with a clear mind, but I am glad to go to my own home. I look forward to cleaning my home and organizing it. Granted I am not working with much, but having my own roof is a great feeling. I gladly accepted Andreas' offer to drive me to work. Riding to work with Andreas was relaxing and much more comfortable than public transportation.

Cersi is at her desk working when I arrive. Her greeting is dry, but I am learning not to allow other people's mood swings to determine the outcome of my day. I work on the itinerary for the next event. I make sure all of my "T's" are crossed and "I's" dotted. I am already under close scrutiny from almost everyone in my life, so I can handle anything Cersi throws at me.

"Thandisha, I thought you finished the logistics for your next book event." I do not know where she is going, but I figure she is indirectly asking me what I am working on.

"Yes, I did. I am working on the next event."

"What event is that?" I smile to conceal my aggravation.

"Ashley Griffith changed plans. She wants her personal trainer and her cook to accompany her. I reserved separate suites on different floors, but she insists they all have rooms on the same floor preferable with adjoining rooms. I could not find a hotel to meet her standards." I am smiling on the outside but on the inside I really want to tell her she can organize the event herself if she does not trust my judgment.

"Where is she staying?"

"She wants to stay in a Bed and Breakfast now. She is willing to pay all of the expenses. She wants it to herself for the weekend.

"She can't do that. That's way too expensive." She walks to my desk, looks at my outline, and goes through Ashley Griffin's file. I think to myself, *"Who is she to say what someone does with their own money?"* Besides, Ashley is not paying for this herself. She provided a credit card that belongs to a gentleman who will pay for the expenses her publisher will not reimburse. The account was verified, so what's the problem?

"Well she obviously thinks she can afford it. I think she is going to stay for a few days. She is always asking questions about the city. I get the impression she may relocate here." I smile in a futile attempt to create a more harmonious atmosphere.

"We do not offer relocation services."

"Okay, I thought if I was accommodating, it would be a plus for CNR's impeccable reputation."

"Just let me do all of the thinking here okay." Her sarcasm is unnecessary, but I manage to keep a smile on my face.

"Sure Cersi, you're the boss." She returns an equally insalubrious smile. Cersi is beginning to get on my nerves. Lately her mood swings are without provocation and often catch me off guard. I want to work long enough to save a little money. It is important I keep this job. I have rent to pay, and this job is good for my self-esteem. Besides, in a few months, I can get the money momma left me and maybe start my own business. I continue to work. I decide not to have lunch; instead, I browse the bookstore and scan through different business books. If I can organize events at CNR, I can put something together for myself.

One thing for sure, Cersi really has her stuff together. The bookstore has a very classy ambience. It's in an ideal location. It is in the heart of Midtown, one of the most ethnically diverse communities in the Atlanta. The median income of the population is one of the highest in Georgia. She has managed to grab and hold on to a loyal clientele. Regardless of her unpredictable mood swings, I am grateful she hired me. After working for CNR this short time, I have learned the ins and outs of operating a business. I often watch Cersi negotiate with vendors, and she always comes out on top.

"Hi," I am sitting on a ladder in the business section reading when he approaches me. I have seen him in the bookstore several times over the past two weeks.

"Hello," I hope he is not going to ask for assistance. I am at lunch, and I really do not want to be disturbed. "Do you need help? There's a clerk at the front. I am on break." I smile and resume reading.

"No, I've been in here every day for the last couple of weeks building up the nerve to approach you. Do you mind if I sit down?"

"Help yourself," I give him a quick, pretentious smile and continue to read.

"You know today is my lucky day."

"Good," it has to be obvious I am annoyed and not interested in carrying on a conversation with him.

"My name is Elliot." He extends his hand. I lightly touch his hand in a soft embrace that Grandma describes as a feminine handshake where you lightly touch the inside of a man's hand with four fingers.

"What are you reading?"

"How to books."

"How to what?"

"How to start your own business. I'm thinking about opening an art gallery and dessert shop."

"Really?" He sounds interested.

"Yes."

"So you like art?"

"Yes. I'm an artist. Did you see the pictures at the front entrance? That's some of my work."

"There is a lot of money in that. I work at a brokerage house, so I know where the money is." I assume I am supposed to be impressed, but I am not.

"That's nice." I give him a quick, fake smile and quickly place my head back in my book.

"Do you go out much?"

"No, I don't."

"I'd like to take you out. What are you doing on Saturday?"

"My daughter will visit this weekend, so I will be doing little girl stuff."

"All weekend?"

"Yes all weekend from Friday night until Sunday night."

"What are you doing tonight? There is a jazz concert in the park." I feel strange conversing with Elliot. Andreas is the only man I have dated. While I was using drugs, I didn't date men. A lot of women resort to trading sex for drugs, but I am thankful to God it didn't take me there. I am sure if I had continued, I would have started trading sex for drugs. The drug is so powerful one hit can erase all moral and values. I didn't have to turn tricks because I stole money from Andreas to support my habit.

"I don't have plans tonight." The idea of getting dressed up and going out begins to excite to me, so I agree to go with him to the jazz concert. I feel giddy. It is too bad I don't have anyone to share my excitement with. Ayanna was the only friend I had since momma was killed, and we went our separate ways after I became pregnant with Kyia. "I will call you, and we can set up a time and place to meet." I did not give Elliot my number; I took his instead.

"Cool, one thing, are you going to tell me your name?"

"Thandisha," I am embarrassed; my lack of experience in the dating game is obvious. He embraces my hand and leaves the store.

"Thandisha," I look towards the front of the store to see who is calling my name. It is Monnighan, one of the front desk clerks. We look at fashion magazines together and talk over tea in the bookstore from time to time. I actually enjoy talking to her. We are about the same age. She is a student at Clark, one of the historically black colleges in Atlanta. She motions for me to come to the counter. "Hey Thandisha, how is it going?" She is smiling as usual.

"Pretty good, I have been working my butt off on this last book signing."

"Really, who is coming?"

"Ashley Griffin."

"Who?" She covers her mouth in disbelief. "Oh my goodness! Thandisha, do you know who Ashley Griffin is?" She does not give me time to respond. "Ashley used to work here. She stole Cersi's husband." It all makes sense now. Cersi has been a bitch since I booked Ashley. I know she is divorced, but I had no idea another woman was involved. I don't understand why she allowed me to book Ashley. I do not understand why Ashley would want an event in Cersi's bookstore. I feel good for the rest of the day. I hate that Cersi would have to endure whatever emotion Ashley's book signing stirred within her, but I am relieved to know I am not the problem. I am also super excited because I have a date. I am on a natural high. My natural endorphins are working again.

I leave work and walk five minutes to my apartment. Moving here was a good idea, and it feels good putting the key in the door of my own apartment. The apartment is cool. It is nice and cozy. I set the alarm on my radio to come on at 5:15 p.m., so I enter my apartment to the sound of cool jazz. I light coconut incense and pour a glass of fruit punch; I no longer drank alcohol for fear of triggering my crack addiction.

After relaxing, watching the news, and tidying up the apartment, I shower, put on my black slacks, and a very sheer black shirt. Grandma used to say I should wear more pastel colors. She used to complain that I always looked as if I were in mourning. I don't know if I am still mourning, but I know I look sexy as hell. I am still very natural. The only makeup I wear is lipstick, and I still wear my hair in the bun pulled back from my face. I probably need to update my hair, but I still look good, damn good in fact.

I hear footsteps coming up the stairs. I hear a beautiful whiny voice. I open the door before they knock. Andreas is standing at the door with Kyia in his arms.

"Momma," she leaps from his arms to mine. She is sweaty and smells like a wet puppy.

"Hey baby." I kiss Kyia in the middle of her forehead. "What brings you guys over here?"

"Momma," she smiles while continuously jumping up and down in my arms.

"We were in the neighborhood, and Kyia wanted to see you."

"You are so sweet. You want to see your momma." She smiles and clings to me.

"You look nice." Andreas steps back and away from me. I turn around in a complete circle, so he can get a good look.

"Thanks. Do you want something to drink? I have fruit punch."

"No, I have to go. I need to bathe Kyia and put her to bed."

"No," she whines and pouts.

"It's almost 9:00. You are an hour past your bedtime." He sits on the chair; his eyes are glued on me. "So how is it going?"

"Everything is okay."

"I see you're painting again." He stands and walks by the window and looks at my canvas. He is still nosey. "You look nice. Did you just get home from work?"

"No, I am going out tonight."

"Who is the lucky guy?" An inquisitive looks flashes across his face.

"A guy I met at the bookstore. We're going to listen to live jazz in the park."

"Do you think you are ready to have a relationship so soon?"

"Actually it's not a relationship. It's a date."

"Same thing." His pitch is elevated. He is one decibel from yelling.

"It's not the same thing." He is pissing me off.

"Well I don't want some random man you meet in the street around my daughter."

"Do you really have control over that?" I would usually get angry when he is controlling but not today.

"Yes, I think I do. I can control who is around my daughter and ain't no street thug coming around my daughter." He is pushing it. I have changed, but I am wise enough to know people, including Andreas, will conveniently use my past against me.

"Actually, he is not a street thug."

"Yeah right." Initially, I was going to meet Elliot at the train station but after Andreas' sarcasm, I decide to allow him to pick me up at my apartment. I go in the bedroom, call Elliot, and give him directions. I am putting earrings in my ear when I walk back into the living room. He is sitting in the chair; His eyes are glued to the floor. "I don't have control of you, but I do have control of what happens around my daughter."

"Yeah I know. I guess that's why I found my best friend's sister naked in my bed with my butt naked man, and our baby was in the house. I guess that was such a high class, non-thuggish thing to do."

"I apologized for that. Remember?"

"Yes I do, and until now, I don't think I ever threw that in your face. Did I?" Elliot's strong, confidant knock startles us. "Oh that must be him. Kyia give momma some sugar. I'll call you tomorrow; maybe daddy will let you spend the night tomorrow." I open the door. Elliot looks surprised to find Andreas and Kyia sitting comfortably in my apartment. I introduce them, and we leave. Kyia is in my arms. Andreas follows behind us. I give Kyia to her father then walk to the passenger side of the black Mercedes convertible where Elliot stands waiting with the door open for me. I do not look back at Andreas, but I can feel his stare.

"Do you and your baby's father still see each other?"

"No, but we are still very cordial. We stay cordial for Kyia. We are still raising our daughter. She stays with him during the week, and I get her from Friday until Sunday. He is more financially able to care for her right now, so this is good for all concerned. Plus, he is a very good father."

"It's Wednesday."

"Yeah I know." I do not feel the need to explain. This is just a date, and I do not owe him an explanation.

Cars never really impressed me. When I think back, material things never impressed me. But it feels good riding in his car. It is a smooth ride and very comfortable inside. We drive to the park with the top down. The park is crowded; it takes ten minutes to find a parking space. The music is nice, and the food is good. We eat wings; he drinks a Stoley tonic, and I drink cola over ice. We eat and dance for most of the concert. I am truly having a nice time.

Elliot has good conservation. He dates a lot. He says he has never found the right woman to settle down with.

"I have never really dated; actually, my daughter's father is the only guy I have ever dated."

"He's a lucky man." Actually we both are lucky. I still have a great deal of respect for Andreas, but I am definitely enjoying Elliot's company. We danced until almost 12:00 in the morning; I wasn't tired, but I still have two more days until the weekend.

"It's getting late." I look at my watch. He looks at his.

"It is only 11:45; you can't be serious."

"I have a busy day tomorrow at work. I have a major upcoming event. Ashley Griffin is coming, and we are expecting a major crowd."

"I understand." His loud, long sigh makes me uncomfortable. "I guess I better get you home." The ride back to my apartment is quiet and relaxing. He walks me to the door and kisses me on my cheek before leaving. "I'd love to see you again."

"We'll see." I thank him for a nice time and lock the door. I shower and put on my nightgown. I am ready to get in bed when I hear a quick knock on the door.

"Who is it?"

"It's me." I open the door cracking it a little. He squeezes his way in.

"Is there something wrong with Kyia?"

"No, she is fine. She is spending the night with momma."

"Well what are you doing here? It's late." He sits down on the chair.

"Are you going to see him again?"

"Yeah I think so. I had a nice time."

"Don't you think it's too soon to start dating? I mean you do know it's not over between us. Don't you?"

"I know. It will never be over. We have a daughter we both love. We still have elementary school, high school, and college for Kyia to work out. Hell one day we will be grandparents." I laugh, but he is very serious.

"I don't want you to see him again Thandisha."

"I probably will see him again because I had a good time."

"What in the hell does that mean?"

"Andreas, I was gone less than two weeks before Dee was in my bed."

"Thandisha, you know it didn't mean anything. Besides, you left. I didn't put you out. You left to be with your crack head friends. Can you imagine the hurt and pain I felt when I found out my favorite girl in the world was on crack? Can you imagine my fear when you left in the middle of the night, and I didn't see you for days?" He places his head in his hands and stares at the floor. "Thandisha, you put me through hell."

"I believe you, but I've been through a lot of pain, and my main focus is to heal myself. I need to become a whole person."

"I can see; Thandisha, you are doing a good job." He reaches for me and pulls me close in his arms. "You are looking really good baby." He places a soft, moist kiss in the middle of my forehead. I feel a pleasant, tingling sensation between my thighs. It has been a while since I made love to Andreas. He is always so sensuous. My temperature rises, and my body begins to quiver. "Who do you belong too?"

"Myself," I kiss him back. I manage to tell him I have to go to bed between kisses, but he acts as if he does not hear me. He puts his hands inside of my panties. It always felt good when he touched me there. "I think you should go Andreas." I pull him closer to me.

"Don't worry baby I have no expectations. I have no demands. I just want to love you right here and right now." He picks me up and carries me into my bedroom. "Does it still feel good to you baby?" I don't speak. I let my body do all of the talking. I stand and pull his pants down below his hips and please him the way I know he likes to be pleased. Damn, I don't know what I was thinking, but love is the best high in the world.

Zero Degrees

I love Andreas, but I enjoy my own space. I love my freedom. I can finally be myself without the stress of living up to others' expectations. When I lived with Grandma, I was expected to grieve the way she wanted me to grieve which really meant I was simply supposed to bury my pain deep inside of me, and act as if the day my father killed my mother never happened. I was unable to live up to Grandma's expectations. I always managed to do something to piss her off. I was not outgoing, a trait she loved in my ex-best friend, Ayanna. I used to get jealous of the way she easily smiled with Ayanna and how easy it was for them to talk to one another. I believe her main issue with me was my genetic makeup. I was my mother's daughter and my daddy's girl. I think we would have gotten along better if she could have erased my paternal DNA. Maybe when she looked into my eyes, she saw daddy's eyes, and maybe that was too painful. Maybe we were all mentally ill because we never dealt with my mother's death. I don't blame her. I am not angry with her. I truly believe she did her best. I simply wished she could have accepted me for who I am and provided the environment for me to grieve my mother's death and my father's imprisonment.

It is 5:15. I am still working because CNR is expecting a large crowd for the Ashley Griffith book signing. I sent invitations to all of the librarians, language art teachers and college English Professors as well as a mass email invite to the clientele on our VIP list. Her book is number one on the best seller's list, and she recently sold her movie rights to an award-winning director. After I place posters at the book-signing table, I go back to the office. Cersi sits with her head face down on the desk. Initially, I thought she was indulging in a power nap. When she raises her head off of the desk, it is obvious she is crying. Her eyes are red, and I see faint traces of dried mucous on her nostrils. I want to turn around and leave the office, but our eyes meet.

"Cersi, are you okay?" I walk close to her desk and gently place my hand on her shoulder. She immediately stands, grabs me and clings to me as if her life depends on some supernatural force I can transmit to her. I stand motionless. I am shocked. I cannot imagine Cersi in this state. I imagine her strong and impenetrable.

"Oh God, Thandisha how could he do this? How could he leave me for that trifling bitch? She was my fucking friend." Between tears and screams, I learn the *"he"* is her ex-husband, and the *"trifling bitch"* is Ashley Griffith. It takes a while for her to get herself together. She talks between sobs, but I can barely understand her.

"Cersi, if this bothers you, why did you allow her to promote her book here?"

"I will not give those bastards the satisfaction of believing they can get next to me." She reaches into her desk and removes a small, brown liquor bottle. She untwists the top and takes a long, hard swallow.

"Cersi, you don't have to prove anything to anyone. If this bothers you, then cancel her signing." She quickly stands and wipes the alcoholic residue from the top of her lip.

"Never, I will get through this." She embraces me again, grabs her purse and leaves. I go to my desk, organize my files, lock up the store, and leave for the day.

I walk to the corner deli for takeout. I am anxious to get home to the nurturing and peaceful environment I have created. It has given me the opportunity to finally begin to grieve the loss of my mother and father. I stop at the mailbox and gather my mail before going inside. My apartment is still relatively bare, which is the way I like it. Space, for me, is therapeutic. I sit in my chair and place the mail on the ottoman. I open each piece, as I gobble down my food. Most of the envelopes contained bills and junk mail. The last letter is peculiar. It is rough with ragged edges. There is no return address. The envelope looks as if it was made of recycled paper that has been recycled over and over again. I slowly open the envelope;

My Dearest Thandie:

It feels quite awkward writing you. Actually I do not feel I have the right to contact you. I understand if you discard this letter without reading it. I would definitely deserve that. It has been a long time Thandie. There has not been a day, an hour, a minute or second you and your brother were not on my mind. The first thing I would like to say is I am so very sorry. I know my apology is almost an insult, but my limited vocabulary does not contain the words that can explain the regrets I have for my selfish act. I would like to say that I did not intend to kill your mother. I loved her more than life itself. If you can go back and try to remember some of the things that transpired before that fatal day when I killed my beloved wife, your beautiful mother, maybe you can see it was truly an accident. I had no intention of killing her. I was trying to scare her into staying with me. I was trying to scare her into loving me again. At that time in my life, I was a very scared and insecure man. My only goal during this time in my marriage was working to take care of my family. I was determined to build an empire so that my family would not have to scrape the bottom of the barrel. In the process of building my empire, I lost my wife. When Riley was searching for and gaining her independence, I became threatened, lost, and scared. I could not imagine a life without her. She was the world to me. The night I accidentally killed her she was going to leave me. She already had an apartment and was packing her clothes to leave. I could not bear it. I initially threatened her, but she would not back down. She continued to pack her things. When I pulled the gun out and pointed it at her, she did not budge. Instead, she came towards the loaded gun. My finger was on the trigger. I was startled, and the gun went off. I make no excuses for my actions. I take full responsibility.

Khalid has kept me abreast on your life. I understand that you have an issue with substance abuse. It slipped out, so please do not be angry with your brother. He was discussing how well you are doing in your own apartment now, and he mistakenly told me of your addiction to crack cocaine. I am sorry, for I take full responsibility for that. I do not want to bombard you, nor do I want to take too much of your time. I will not write you again until I hear from you. You are forever in my prayers.

I love you Thandie
Daddy

My heart begins to beat rapidly. I am so emotional, I can barely breathe. The tears begin to flow uncontrollably. I run to the phone.

"Hello."

"Andreas...please," I can barely talk between screams.

"Thandisha! Thandisha, calm down! Are you okay? What's wrong? Baby slow down and talk to me." I cannot speak. I am a ball of emotion. "Thandisha, I am on my way."

I sit absorbed in my pain, feeling every emotion. I long to see him, to touch him, to slap him, and maybe even shoot him too. I am happy to read words from daddy. I am angry with him. I love him. I hate him.

"Thandisha, open the door!" I feel so many emotions. Initially, I do not hear the knock at the door. "Open the door baby!" I somehow pull myself off of the floor and open the door. I collapse in his arms. He carries me to the chair. "Baby what the hell is wrong?" I cannot speak. I simply give him the letter. He reads the letter silently. When he finishes reading the letter, he places it down on the floor. He pulls me out of the chair and carries me to the bedroom. I lay in bed with his arms tight around me. I still cannot speak. I do not have words. I can see the beginning of tears forming in his eyes. He is speechless. I do not need to hear words. I want to finally feel all of these emotions. I cry myself into a long, relaxing, and peaceful sleep...

The door makes a loud noise, as she walks in and out of the house each time carrying a box of her things. I wonder where Khalid and I are going to sit in the car. She places her things in the front and back seats of the new Volvo Station Wagon daddy bought her a month ago. Daddy continues to beg her to stay.

"Jikki, I am tired of your shit. I told you when I finished my GED I was going to school. I told you when I finished the certificate program, I was going to get a job."

"Riley, what about my kids? Who is going to take care of them? You don't have to work. You don't need to work. I have enough income from rental property, so you

don't have to work. I have a successful business. Why do you think I worked so hard all of these years?"

"So you can maintain all of the damn control!" She walks close to him and screams in his face.

"Baby, you can work for me! Don't allow that fool to disrupt our family."

"Are you fucking deaf? I don't want to work for you. I don't want this damn house. I want me. I want to get to know me. I have been with you since I was fucking 14 years old. If it weren't for the abortions I've had, I would have stayed barefoot and pregnant.

"What fucking abortion? When did you have an abortion?" He grits his teeth so hard his jawbones protrude.

"Oh baby not an abortion try three or four!" She sounds as if she is enjoying her performance. She acts as if she has been harboring feelings for years and now rejoicing with an almost violent release.

"You fucking bitch, how could you..." I hear loud, stinging slaps alternating with screams from momma.

"Go on hit me Jikki. It doesn't matter now. It's over. Their bedroom door opens then abruptly closes again. Momma and daddy are screaming at each other. Khalid runs into his room. I sit quietly on the sofa in the den. I hope they will stop fighting and instead make those weird sounds they make at night and sometimes in the early morning.

Instead, I heard a loud, hollow pop followed by an eerie, echoing silence. I slowly walk into my parents' room. Momma is a folded heap in daddy's arms; blood oozes...

Also by
Regina Neequaye

" *Urban Tango*"

CHAPTER 1

I stand in front of the bathroom mirror in awe of Stacy's reflection. She lies on her stomach in the middle of my bed. Her full breasts are almost flat to the mattress. Her thick, black hair is haphazardly spread across the fluffy, down pillow. The covers have slid down exposing half of her rotund, firm chocolate bottom. I flush the used condom down the toilet and wash my hands. I am en route to her, holding my hard-on in my hand, ready for round two when her phone rings. She quickly leaves the bed and retrieves the phone from her purse. The curve of her hips, her toned, slightly bowed legs, and her firm, round breast turn me on. I stand close behind her and attempt to get her in the mood again. She moves my hand from between her legs and quickly grabs her robe.

"Shush," she places her index finger in front of pouty, succulent lips and whispers, "it's Ming Lee." I quickly move to the side fully out of view of the phone's camera. She accepts the request for a video connection and places the phone on the desk. The thin face Chinese woman with a British accent appears on the tiny display. She and Stacy trade a few niceties before quickly getting to business.

Mr. Ye is requesting an impromptu date with his personal companion. He has developed a strong affinity for his special young friend. He normally visits once per month; however, this will be the second for the month. I have never met Mr. Ye. I have never spoken to him. All communication is through Ming Lee and Stacy. Stacy informs me of the time and date of his arrivals, and I

1

coordinate the transportation with one of my drivers.

Mr. Ye is my favorite client. He receives special services. He transfers twenty-five thousand dollars to my offshore account in the Caymans every month to keep his companion personal. He is a top shelf client who pays for top shelf service. I immediately call Courtney. The phone rings three times and goes directly to her voicemail. I hang up and dial her cell. Again, the call goes straight to voicemail.

"Fucking bitch!"

"What's wrong?" Stacy ends her call with Ming Lee, quickly strolls through her text messages, and places her phone back in her purse.

"We are going to have to do something about Courtney!"

"Besides you and me, who do you know is awake at 5:00 o'clock on a Saturday morning? She is probably asleep. Mr. Ye's plane does not land until 8:00. He is not expecting Ashleigh until 9:00. That is five hours from now. We have a lot of time. Calm down." She walks to the bathroom and stops in the middle of the threshold. "Do you want to join me?"

"You know I do not do romantic and mushy." She laughs; she and I both know I am not joking. I have made it perfectly clear on more than one occasion this is a business with benefits arrangement. We both agree this works for us since we are together so much. Due to our line of business, we cannot afford serious outside relationships with people who will need accounts of our time. She sometimes forgets, but I have no problem reminding her and keeping her on track.

I lean back deep into the pillow. I am restless. My mind is occupied with Courtney. I replay Courtney's behavior for the last month or so in my mind. My anger bounces between Courtney's fuck ups and Stacy for not keeping her cousin in check.

The sound of the shower annoys me. She has the acupressure massage at full blast. The bathroom door is closed, but I can still hear the sound of the water hitting hard against the stone walls in the shower. I can only imagine what it is doing to her flesh. I dial Courtney's number again. She does not answer. I throw the phone hard against the mattress and leave the bed.

"What are you doing?" I open the bathroom door and find Stacy squatting in front of the vanity.

"I am looking for shampoo. I need to wash my hair."

"I don't have any!" I push her away, close the vanity door, and turn the shower off. "Don't go through my things!" I step over her wet body and walk to the toilet and relieve myself. "I am not going through your things. I need to wash my hair." She pulls strands of her hair from the shower cap and brings them to her nose. "My hair smells like your sweat." She laughs. "I have a few days before my next salon visit."

"Don't go through my shit!"

"You are uptight. You should calm down. Call another driver."

"They are all tied up." Her nonchalance fuels my agitation. I flush the toilet and wash my hands. She follows me to the bedroom. She removes the shower cap from her head; a mass of thick, jet black hair falls out of the cap and down her back. She bends forward and gathers her hair to the top of her head and wraps a rubber band around it. The long, bouncy ponytail makes her look like a teenager. She loosens the towel; it falls to the floor. I expect to see bruising and discoloration from the massage jets, but her chocolate skin is flawless. The sight of perfect, firm melons on her chest makes my nature rise. I am too focused on Mr. Ye, his companion, and Courtney to do anything about it.

"I am going to leave now. I have errands to run. I will catch you around noon at the Chicken Shack. You do not have to pick me up. I will drive myself." She squeezes her perfect body into tight jeans, pulls her T-shirt over her head, and throws her bra and panties in her purse. I grab my robe and walk downstairs with her. She hugs me; I am uncomfortable but reluctantly return the embrace. She gathers her shoes and leaves.

I call Courtney again as I crack two eggs and drop them in the hot skillet. The call goes to voicemail. She has no more times to fuck up. I get rid of trouble before trouble starts. According to the rumor mill, she is using street pharmaceuticals again. I started to take care of her when the rumors first surfaced, but Stacy pleaded her case and convinced me the rumors come from people who do not want to let go of the past. I agreed with Stacy for a while, but I could no longer ignore the rumors when she almost fucked up a thirty thousand dollar deal a couple of months ago. She was a no-show for a very wealthy new client who paid fifty percent down for a companion for a five-day Mediterranean cruise. Lucky for Courtney, Stacy found a replacement. The replacement was not an

3

exact match. The skin color was a half-shade darker than Courtney's. Her no-show cut into our profit, as I gave the customer a twenty percent discount for his inconvenience. This business thrives on repeat customers, and customer service is my number one priority.

My goal is to give our customers exactly what they want. I hired one of the best programmers in the world to build and maintain an encrypted website so secure, the government's best programmers cannot hack into it. With the exception of Mr. Ye, my first and favorite international client, our clients log in, enter the desired dates to meet with their companions. The client has the option of choosing from a variety of characteristics, including eye color, hair color, hair texture, and skin pigmentation. Profiles of available companions and their sexual specialties populate. The client chooses his companion and wires the money to my off-shore account in the Caymans.

I guarantee my services. I would have made Courtney disappear for fucking up, but she is Stacy's cousin. I gave her a second chance. I limit her job to transportation, and she is fucking that up. I run a tight ship. My staff knows I don't play. In this business, everyone has to be on their game one hundred percent. Drug addicts and alcoholics lack discipline and have no place in this business.

I check my text messages as I walk up the stairs. Lailah, my children's mother, thanks me for the extra five grand I deposited in her account yesterday. She texts a picture of Kaycee, our eight-year-old daughter, and Jonathan our four-year-old son. I stare at my children's pictures and sometimes allow myself to dream, for a moment, that one day I will share a home with Lailah and my children with the white picket fence, the two car garage, and a dog named Fido. In reality, I know I am not equipped to be a husband or father. I see them when time permits. Besides, Lailah is too special to be affiliated with this game. I don't want her or the kids exposed to this life.

I straighten the covers, sit on the bed, and catch the last of the morning news. I am restless and cannot sit still. I pick up Stacy's wet towel from the floor and make a mental note to remind her to pick up after herself. I stare at the phone and contemplate dialing Courtney's number again. She has my mind fucked up. She is a distraction. If she is using, she risks bringing unwanted attention to our organization. Something has to be done before she fucks it up for everyone. We have a multimillion dollar business. If the business continues to grow, I project in a year or so we will have a billion dollars in sales. Several national and international players depend on our business to stay discreet. A drug addict is unpredictable and has no place in this type of business. I take a quick shower and slide into an old pair of jeans. I open the vanity, slide the fake backing to the side, open the safe, and remove a few bills from a stack of cash hidden under a small manila envelope.

I have been out of the street game for years, but I never gave up my pass. I drive to Buckhead and stop at an old acquaintance's house to make a quick purchase, then drive to the train station. I park my car at the Lindbergh station and ride one stop to the Buckhead Station. I exit the train with my sun visor pulled close to my head. My sunglasses cover my eyes. I stop at the neighborhood store and pick up bread, milk, eggs and enough canned goods to fill two grocery bags, and walk three blocks to her sky rise apartment. I walk towards the side of the building, careful to keep my face away from the cameras. I inconspicuously wait with the two bags filled with groceries in both of my arms for a resident to enter or exit the building. I have digital access, but I don't want this visit recorded. I walk the ten flights of stairs to her apartment with my head turned away from the security cameras. I knock on the wooden door, but she does not answer. I pull my sleeve over my finger and press the numbers on the keypad to unlock the door.

The smell of rotten food hits me like a ton of bricks as I enter the foyer. I am filled with anger when I notice a sink filled with dishes and a sea of empty takeout containers on the counter. I kick a plastic garbage bag half-filled with trash to the side as I make my way to the living room. I walk to the front of the leather sofa and find Courtney sprawled out in her bra and panties. Her hair is wet and slick to her head. Mascara is smudged around her puffy eyes. I look at my watch; it is 8:00. She should be dressed and ready for the day. I stand in front of her. She does not notice my presence until I raise her arm. Tiny black holes the size of a pin head mark the inside of her arm and the back of her hand.

"Jefferson" It takes several minutes for her to focus. She attempts to stand; she grabs the side of her head, then slowly sits down. "What's up baby?"

"You tell me; I had a job for you. I have been calling you all fucking morning!"

"What time is it?" She uses her fingers to remove thick, crusty sleep from her puffy eyes. She struggles to focus on the crystal clock on the side of the table. "Damn, baby I am sorry. It won't take me long to get ready." She slowly stands and pulls her arms high over her head exposing unshaven armpits. I step back and away from her as the putrid smell of musk from her underarms mixed with the stench of unwashed ass assaults my nostrils. "You have a job for me?"

"Don't worry about it baby. The client has been taken care of."

"I am sorry, Jefferson. I had a late night. I hung out with some friends from Vegas I have not seen in a while." Her apology is sincere, but much too late. "I will be on it next time." She stands, stretches, and walks to the bathroom. She appears to not notice she is half-dressed; her only clothing is her bra and panties. I follow close behind. She opens the medicine cabinet, removes a white pill from a folded napkin, and pops it in her mouth. She grabs an open bottle of water from the shelf over the commode. "It's a muscle relaxer."

"You need something stronger? I got what you need right here." I reach in my pocket and remove a baggie of uncut heroin and dangle it in front of her.

"Jefferson, you got me wrong." Beads of perspiration congregate on her forehead. She scratches the inside of her arm incessantly. Thick saliva forms in the corners of her mouth. "You know I know better. I don't do that shit anymore." She is so focused on the baggie in my hand, it is as if she is talking to the baggie instead of me.

"That's not what I heard. My Buckhead connection says you are a regular for heroin and ecstasy." She turns away. Her nervous tics confirm she is a heavy user. "I hear you got fired from the nonprofit for not calling and not coming in for an entire week. Everyone has to keep a job to look on the up and up!" I look around at the upscale downtown condominium she rents on paper from my offshore corporation. "How will you explain your ability to pay this high ass rent if you are ever questioned?"

"You're right, Jefferson, but it wasn't my fault. Those people…" She cannot complete a thought or finish a sentence. "I don't know what you heard, but I am not using." I step closer to her. The stench of metabolized heroin seeps through her pores. She steps back and away from me. She loses her balance and falls in the bath tub, landing with both feet in the air. I grab her feet and spread her toes. Black marks surrounded by puss-filled blisters sit in the cracks between her toes. "Courtney, you know better!" I throw her foot to the side. We are both startled by the loud echo as her feet hit the shower.

"I am so sorry, Jefferson." She puts her hands together as if she is praying. "Shit got so hard. You know my mother will not allow me to visit my kids and…"

"It is okay; don't worry about it. Has anyone been here?" I look around for evidence of lowlife drug dealers and desperate drug addicts. I open the bathroom closet and find size 12 men's Timberland boots. I look under the cabinet and find two different bottles of male cologne. An oversized men's Obey sweat shirt and a dingy pair of hi-end designer jeans lay unfolded on top of the hamper.

"I swear on everything, I am sorry, Jefferson!" Her lips quiver as she speaks. Her carotid artery beats so hard, it looks as if there is a jumping bean in her neck. "I will pull it together; ain't nobody been here but my brother. I never cop here." I feel like smacking her across the face for insulting my intelligence. Her only brother is locked up, doing a ten-year bid for stupid shit.

She grabs the handle on the side of the bathtub and attempts to pull herself out. I stand and watch her struggle. After several unsuccessful attempts, she lets go of the handle and falls back in the tub. I offer my hand; she takes it. I pull her out. She stands close in front of me. "I am really sorry." She flirtatiously bats her eyes. "Let me make it up to you." She smiles, showing yellow, decaying teeth as she rubs her thin body against me. She takes my hand and leads me to the bedroom. I grab the open bottle of water and willingly follow. She grabs what looks like a month of dirty clothes from the bed and throws them on the floor. The drugs have made her lose her mind. She knows, and everyone who works for me knows, with the exception of Stacy, I don't get down with employees.

"Don't worry about it, Courtney; everything is cool." Dark circles surround her eyes. Stress lines cover a prematurely aging face that was flawless two months ago. "I am going to make you feel good; take your mind off of everything." She lies on the bed and leans back on two oversized pillows. I sit next to her and open the small baggie filled with uncut heroin. She quickly opens the night stand and pulls out her gear. She is so anxious she doesn't notice the thick black leather gloves that cover my hands. Her hand trembles as if she has a neurological disorder. She struggles to get the rubber band around her arm.

"Let me help you, baby." I take the rubber band and tie it as tight as I can. I remove the syringe and metal spoon from my pocket. I place the heroin on a spoon, mix in a couple of drops of water, melt it with a lighter, and fill the syringe with as much of the warm, bubbly liquid it can hold. I rub my thumbs over her desecrated veins, find a good injection spot, and insert the needle.

"Slow, baby, you got to do it slow." I ignore her and quickly push all of the poison in her arm. She leans back against the upholstered leather headboard. Her eyelids flutter and slowly close. A euphoric smile stretches across her face. After several minutes, she slowly opens her eyes and stares at the wall. I almost pity her. She was never smart, but she had a perfect body and a beautiful face. Small craters now cover her honey brown cheeks. She lost a lot of weight much too quickly, causing the elasticity in her skin to diminish. Courtney very much needed her good looks to make up for her lack of intelligence and common sense. She has no self-confidence and is a magnet to losers.

Her head falls to the side. She struggles to hold meaningful conversation. The heroin that flows through her veins is pure and uncut. Her eyes slowly roll back in her head. Her gaze is peaceful. She mumbles, but her words are inaudible. I sit in the chair next to her bed and watch the clock.

"This is some good shit! You got a little more?" The high is wearing off. Her speech is still slurred and labored; it is as if the space in her mouth is too small to accommodate her tongue.

"Sure, baby, anything for you." I sit on the side of the bed, tighten the rubber band around her limp arm, empty last of the poison from the baggie onto the spoon, and melt it. I siphon the liquid in the syringe and stick the needle in her arm. Her mouth curves into a slight smile. Her head slowly falls back against the headboard. Her breathing is soft and slow, almost like a sleeping baby. I look at my watch. Five minutes have passed. Her body jolts forward and begins to shake uncontrollably. She is stiff as a board. Spittle, thick like milk, flows from her mouth. Her head falls forward; her chin sits awkwardly on her chest. Her eyes are wide open; I take my glove covered hand and close her eyes. I leave the needle stuck in her arms and turn off the lights. I grab the empty baggie and cigarette lighter and place them in a pocket of the jeans that lay on the hamper. I wipe down everything my hands touched and leave with plenty of time to transport the companion to my favorite client.

Chapter 2

It is 4:30. I have completed five of the ten tasks on my "Things To Do" list. Osei hates when I bring work home, but I have to do what I have to do. He used to be my biggest supporter and number one fan. He has changed and become resentful of the time and energy I spend advancing my career. I reluctantly shut down my computer and shove files in my briefcase. My cell rings. I ignore it and organize my desk for next week. It has been ringing off and on for the last hour. The constant ringing is annoying. I grab the phone, change the setting to vibrate, and drop it in my pocket, but the caller is persistent. The vibration from the phone drives me crazy. I reach into my pocket, feel for the decline button, and forward the call to voicemail. It is killing me not to answer. It's Friday; I meet Osei and the kids for dinner every Friday after work. I should have left thirty minutes ago to avoid rush hour traffic. I lock my file cabinet, grab my things, and walk to the elevator. I reach the parking deck, and the phone begins to vibrate again. I remove it from my pocket and look at the display. It is Detective Davis. I throw my things in the backseat of my car, sit in the driver's seat, and reluctantly return the call.

"Detective Davis," he answers after the first ring.

"Why are you blowing up my phone? It's Friday, and it is almost five o'clock." I glance at my watch. I should not have returned the call. Time is quickly passing, and there is a pit bull waiting for me with my children at Benihana's.

"Ayanna," he chuckles. "You are just as married to that chair in the District Attorney's office as I am to mine at Precinct East." Unfortunately, my husband will probably agree with him, but the truth is that chair in the District Attorney's office will lead to greater opportunities.

"Quiet as it's kept, Detective Davis, I have a life, and it is waiting for me at Benihana's."

"I know; but give me a few minutes. I have a surprise for you. I will be at the detention center in two minutes. Meet me in front of the Intake Desk at the female entrance. You will not believe who is sitting handcuffed in the back of my car."

"Who is it?" I turn my wrist inward and glance at my watch again. Time is quickly passing.

"It is a surprise, a big one; I will see you in two minutes." If I am late for dinner, there will be hell to pay, but business is business. I leave my car in the garage, grab my purse and clipboard, and jaywalk across the street to the detention center. Davis is at the Intake Desk when I arrive. A handcuffed female dressed in high end fashion stumbles in front of him. She looks out of place amongst the other female detainees waiting in line to be processed into the jail. "This is one of my presents to you." A female detention officer escorts Davis' prisoner through the X-ray check point. Detective Davis instructs the detention officer to pat her down and take her to an interrogation room on the female side of the jail.

"Who is she?" I don't know where he is going with this and wonder why he believes his detainee is a present to me. "Where did you find her?" The handcuffed female with blue eye shadow and two shades too light pink lipstick smudged on her lips looks more like a child than a woman. Her body looks out of place in the high end Gucci Stilettos and the body fitting black dress. I can't think of the designer, but I have seen this dress in one of the high-end fashion magazines I subscribe to.

"We detained her during a prostitution sting at one of the five star hotels in midtown; an undercover officer saw her leave the hotel with a suspicious, middle-aged Asian male before getting into a white Range Rover."

"She does not look like a typical streetwalker." I inconspicuously glance at her shoes and examine the intricate stitching and the logo; they are authentic. Her high end, sexy and classy attire is not usually worn by common prostitutes. "I hope you arrested the men as well."

"We arrested the man in the white Range Rover."

"Only one of them?"

"We tried to detain and arrest both men." I look over my glasses. Davis looks over his. "The Asian gentleman is a foreign diplomat. He refused to answer questions. Within minutes of detaining him, a representative from the Chinese embassy was on the scene. After he flashed his credentials and requested diplomatic immunity, we had to release him to his embassy. We believe the white Range Rover belongs to her pimp."

"Oh." I try not to be rude, but I hope like hell he has not interrupted my evening to inform me of a pimp and his hooker's arrest. The pit bull and my kids are waiting for me. I am in no mood for confrontation. Last Friday, Osei blew a fuse because I was 15 minutes late.

"And guess who the pimp is?" I balance my weight on one leg, fold my arms across my chest, and wait for disclosure. "Jefferson Thomas." My thoughts travel from zero to a hundred in minus two seconds. I quickly glance at my watch. Osei and the kids are expecting me in less than ten minutes, but this is the best news I have had all day. Jefferson Thomas, as he is now known, is one of the cockiest, ruthless criminals that have crossed my path. He seduced many of the occupants in City Hall with campaign funds and monetary bribes. He is Ivy League educated with a thuggish modus operandi.

He, along with his suit wearing crew of thugs, turned Mason Hills, Dixie Falls, and half of the Fourth Ward into a zombie land of oxycodone, crack, and meth addicts. He and his cohorts single handedly destroyed what was once a strong and affluent, upper middle class, African American community. Most of the businesses in the communities were owned by black people who actually resided in the community. The community was home to the largest concentration of educated blacks in the nation; however, education and affluence could not compete with residents who became the dope fiends that lived in the community or the fiends that came into the community from the suburbs to purchase illegal drugs. The dope fiends ran customers of once thriving businesses away. Jefferson and his cohorts used politicians he bribed with campaign contributions and City Hall staff on his payroll to change zoning codes. Locally owned boutiques, bookstores, and flower shops were replaced with pawn shops, liquor stores, and other cash-based businesses that were fronts to funnel proceeds from illegal activities. Between the constant thievery and the turf shootouts, many family-owned businesses that were part of the community landscape for decades were forced to board up and close shop. The demographics of the community quickly changed. Residents who could afford to leave left in droves. Many high-priced homes were boarded up and abandoned. Those that remained lived in self-made prisons. Security firms made a fortune. Windows covered with burglar bars and steel doors became the norm. Because of his connections, Jefferson got away with his illegal enterprises for many years.

He travels in the right circles amongst politicians, bankers, and big money investors. He inconspicuously slithered his way onto many civic boards and charitable organizations. He is able to disguise his nefarious ways by sponsoring events for underprivileged youth and the elderly in the community. His enterprise would have continued to thrive until the neighborhood was zoned a weed and seed community. An influx of mostly white, upper middle class to wealthy homeowners desiring quick and easy access to downtown purchased properties and became active in the community and eventually voted the old guards out of political office. The politicians that remained realigned themselves with the new guard and were forced to act as he expanded his enterprise and drug addicts started showing up in classrooms in some of the most prestigious, private schools in town.

The District Attorney's office worked with the police department and spent hundreds of thousands of dollars trying to build a case against him. When we finally had enough evidence to get an indictment, the witnesses began dropping like flies. Those he did not manage to kill or have killed were so afraid that even under the threat of racketeering charges and possible federal indictments, they refused to testify. Without crucial testimonies, there was no choice but to withdraw the indictment.

I was crushed. Jefferson Thomas was my first unsuccessful prosecution. He became an instant celebrity. He slandered the District Attorney's office and the police department in the many media interviews after the dismissal. His lawyer filed over two hundred ethics complaints against me and the District Attorney's office. Answering each complaint was extremely time consuming and stressful. The grueling hours of interrogation from the ethics boards were so overwhelming that I was prescribed three different medications to deal with the stress.

"So we get another shot?" I glance at my watch as I walk down the hall to the interrogation room. At this point, I am ten minutes late to dinner. Ten minutes or an hour will not make a

59521774R00133

Made in the USA
Charleston, SC
08 August 2016